PIECES
OF YOU

JAY McLEAN

PIECES OF YOU

PIECES DUET **BOOK ONE**

Editing: Rebecca Fairest Review

Cover Design: Books and Moods

Formatting: Jay McLean

For Myrtle aka Mary

PROLOGUE

I hold on to pieces of her.

Segments of the life she lived, fragments of a girl I'd fallen in love with.

She flew in like a hurricane, forcing me to drown in her depths while shaking my foundation and tearing down my walls. And then came the aftermath: the never-ending storm—like constant cracks of thunder and blasts of lightning that paved a path toward our destruction.

She was frustratingly defeating,

and devastatingly desolate.

Completely unforgiving.

And *beautiful*.

God, was she beautiful.

Even when shattered to pieces.

CHAPTER
ONE

JAMIE

My lungs burned as the hand covering my mouth shifted, making sure I couldn't breathe, let alone speak. Or scream. I don't know why she always went to that extreme. I *never* spoke when I was home.

It was one of the rules.

Don't make a sound.

Don't *exist*.

"Good girl, Jamie. Just stay quiet." Mom's warm breath fell on my shoulder while anger raged through me.

I squeezed my eyes shut, hiding the heated tears that were forming, and repeated over and over in my mind: *I will not break. I will not break. I will not break.*

I was nine years old, and this wasn't the first time it was happening. I knew it wouldn't be the last. I also knew that it wouldn't kill me—but sometimes…

Sometimes I wish it would.

"I don't know what to tell you, ma'am." I could barely make out

Beaker's voice through my pulse pounding in my eardrums, rapid, *manic*. "I'm not sure where they went, but they're not here."

"Can I come in?" Even at nine, I knew it wasn't normal to know who was at the door based on the car in the driveway and the type of knock used. But I did. The woman at the door was the third social worker to come to the house that year, and every time one would show up, Beaker—my mom's boyfriend—would have a story to tell.

A *lie*.

"Do you have a warrant?" That was Beaker's go-to line. The final nail in my so-called coffin.

Head spinning from lack of oxygen, I reached up, tapped Mom's forearm—my signal that I just needed one tiny breath. She gave me a second's reprieve before placing her sweat-covered palm over my mouth again.

It was dark in the closet where Mom held me to her, but I could feel her bones trembling against her flesh. Against mine. She was more afraid than I was, which made sense. Her punishment was far greater than mine.

At the sound of the door closing and heavy footsteps approaching, Mom's grip tightened. Through the cracks of light in the closet door, I knew he was there. Watching. Waiting. He wouldn't do anything—not until he was sure the social worker's car had gone and she'd left entirely. When the closet door opened, I didn't move, didn't make a sound. And even though nothing was blocking my airways anymore, I still didn't take a breath.

That day's weapon of choice was a leather belt already wound around Beaker's fist. "Disappear," he ground out. The devil's eyes were the shade of slate, and he focused them on my mother, even though his order was for me.

I looked up at my mom, finally releasing the tears I'd been holding onto, but I didn't make a sound. I begged with my eyes, pleaded for her to come with me. We could disappear together. We could leave the hell of Satan's wrath and just go.

She didn't move. Not until I caught a flash of movement from the corner of my eye. Beaker raised his fist, aimed at me, and my mom blocked the blow just like she always did. "Run, baby!" she cried out, and so I did.

I ran out of that room and out of the house, and I cried silent tears along with my silent shame and regret, and even then, when my life was filled with nothing but lies—there was one thing in the entire world I knew to be true: my silence would kill us both.

CHAPTER
TWO

HOLDEN

"**N**o fucking way." Probably not the best words to throw out the day before I start my senior year of high school, especially since I'm sitting in the principal's office with both my mom and said principal, but still: No. Fucking. Way. am I doing what they're asking of me.

Next to me, Mom gasps. "Holden, you can*not* speak like that!" She actually has the audacity to sound serious. She's the one who taught me to swear like a sailor. Not on purpose, obviously, but I'm pretty sure the first word out of my mouth was *shit*, and I sure as fuck didn't get it from Sesame Street.

"Your mother and I have spoken, and we both agree that this is a great opportunity for you," Principal Hemmings says, his cheeks blushing red when he finally trails his eyes from my mom's chest to me. He knows I've caught him leering at her, and it's not like it doesn't happen on the regular. It's the only downside to having a young mom. Still, if he doesn't check himself soon, I have no problem climbing over his desk and pulling his teeth out one by one.

"I'm sure you'd agree with anything my mother says," I mumble, earning another gasp from Mom. "Especially when you're looking at her tits when she's speaking."

"Holden!" That came from both of them, in sync.

Shaking my head, I sit up taller. "I'm not doing it."

"You are." Mom's words come with a tone of finality, and I can't help but narrow my eyes at her.

"I know you have a busy schedule, with football and basketball and baseball, and who knows what else, but I think this would be good for you," Hemmings says, resting his elbows on his desk, his eyes on me, and *nowhere* else.

After clearing my throat, I strum my fingers on the armrest of the cheap-ass chairs and say, my tone even, "I don't know how many ways I can say this, but *No. Fucking. Way.*"

The pain starts at my ear and quickly makes its way down my neck and then my entire face. A second later, I'm on my feet, *screeching,* and it takes a moment to realize that my mother is literally dragging me out of the office by my ear. I'm officially calling bullshit on all the times she's asked me to open jars for her because the woman is *way* stronger than I've given her credit for.

We're standing in the foyer right in front of the office desk when she finally releases me. I'm quick to rub at the spot she'd just attacked; my eyes thinned to slits as I glare down at her. Then I take a quick glance around the space. Usually, the day before school starts, the office area's filled with students checking their subjects and schedules and whatever else it is people who care about school do. Luckily for me, there's only the office lady behind the desk and a girl I don't recognize sitting in the short row of waiting chairs.

If I were the type of person to get embarrassed, this would be one of those moments.

The girl doesn't even bother hiding the fact that she's watching us, eyebrows drawn, her hazel eyes flicking between Mom and me. I wonder what she's thinking. *If* she's thinking at all. She sure as hell wasn't when she got dressed this morning. She's in a tweed skirt down past her knees and a white short sleeve blouse with the buttons done *all* the way up to her collar. Back straight, hands

14

folded on her lap, and next to her black old-lady shoes is a worn, brown, leather messenger bag. She dresses like she's eighty, but she doesn't look a day over eighteen. Her eyes catch mine and widen slightly. For a moment—a split second—we just stare at each other. And, because I like to play games, I throw her a smirk and then a wink.

Because why the fuck not?

JAMIE

"What the fuck, dude?" the woman standing in front of G.I. Jock whisper-yells, but he doesn't hear her because he's too busy trying to… what? *Flirt* with me? Intimidate me? He'll have to try a lot harder than that to get under my skin. After waiting a few seconds for a reaction from me and not getting one, he finally looks back at the woman.

Going by their possible age difference and the way she's speaking to him, I assume that she's his much older sister. For a moment, I wonder where his parents are. I push away the question, annoyed that I even went there. G.I. Jock's sister sighs, shaking her head. "I need you to work with me on this, Holden."

Holden. I flip the name over in my mind for no other reason than I *like* it. It's a good name. Solid. Strong.

"What is this even about?" Holden says, crossing his arms. "You've never cared about what I do before. Why start now?"

"Because it's your senior year and—"

"Bullshit," Holden cuts in.

The middle-aged lady behind the large reception desk clears her throat, giving the siblings a look that clearly states *this is a school, dipshits, and you're being inappropriate.*

They both roll their eyes, moving two steps away from the desk and closer to me. Holden's sister keeps her voice low when she says, "I need to start being more present in your life, and this is how I'm choosing to do it."

"How is this making you more *present?*" Holden retorts, his broad shoulders shifting when he shoves his hands in his pockets. "This is just giving me something *more* to do on top of—"

"At least I'll know where you are instead of you disappearing at all hours of the day and night doing God knows what to fuck knows who." Ah, so Holden's a player, and his sister doesn't like it. I should've picked up on that the moment I laid eyes on him.

"This has nothing to do with me, does it?" Holden's tone changes when he says this. He's no longer combative, no longer fighting her. It's as if he's accepting whatever fate his sister is asking of him. "It's about Mia, right?" *Mia?* Hmm. I'm intrigued. This is the most drama I've witnessed since Mom used to make me watch a bunch of housewives on reality television.

They have the same eyes, I note, and they use those eyes to stare each other down for way too long. The difference? Holden's eyes get clearer while his sister's fill with tears. "Stop it," she whispers, teeth gritted.

Holden doesn't stop. "Because you didn't know what was happening with her, and so you're projecting that fear on me?"

"That's enough, Holden," she says, only this time, her tone is authoritative. It's impressive, really. She's quick to wipe at her tears before lifting her chin defiantly. "So what if I want to keep a closer tab on you and—"

"So just say that, Mom," he cuts in, bringing her in for an embrace. Whoa. *Mom?* This is a plot twist I was not expecting. And neither is the sincerity in the way he holds her, the way he strokes the back of her head as he brings her into his chest. "If you need me to do this to take away your guilt, Ma, then I'll do—"

The office door opens, and a man appears. From the research I'd done on the school, I assume this is Mike Hemmings, the principal. Hemmings' eyes go from Holden and his mom to me sitting here, completely enthralled in what's happening in front of me. "I'm sorry to interrupt," Hemmings tells them. "But I have other students I need to see today, so…" He looks as awkward as I feel, and he didn't even witness what I did.

Holden's mom pulls away while Holden nods and states, "I'll do it."

Hemmings returns his nod with a flat, "That's good." Then he smiles, first at them, then at me. "Jameson?" he questions.

I get to my feet, run a hand down my skirt. "Yes, sir."

He opens his door wider. "Come in."

"Thank fuck that's over," Holden murmurs as I pass him, throwing an arm around his mother's shoulders and spinning her toward the exit. Right before I step foot in the office, I hear his mom's reply, "No shit."

"I'm Principal Hemmings," the man dressed in a neatly pressed suit introduces himself as I move around him. He closes the door after me and points to the chair on one side of his desk as he makes his way to the other. I notice the shine on his black dress shoes while his cologne wafts through the air. Sitting in his high-back chair, head bent to look down at what I assume is my file laying open on his desk, he asks, "Are your parents here with you, Jameson?"

My heart skips a beat. Two. "Jamie's fine, and no," I sputter, my voice barely audible as I link my fingers on my lap and push my palms together. After clearing my throat, I add, "I take it you haven't read my file?"

Hemmings glances up but keeps his head down. "No, I'm sorry." He seems sincere enough. "It's been a helluva day. Can you give me a moment to skim it?"

I press my lips tight and nod once. When his eyes start shifting from side to side, reading the cliff notes of my academic life, I take the chance to get a good look at him. He's in his late forties, with dark-brown hair combed and styled to the side. His desk is immaculate, just like his clothes. I wonder if the way he displays himself for the world is an extension of who he is—or if he's faking it just like I am. I don't have a lot of time to ponder that thought before I notice his eyes widen, and I know he's just read the part in my file that will no doubt label me for my last year of high school. When he looks up, frowning, his eyes can no longer focus on mine. "*Emancipated*?"

CHAPTER
THREE

HOLDEN

"I'm proud of you," Mom says, sitting opposite me at the kitchen table while we try to fake some form of normalcy over our bowls of cereal. I can't even remember the last time we sat down for breakfast together, but it's important to her, so I'm *trying*—which is all I could promise her. She's either going through some form of a mid-life crisis, or everything that happened over the past few years is catching up to her. From the divorce and the relocation to the death of someone she considered a second father to the downfall of my best friend—a girl who my mother *wishes* were her child.

I get it. It's a lot to take in, and besides my grandparents, there aren't many people in her life. When my parents split, Mom moved us to Tennessee, where her parents were, and Dad stayed in North Carolina to continue running the family business. She has no real friends. No real *life*. I'm all she has. So, I sit, and I smile, and I watch her eyes cloud with tears as she looks over at me and says, "I can't believe I have a high school senior."

I *want* to roll my eyes. I don't. Instead, I plaster on a smile. "It's crazy, right?"

"It seems like only yesterday I pushed you out of my vagina and held your conehead, alien body for the first time."

A chuckle bubbles out of me. This is the mom I know—the one who raised me. "That's not gross at all, Ma," I murmur.

Her lips kick up at the corners as she pushes her bowl to the side, replacing it with the felt mat displaying the half-completed jigsaw puzzle we'd started a few weeks ago. I can't remember a time in my life when puzzle pieces didn't take over a section of the kitchen table. It had always been our thing—Mom and me. When I was a kid, it was our after-dinner activity, and when Mia wasn't around, or Dad was busy working, we'd settle at the table with a hot chocolate each and spend hours focused on hundreds of pieces of tiny cardboard shapes.

My eyes catch on a completely blue piece, and I move it to the part of the puzzle where it's nothing but the sky. It connects perfectly, and I smile when Mom says, "I hate that you can find them so fast."

"It's not a competition."

She quirks an eyebrow at me. "Says the most competitive boy I know."

I shrug, down the rest of my cereal, and get up to dump the bowl in the sink. "I have to go. Coach set up a morning weights session." I drop a kiss on the top of her head. "Maybe you're just getting old, Ma. You should get your eyes checked."

Gasping, she holds a hand to her chest in mock horror. "I'm thirty-four, you smartass." When she stands, I can't help but look away. Even beneath her robe, it's clear how much weight she's lost over the past couple of months. Her cheeks are hollow, dark circles are under her eyes. She's tired and worn, and maybe even a little broken. I'd never seen her like this. Even during and after the divorce, she'd been a pillar of strength. Not just for herself but everyone around her. I hate this version of her. And the problem... the thing I'll never admit to anyone but myself... I don't think I have the strength to fix us both. "I told your dad I'd get a photo of you on your first day," she tells me, grabbing a sheet of paper off the kitchen counter. It's one of those lame first-day signs kids in elementary school hold up so their doting parents can share it all over social media for friends and family to coo over.

I hold back another eye roll, force another smile. "Sure."

After collecting my shit, I stand on the front porch, the stupid sign held out in front of me, and wait not-so-patiently for Mom to take all the pictures she thinks she needs. She sends them to Dad, and after I promise to call him, she waves from the front yard while I reverse out of the driveway, the speakers in my truck already sounding with a ringtone.

Dad answers the call after a few rings with a single word: "Son."

"Dad."

"Ma's still making you take those pictures, huh?"

I shrug, even though he can't see me. "It makes her happy," I mumble.

Dad's silent for a beat. "She sure could use a little happiness right now."

I don't respond. I don't know how to. My dad is a good man, was a great husband, and *is* a phenomenal father. The divorce didn't come from the usual reasons: constant arguing, financial problems, or infidelity. There was, however, another man.

A man I *hate*.

"How are you, son?" Dad asks after seconds of my silence.

"Good," I lie. "How's the farm?"

"Great." He's lying, too. I spent most of the summer at the farm going through the numbers, and there's not a single piece of evidence that things are *good*. He must sense what I'm thinking because he adds, "You just worry about taking care of your mother and getting through your senior year, okay?"

I heave out a sigh, let my shoulders drop with the burden of his and everyone else's expectations. "Yes, sir."

———

There's no denying that I've always had a pretty decent life. Even with my parents' divorce and moving out of state, it didn't affect me as much as it probably should have. Back home, we lived too far away from any schools that made the commute worthwhile, so I was home-schooled my entire life—right until high school when we up and moved. My best friend, Mia, was my only classmate, and my mom was our teacher. From sunrise to sundown, wherever I was, Mia was, too.

I never would've thought that my moving away would break her more than it broke me.

We were both raised on farms. Her grandfather had a dairy farm, and my dad took over Eastwood Nursery. Along with my mom's "fuck what people think" attitude, I was raised on hard labor that involved heavy machinery and even heavier lifting. So, it's no real surprise that I got a lot of attention when I first stepped foot in public school freshman year. I was a fourteen-year-old boy in a grown-ass man's body. It didn't take long for the girls to notice me. And then the coaches. I'm not all that great at any one sport—unless sex counted as a sport—but I was good enough. I don't *love* organized team activities, but I appreciate a good game.

I guess you could say I like *challenges*.

Physical.

Mental.

As long as I win.

Add that to my height, my size, and here I am: Monday morning, the first day of senior year, doing what I'd grown up doing—lifting heavy shit. Only now, the bags of sods are replaced with barbells, and I'm not on acres and acres of land. I'm in the school's weight room, one headphone in, ignoring everything else around me. This is my zone, my sanctuary. The one place in this suburban shitshow where I can think my own thoughts, let my pulse pound to its own rhythm.

It's where I can get lost and feel found, all in a single exhale.

"Two more, and you're good," Dean says, spotting me while I finish the last set of reps on the bench press. Besides Mia, Dean's the only other person I'd consider an actual friend. Sure, I'm always around a ton of people who know my name, and I know theirs, but those relationships are all superficial.

Isn't that what high school is?

If I needed someone to talk to, to dump what little emotional baggage I have, I'd call Mia.

If I needed bail money because I was pulled over while having inappropriate things done to me, Dean's my guy.

To most people, Dean's the quiet, respectful, people-pleaser type, and I... am not. If it weren't for football, we'd probably never have crossed paths. He keeps me grounded while I get him high. On paper, we don't make sense. In reality, paper doesn't mean shit.

"All right, ladies, you're done for the day!" Coach Griffith yells, and I push myself to the edge of physical pain twice before calling it quits.

Chest and triceps burning, I sit up, towel the sweat off my brow, and look toward Coach, where our teammates are already huddling around him. "I feel like you've gotten weaker," Dean says as we go to join the rest of the team.

I shrug. I didn't work as much as I usually do over the summer, so yeah, he's probably right.

Coach eyes us both, glaring because we're taking our sweet ass time getting to him. He's already losing his patience with us, and the season hasn't even started. "You're all out of shape," is the first thing he says. "You've had all damn summer to get your asses straight and —" he cuts himself off, huffing a frustrated breath. "We might have a shot this year, gentlemen," he announces, then pointedly glares at my friend beside me. "Especially since Dean's girl dumped him."

A united hiss fills the room, and all eyes go to Dean. I don't know how he's kept the whole breakup a secret, but good for him. Three weeks ago, he'd called... and called and called and called, and no matter how many times I rejected it, he kept calling.

I was still in North Carolina, trying to keep Mia in one piece, and when I finally felt comfortable enough to pull away for a few minutes, I called him back. He told me that Bethany—the girl he'd been with since middle school—had broken up with him. He was a mess; it was evident in his voice. A part of me wished I could be there for him, but there was no way I was leaving Mia's side. Or my mom's. Especially since Mia's dad was the only one there to take care of her… and I didn't trust that motherfucker as far as I could spit.

Dean didn't tell me why he and Bethany broke up, and he still hasn't. A couple of weeks later, when I got back into town, I took him out and filled his bloodline with enough weed to help him forget. It was the only thing I could think to do. I'd never been in his situation. Never even cared enough for a girl that I thought about her when she wasn't around. Love… love, at this age, is bullshit. It's deceitful and vicious and cruel, and it exposes the weakest parts of the strongest people. And I've been witness to the destruction love can cause too many fucking times that I want nothing to do with it.

"Well, it's out now," I say, adjusting the strap of my gym bag as Dean and I walk toward our lockers. "Honestly, I'm surprised Bethany hasn't told everyone."

"I guess it's not something either of us wanted to announce." Dean shifts to the side to avoid a rushing student walking with his head down. "She has her reasons. Trust me," he mumbles, stopping in front of the same lockers we had last year, side by side—the same way you can generally find us when we're not in class.

"I give it to lunch until every one of these assholes is talking about it."

"I give it five minutes," he scoffs.

He opens his locker while I lean against mine. "You still haven't told me what happened." Not that I *really* care. It's just that Dean and Bethany had that whole picture-perfect, destined for eternity thing going for them. I shouldn't be surprised, I guess. My mom had that with Mia's dad, and the fact that Mia and I *aren't* siblings speaks for itself.

"It's just weird," I add with a shrug. And it's not like Bethany and I are friends. At best, we're acquaintances by association. Personally, I don't have a problem with her. What she thinks of me, however, is questionable. I'm pretty sure she only tolerates me because I'm friends with her boyfriend.

Ex-boyfriend.

"I don't want to talk about it," Dean says through a sigh, his eyebrows raised as he shifts his tired eyes to mine.

"Got it." I press my lips tight and push off my locker to open it—accidentally bumping into something behind me.

Or some*one*.

I spin quickly, ready to apologize, but the girl's words cut me off. "Who the fuck taught you to stand?"

Well, well. If it isn't the teenage grandma from yesterday. Her words do not match her appearance. Neither do those hazel eyes currently burning with fury as she adjusts her overly modest clothes. When she flicks those eyes to me, a wise-ass crack forms, but before I can get it out, Dean says, "*Jameson?*"

Grandma Jameson.

Suits her: checkered skirt past her knees, blinding white blouse, and a bullshit attitude.

Jameson's gaze shifts from me to Dean, her eyes widening slightly before she lets out a disbelieving scoff. Ignoring him, she focuses on me again. "You're in my way."

"Jamie," Dean repeats, trying to get her attention.

Jamie reaches up, grasps my shoulders, and not so gently moves me to the side so she can access the locker beside mine. Without another word she opens it, shoves her bag inside.

"Jamie!" Dean again, and I should really ask how the hell he knows this girl because she sure as shit doesn't run in our circle. "Are you just going to pretend like I don't exist?"

She doesn't respond, and I can't see her reaction because her locker door is blocking her from view.

"Yo, Grandma! Turn up your hearing aid!" I quip, but no one laughs. Well, shit. *I* thought it was funny.

A moment later, her locker door slams shut. "I can hear just fine," she seethes through clenched teeth. And then she steps past me and toward Dean, and before I can blink, she's slapping a sticky note on his forehead with a single word in thick black marker: *LIAR.*

CHAPTER
FOUR

JAMIE

have no visions of my future. I only have plans. One to be exact: to recreate my past. Recreate *me*. That won't be for at least another year, and so for now, I'm stuck somewhere in the middle.

I don't make a conscious effort to think about the things I left behind, but sometimes a single, insignificant item will spark a memory, like the pearl buttons I'm currently doing up on my blouse. Some people might call it vintage. I call it a gift. *"This one will do,"* *Gina had said, her light gray eyes on mine as her hand trembled while she held out the crisp, white top between us.*

Gina's the only thing I miss from my past, the only thing that brings joy to my constant loathing. When I think about it, *really, truly,* think about it—I wish I'd brought Gina here instead.

———

I've officially made it through my first week of school. Sure, I was in a zombie-like state, but I showed up, and that's all that counts. With work and *life* and the last-minute decision to join the world of public schooling, I didn't give myself enough time to adjust my sleep schedule. For years, I napped between work and was forced to stay up all night.

See, my mom was afraid of the dark.

She wasn't scared of monsters, or evil, or the typical things people fear. She was afraid of herself. So, most nights, when the sun went down and darkness took over, she'd rely on me to keep her straight, keep her focused. We'd stay up all night watching reality television while I sat at the coffee table doing the bare minimum amount of work that home-schooling required. I'd have preferred to spend my senior year doing the same. Unfortunately, according to the program's "guidance counselor," if I wanted to further my education, I'd need to do more than what I was doing, and that's when she mentioned public school. My "situation" had changed, the counselor had said. "So, what's stopping you?"

Nothing.

Nothing was stopping me, and so in a last-ditch effort to save whatever I could of my future, I enrolled at Townsend High School. It was the only high school in my district. The only problem was my car was sitting unusable in the driveway, and I didn't have the funds to fix it. So here I am—most likely the oldest person riding the school bus.

It's a metaphorical hell on wheels.

But, for a few minutes every morning, I have to be in the presence of two idiot jocks whose lockers just so happen to be right next to mine—those few minutes are *literal* hell.

After the first three days of ignoring Dean, he finally got the message. G.I. Jock, on the other hand, greets me most mornings with a "'Sup, Grandma?" Clever, right? On Friday, I accidentally dropped a textbook as I was pulling out another one, and when I squatted down to collect it, the dumbass said, completely serious, "If you want to drop to your knees in front of me, you'll have to get in line."

Contrary to how I dress, I'm not a prude—not even close—but even that was too much. I physically gagged, and he smirked, of course, and I knew what stupid sexual innuendo-filled crack was coming next. So, I beat him to it. I told him I'd rather swallow razor blades than have his dick anywhere near me.

It was the second set of words I'd ever said to him, and it was about his penis. *Nice.*

His eyes had widened, and a second later, Dean was pulling him away.

In one week, I have made a total of zero friends.

Surprised?

Yeah, me neither.

The weird thing is that the lack of friends hasn't come from a place of malice, like I'd expected the moment I realized Dean was now my classmate, and I assumed Bethany was likely to be, too. That assumption was proven the second I stepped foot into first-period English. We both gasped when we saw each other, then quickly looked away. Panicked, I could barely hear a word the teacher said over the thumping of my heart. It's been four years since I stepped foot in a school, and I was suddenly preparing not only for my last year but also having to fight off or ignore the constant name-calling and accusations.

Strangely enough, no one seems to know who I am.

Either that, or they just don't give a shit.

———

When I get to school on the second Wednesday of the school year, Tweedledee and Tweedledipshit are at their lockers like they are every morning. Dean's the first to see me walking toward them, and he stops talking mid-sentence, his eyes catching mine. "Jamie," he says, tone flat.

Like always, I ignore him, turning my back to open my locker.

"You're not going to talk to me? Ever?"

I heave out a sigh. And then I let my shoulders drop, along with my facade. It's so draining—trying to be this person I'm not when-ever I'm around him now. And I'm *tired*. Physically spent. I got a total of two hours of sleep last night, and I don't know if it's my exhaustion or my weakness that has my walls dropping. Slowly, I face him, the dark-haired boy with big brown eyes… eyes I'd spent most of the summer getting lost in. "What do you want?"

His cheeks flush as his eyes widen, surprised I'm even acknowledging his existence. He steps forward, leaving *Thing 2* behind. "To talk." His hands are up between us, palms out in surrender. "That's all."

"I have nothing to say to you."

"Well, I have a lot to say to you," he replies.

I can feel my anger brewing—a reminder of the humiliation he'd caused. And because I can't look at him anymore, I look over his shoulder. A mistake. Because I catch Holden watching our exchange with unabashed curiosity. The kid is *smiling* as if he's privy to a secret. An inside joke. And that joke is *me*. His stupid grin widens when the warning bell sounds, and he slaps his friend on the shoulder, saying, "I love a good daytime drama. To be continued, right? Don't hit play without me."

Dean curses, and my gaze snaps to his. Shaking his head, he keeps his eyes on mine when he says, "I'll see you after school."

I scoff. "Un-fucking-likely."

Welp. The last words I said to Dean come back to bite me in the ass. As part of this whole enrolment into public school plan, my guidance counselor suggested I join some clubs to help with college applications. It's why I was here the day before school started—so Principal Hemmings could tell me what a good fit would be. He suggested the Outreach Club —a kind of community service program organized by a student and overseen by a faculty member. I didn't have to think twice about it. I mean, how hard could it be? Take the elderly on walks? Read to a bunch of toddlers? Pick up trash on the side of the highway? I could do all that.

By the time I find the classroom where the meeting's held and rush inside, I'm late—and *pissed*. Because the person holding the meeting, standing front and center, is none other than Dean Griffith.

Because, *of course*, he is.

And there's no doubt he saw my name on the list of participating students, which is how he knew he'd see me here. *Asshole.*

The man standing beside Dean, dressed in a blue polo, khaki shorts, and whistle around his neck—obviously a coach of some kind—grunts at me, followed by "Take a seat, young lady."

Young lady? Yeah, this isn't the place for me, and as soon as I get the chance, I'm bailing.

"I got a seat right here." My stomach turns at the sound of a familiar voice, and I glance around the room filled with twenty or so students—until I find Holden, who's sitting on a desk, patting his lap like the cocky little germ he is.

"Shut it, Eastwood!" the coach booms. Then lowers his voice to a more appropriate level. "As I was saying… I'm Coach Griffith." Griffith? *Nooo.* I slump down in the nearest empty seat, doing everything I can to avoid slamming my head on the desk over and over. "And you all know my son, Dean." This can*not* be happening. I inconspicuously look around the room, searching for the hidden cameras, because this *must* be a joke—a *sick* one. Just when I think things couldn't get any worse, I lock eyes with *her.* Dull blue eyes on my hazel ones. Bethany frowns, but she doesn't look away. I do, though, and this time, I drop my head on the desk. Once. And then again. It's merely a tap, but it's enough to have Coach Griffith singling me out and asking, "What's wrong with you?"

I reply, "Nothing," at the same time Holden cracks, "I think she swallowed some razor blades."

I hate him.

And Dean.

And this entire school.

Minus Bethany.

Sitting taller, I lift my head and force a smile. "Sorry," I mumble. "I'm just tired." *So* tired.

"Well, buckle up, princess, because it's just getting started." Young lady *and* princess. This man is going to kill me.

I force a nod. "Yes, sir."

"Now..." He tears off a sheet of paper from a notebook and asks, "What's your name?"

"Jameson."

Coach Griffith makes quick work of writing what I assume is my name on the paper, then folding it up and dumping it in one of the two ball caps on the desk in front of him. "Let's get this started then."

"Why can't we choose our partners?" some guy in the back of the room asks.

"Because we don't want you goofing off and collecting hours for smoking weed in the back of your van, *Dwight.*" Laughter fills the air and dies down just as fast when Coach grunts. I have a feeling I'll be hearing that grunting a lot this year. He reaches into both hats with each hand, taking out two names, then unfolds the first one, his lips turned down in concentration. "Holden," he states.

Whispers, mainly from girls, float across the room while I send out a silent prayer.

Please, not me.

"You're going to be paired with..."

Please, not me.

Please, not me.

Please, not me.

"Jameson."

This time, I *slam* my head on the desk, and I don't bother lifting it back up. Not even when Holden busts out a laugh. "Game on, *Grandma.*"

CHAPTER
FIVE

HOLDEN

I'm pretty sure Jamie hates me, which is bullshit because she doesn't even know me. Of everyone in the club, besides maybe Dean, I'm positive I'm the absolute last person she hoped to be matched with. Sucks for her. Me too, I guess. I'd prefer to be paired with any other girl in that room. At least then, there might be an extra *benefit* to the outreach we'll be providing.

We're sitting on one of the tables in the school's courtyard, going through the notes provided by Dean about our upcoming project. This club was Dean's idea, and it goes with all the charitable work he does through his church. Again, Dean and me, on paper, are complete opposites.

"So, I guess we'll be doing yard work for some old lady." I look up from the notes and quirk an eyebrow at the girl sitting opposite me. "Maybe you know her from bingo."

Jamie's eyes are on me, void of a single emotion, and I've concluded that she genuinely gives zero fucks about anything I have to say to, or about, her.

Of course, I've asked Dean who she is to him, but he won't tell me, so I highly doubt she will either. I'm curious, though, and the few minutes we're around each other every morning don't give me many opportunities to get to know the girl behind the filthy mouth.

Not that I *want* to.

It's not like I was instantly attracted to her, because let's be real— she hasn't an iota of sex appeal, at least not that she openly displays. But I'm… perplexed, maybe?

She's still watching me, wordlessly. Is this a game to her? This little stare-off she's having with me? Because if so, I'm down.

With an exaggerated sigh, I shut the folder, rest my elbows on top of it and lean forward, saying, "I have a question. Well, two questions. A two-part single question. Statement, maybe?"

She blinks. Once. Twice. But those eyes stay on me.

I add, pinning her with my glare, "How far is that stick stuck up your ass, and do you need help getting it out?"

Her lips twitch before leveling out again. The movement was so quick, I don't know if she was about to smile or snarl. Either way, I got a reaction, and that has to be a point for me.

Rubbing the back of my neck, I settle in my seat and get more comfortable. "Want to know what I think happened between you and Dean?"

She shakes her head and sits taller. "We're not talking about Dean."

"Ah, she speaks in full sentences *and* without cursing or insulting. Who'd have thought?"

"Contrary to what you think of me, I actually enjoy talking. Just not to morons who think their dick activity defines their worth."

"You talk about my dick a lot. Can't imagine how much you think about it when I'm not around." I throw her a smirk. "Obsessed much?"

Her eyes narrow. "I really don't like you."

"I'm fully aware." I chuckle. "Which is a shame since you don't know me."

"I know enough." Hand held out between us, she demands, "Pass me the folder."

I pull the papers closer to me and cluck my tongue. "Say please."

And now she's back to passively staring. It *should* make me uncomfortable, but I kind of dig it. The longer she stares, the wider my smirk gets. She's the one to break first. "You do realize I'm immune to… to…"

I hold back a laugh. "My dick activity?"

She drops her head back, eyeing the sky, and mumbles something incoherent under her breath.

"You know…" I say, standing, "You might hate me for whatever unknown reason, but I actually *like* you."

Her eyes meet mine again. "In what world could you possibly *like* me?"

I wait for her to get up and lift her bag strap across her torso before stating, "In a world where I like to be challenged."

"I'm not challenging you to anything."

"That you know of." I shrug, then motion toward the student parking lot. "Let's go pay your knitting buddy a visit."

Sitting cross-legged in the passenger seat of my truck, her granny skirt covering her legs, Jamie focuses on the file that Dean had given me a few days earlier. When he found out that I'd signed up to the club, he'd given me the first choice of what to do. Yard work I could do in my sleep, and even though it's hotter than Satan's asshole, working outside is what I've spent my life doing. Jamie, on the other hand, I don't know how she's going to handle it.

"It says she's a widow," she murmurs.

I glance sideways at her.

"Her husband passed away, and he used to do all the upkeep," she adds, her thumb working at spinning one of the few mood rings on her fingers.

When we're this close, this confined, I can smell her shampoo or perfume or whatever it is. It's a natural scent—flowers and citrus, and it reminds me of home. Of the farm. "That's sad," I respond.

She sighs. "This is why you don't rely on men to do anything."

I scoff. "So… it's not *me*, specifically. You hate all men?"

She shakes her head, her loose black hair shifting with the movement. "No, I hate the idea of dependency."

"Jesus Christ," I huff out, my brow bunched. "It's just yard work. The man *died*."

"People die all the time," she states, tone flat, distracted with reading the notes.

Dang. "You're a little cold, don't you think?"

"I'm actually really hot," she says, lifting her eyes from the folder and toward the dashboard. "Do you have AC?"

"It's busted."

With a groan, she starts undoing the buttons of her blouse while simultaneously tugging the ends from beneath her skirt. I struggle to pay attention to the road because I'm too busy focused on her. Beneath her top, she's wearing a tight, white tank, the straps of her hot-pink bra visible.

Dudes and boobs. Why we're so fascinated with them is an enigma, but I have to admit—

"It's rude to stare," she mumbles.

I shrug. "You have a nice rack."

She turns to me, and I expect her to scold me. Instead, she chews her lip and says, "Thank you."

What the fuck? "You're welcome," I say, but it comes out as a question.

She nods toward the windshield. "Focus on the road, you pervert."

"Right." I do as she says, realizing that this girl is far more complex than I'd expected. Maybe we've both jumped the gun with the judgment of each other because she's cold one minute and hotter than hell the next.

Either she knows exactly who she is and what she's doing, or I'm way, *way* off my game.

It takes only ten minutes to get to the house, where we'll be spending one afternoon a week for an entire semester. When we pull into the driveway, the first thing I notice is how much work there is to do in the front yard alone. Almost every visible area is covered in weeds and out-of-control vines. It's nearly impossible to see the paved path to the front door, but I manage, and waiting for us at the entry to the closed-in porch is an older woman.

"Hey, look." I motion to where the woman's opening the door. "It's your best friend, Gladys," I quip.

"Her name's Esme," Jamie mutters.

"I know." I sigh. "It was a joke."

"I know," Jamie echoes. "It wasn't funny." *Cold* Jamie's back. Good to know.

Once the truck comes to a complete stop, she starts to open the door, but I stop her with my hand on her arm. "Be nice, okay? She's... *old*."

Her entire face scrunches in annoyance. "I am nice."

The *audacity.* "Are you, though? Because you just told me she was a loser for relying on a man, and you gave zero fucks that her husband had just died."

"I didn't say that," she says, shaking her head. And the girl might just be insane. Like, certifiable. I'm getting goddamn whiplash from being around her.

I say, slowly, enunciating every word, "You literally *just* said it."

"No." She shakes her head again, seeming agitated that she even has to talk to me. "What I said and what you *heard* are two completely different things." She yanks her arm out of my hold, and a second later, she's out of the truck and walking toward the porch. I rush out to join her because the last thing I need is someone's grandma complaining about some crazy, unstable high school girl ripping into her about her dead husband while I stood by and did nothing.

When I catch up to Jamie, walking only a step behind her, Esme waves, smiling from ear to ear. Then calls out, "What's poppin', bitches?"

Jamie stops so suddenly I almost run into her. Whatever look must be on our faces has Esme's smile fading. "Isn't that how kids talk these days?"

I stifle my guffaw, but Jamie—she lets out a bark of a laugh. And because I struggle to believe what I'm hearing, I step beside her, just so I can see her face—make sure the sound is actually coming from her. It's loud, and it's free, and it's as odd as it is fascinating. After a while, she silences the sound, but her expression is still there—her smile still present. She has a tiny gap between her two front teeth, something I never noticed before, and her eyes—her eyes meet mine, crinkled at the corners. Seconds pass, neither of us breaking the stare, but her smile is waning, and maybe she's better at this game than me. "What?" she croaks out, her throat moving with her swallow.

Shoving my hands in my pockets, I tell her the truth, "You're kind of cute. I mean, when you don't look like you want to knee me in the nuts."

Her breath hitches right before she catches herself. And just like that, she blinks, and she's void again. Completely empty. Expressionless. "Thank you." *Weirdo.*

I shrug. "You're welcome."

CHAPTER
SIX

JAMIE

'd spent most of the car ride going through the notes that Dean had provided, so I thought I knew what I was walking into. Sitting on Esme's porch, gripping an ice-cold lemonade, while listening to her speak with shaky hands and a constant wobble in her voice—it's kind of heartbreaking. And regardless of how I acted or what I said to Holden in the car, I'm not the cold-hearted bitch I've unintentionally portrayed myself to be. After the initial shock of her welcoming words wore off, she apologized no less than four times for them. And no matter how many times Holden and I said that it was *fine*, that it was—in Holden's words— "a good icebreaker," I could tell that it embarrassed her. When Holden asked if one of her grand-kids had told her to say it, Esme had us sit down at a little table on the porch, a pedestal fan blowing hot air on us, and told us her life story.

She didn't have any kids, so grandkids were non-existent. She and her husband, who died almost three years ago to the day, spent a lot of their lives trying and failing for a family they both wanted more than anything. Eventually, they realized it wasn't in God's plan for them, and so they focused on their love and their home. Wesley, Esme's late husband, spent most of his days in the yard. And while he didn't have the sons he wanted, the football team he'd dreamed of coaching or his children's achievements he looked forward to boasting about, he was proud of two things in life: his wife and his yard. And that was who Wesley was right until the day he died. He collapsed in the front yard of a heart attack, doing what he loved. And Esme—she's never been the same.

She became a recluse after his passing, and it's only been the past couple of months she's found the courage to leave the house for anything other than essentials. For over two-and-a-half years, she didn't speak to a soul, so when the opportunity came up at the church, she'd just started attending, to have a couple of high school kids help around the house, she jumped at the chance. And then she panicked, feeling as though she'd forgotten how to interact with people in general—let alone kids of our generation—so... she googled it.

The Internet, she said, had been the only thing to keep her sane for the past three years. That, and Netflix...

... and *porn*.

That last part had Holden spitting out his lemonade and spraying it all down his *Townsend HS Athletics* t-shirt.

"You're right," Esme said, smirking as she winked over at the six-foot-four behemoth of a man-child who seemed to take up the width of the entire porch. "I *am* good at ice-breakers." Then her eyes slid to mine, her cheeky grin revealing her lipstick-stained teeth, and she said, "It's so easy to get to him, huh?" And then she laughed, and I laughed with her, and I forgot—just for a moment—how much I missed my only friend in the world, Gina.

Esme then asked us about our lives. Holden seemed to be an open book, telling her he's from North Carolina and how he grew up on his family's nursery, thus assuring her she's in excellent hands. He also told her he's an only child to divorced parents and that he takes part in almost every sport under the sun—a fact that has Esme smiling and mentioning how much her Wesley would've loved him.

I didn't realize how enthralled I'd been in their conversation and all the additional information I was learning about Holden—as his own person—rather than just Dean's friend, that when the questions came at me, I wasn't prepared. The only things I told them are that I grew up about four hours north of here, that I'm an only child, too, and that I don't have as much experience as Holden does, but I do love flowers. One of those things is a fact. The other two are questionable.

Once the entire jug of lemonade's gone and our time's almost up, Esme stands and offers to show us the yard and all the work she's hoping to get done, which is where we are now: me, following behind as Esme and Holden walk side by side, her hand in the crook of his elbow.

I will say this, for such a giant, cocky douchebag, when it comes to Esme, Holden is polite and respectful and full of yes ma'ams and no ma'ams and whatever you want ma'am.

It's weird. And I don't like the way it's making me feel. Like I have to second-guess the revulsion I have for him.

In the large back yard, we head toward a swamp that I'm sure was once a pool, and Esme stops beside it, her shoulders dropping with her heavy sigh. "We spent many a lovely day in that pool—my Wesley and me." I like the way she says *my* Wesley. Like he was hers and hers alone.

Must be nice.

"And that," she adds, pointing to a building crawling with ivy, "is my Wesley's workshop. Well, it was the pool house, but he filled it with all his gardening tools, so that's what it became." She hands Holden a set of keys and backs away, saying, "I'm not quite ready to go in there, so…"

I frown while Holden's gaze flicks to mine. "*Your* Wesley's yard and tools are in excellent hands, I promise," he tells her. His tone is gentle, comforting, and I almost want to shake him because *Who Is He* right now?

Esme smiles at him, but it doesn't reach her eyes, and a moment later, she's moving toward the back door. As soon as she's inside the

41

house, Holden steps beside me, keeps his voice low when he says, "Don't think I didn't see you thawing on that porch, Ice Queen."

I roll my eyes.

He pokes my side. "Admit it, Nanna Nelly. It's sad."

"It is," I reply with a shrug, leading us to the workshop.

After sliding the key in the lock, Holden turns to me and whispers, "Hey, you really think she watches porn?"

I don't give him the reaction I'm sure he's expecting. "I bet her drawers are filled with vibrating toys."

He lets out a disbelieving scoff. "You're a little twisted, Jameson." And then his lips kick up on one side. "And I'm into it."

"Shut up." I move past him and enter the space, stopping just a foot inside. Tools cover an entire wall, and a workbench spans the length. There's a couch on the opposite wall, facing the workspace, and I imagine Esme sitting there, watching *her* Wesley work for hours and hours. And then there's the dust—so much of it—covering every space, every surface, floating through the air, completely *unwanted*.

"She's like dust, Dahlia! Always around and fucking useless."

"I gotta make a quick phone call," Holden says from behind me.

I turn to him, notice his phone already held to his ear. "Lining up tonight's booty call?"

The boy *winks*. Gross. "I got my booty call right in front of me." Then he's walking away, backward, his stupid smirk leaving me annoyed… and maybe a little breathless.

There's no denying that Holden's hot in a way that makes girls want to rip off their panties and do dirty things to themselves with the lights out. He's tall, muscles upon muscles, and never without a cap that covers his dirty blond hair, hair that's long enough to curl over the edges. But it's his eyes I worry about the most. Green, like a lively forest. But when he looks at you—*really* looks at you—there's nothing *alive* about his stare. Even when he's cracking one-liners, they never brighten, never flash with anything other than indifference.

It's as scary as it is captivating.

Kind of like serial killers.

Not that any of this matters, because I've fallen for the hot guy before, and that turned out *peachy*. Truly. It's not as if he broke me down, piece by piece, only to shatter what strength I had left and leave me questioning who I am and what my purpose is.

I'm being dramatic.

Probably.

I try to push away the sudden ache in my chest, but the tears come too fast, and I hate that they do. Of everything in my life I could've shed a tear over, dickhead Dean Griffith shouldn't be it. I've spent the past year on the verge of breaking, and now? Now I decide to crack? *Outstanding.*

"Okay, let's do this!" Holden shouts, clapping his hands together as he steps into the workshop.

I'm too surprised by his presence that I face him without thinking.

"Oh, shit." He grimaces. "I don't do crying girls."

I sniff back my heartache and wipe the wetness off my cheeks. "Good. I don't do idiot boys."

"Liar." His grin is stupid. "I give it three weeks until you're begging me to bend you over this workbench and bone you from behind."

"Two things," I start, focusing on the tools again while I attempt to keep my voice even. "You just called yourself an idiot. And *bone*? Who says that?"

He stops beside me, mimics my position. "Right, I forgot you were from a generation when dinosaurs ruled the Earth." After taking out his phone, he makes note of what we'll need to get the job done. He goes through a rough timeline with me, and I listen to every word he speaks. When he's like this, when it's just him and me, and there's no innuendo to fall back on—it almost seems normal. *Almost.* And I don't miss the fact that he skimmed right over the whole me crying incident. He didn't ask why, and I don't know if it's because he's genuinely uncomfortable or because he knows I wouldn't tell him. Whatever his reasoning, I'm grateful.

When it's time to leave, I check the nearest bus stops and their schedules on my phone. I don't know where Holden lives or is planning to go, but I know for sure that it's not anywhere near me. "I'll see you tomorrow," I call out, walking down the driveway past his truck. "Unfortunately."

"You calling for a ride?"

I keep my head down, eyes focused on times and routes. "Bus schedule."

"My truck's right here," he shouts.

"I'm good." I don't turn to him, not even when I hear his rushed footsteps catching up to me.

"Quit being so stubborn. I can give you a ride."

"No."

"Yes."

I make it to the sidewalk before stopping and facing him. "It's out of the way."

A single eyebrow arches. "You know where I live now, Stalker Sadie?"

"Where the hell do you come up with these names?"

A burst of laughter falls from his lips. "*Please* get in my truck, so I can say I'm driving Miss Daisy."

"You need that one-liner more than you need your next breath, huh?"

"I really do," he says through a chuckle.

I contemplate his offer for less than a breath. "Look, it's one thing to get in a virtual stranger's car to go to a designated destination where a ton of people know where I'm going and who I'm with, but driving me home? That's another level. You could kill me and dump my body on the side of the road." Or a lively forest. It would go with his serial killer eyes.

For some reason, he finds this funny—made clear by his laughter. And his smile. And I *don't* like his smile.

Maybe.

"So, let's not be strangers then."

My nose wrinkles at the thought, which only makes him laugh again.

"Ask me anything, Agnes. You want to see my driver's license?

Address? Date of Birth? No, I know," he says, and he's such a rambling idiot; I don't even know if it's worth stopping him at this point. "Want to post it on social media? Tag me. Everyone will know then."

"I don't have social media."

His smile is *wiped*. "Can I ask you a dead serious question?"

Oh, God.

"How fucking old are you?"

I sigh the loudest, longest sigh in the history of sighs.

"Fine then," he says. "Get your parents on the phone, and I'll tell them what an upstanding, young man I am. Preferably your mom." He smirks. "I'm *real* good with moms."

"I'm sure you are," I reply. I don't bother telling him that unless he's proficient with a Ouija board or possesses some out-of-this-world hallucinogens, we're both shit out of luck with that idea.

At my silence, his brow dips in concentration, and he watches me, *scrutinizes* me, as if he's trying to memorize my face. Serial killers probably do the same thing right before they finish the deed. "Okay, I'll post on my social."

He wouldn't.

Before I know what's happening, he takes out his phone and snaps a picture of me. "What the hell are you doing?"

"Posting your scowly little ass on Instagram."

I'm so quick to grab his phone from his hand, he doesn't even have time to stop me from deleting the image completely. "You cannot post my picture on the Internet."

He barks out a laugh. "What are you in witness protection?"

My eyes snap shut. "No," I breathe out, unable to look at him. "I just don't want my picture out there, and you shouldn't either." It's supposed to be a warning, though I'll never tell him why.

At his silence, I finally peer up at him through my lashes, my palm sweating as I clasp his phone tight in my grip.

"Because of Dean?"

Not even close, but I'm relieved that's where his mind went. I release the breath I'd been holding and hand him back his phone. "Yeah, because of Dean," I lie.

"Fair," he responds, then motions to his truck. "You coming?"

At this point, I don't think I have much of a choice. "Okay."

I get in his truck and hold back an eye roll when he gets behind the wheel, all giddy-like, and says, his smile wide, "Look at me, I'm driving Miss Daisy."

"Feel better?"

"So much better." He brings the engine to life and settles both hands on the wheel before facing me. "Where to, Thelma?"

"You know how to get to Parkway?"

He thinks about this a moment as he eyes the ceiling of the cab. "Yeah, but there's nothing there besides—" He stops himself there.

"The trailer park," I finish for him.

He's quiet as he reverses out of the driveway and stays that way for minutes that feel like suffocating hours. I don't need to overanalyze what he could be thinking. Living in a trailer park comes with a cliché stigma that isn't fair to anyone. People do what they can to survive, to put a roof over their heads and food on the table, and that's exactly what I'm doing. And, the possible judgment, coming from him, a boy whose—I'm willing to bet—parents are *actually* parents and do what they can to shield him from the bottom of the barrel, is… expected. And I don't have the energy to be mad about it. Agitated, maybe. But mad? No.

People don't know what they don't know, and Holden? He knows nothing about me. "I'm not ashamed of where I live," I murmur over the humming of the truck.

His gaze flicks to mine. "Who said you were?"

"You went all quiet after I told you where to go," I tell him. "You're being weird, and it's making me uncomfortable. Just tell me you're going to *bone* me again."

He shakes his head, chuckling. "Nah, I'm just trying to think of an old lady name to go with trailer. I keep coming up with Trailer Tammy, but that's my mom's name, so…"

"Sounds like a stripper name."

He gasps in mock horror. "You take that back!"

I giggle—such a contrast to the whirlwind of emotions that had taken over my mind, my heart—only minutes earlier. "Are you a mama's boy, Holden?"

His shoulders square, no hint of embarrassment when he says, "So what if I am?"

Well, *shit*. "Trudy," I say.

"What?"

"Trailer Trudy."

He grins over at me. "I like it," he tells me. "But it doesn't have the same impact when you self-deprecate. I insult you. You insult me. That's the way it works, Trailer Trudy."

"Noted." I nod. And before I can retort, his phone goes off through the car speakers. The name *Mia Mac* appears on the stereo, and Holden veers off the road and brakes so fast, I have to catch myself on the dash.

"Sorry," he mumbles. "I gotta take this."

Taking his phone from its holder, he answers, opening his door as he does, "Mia. When I call, you answer. That was the deal." I don't hear anything else he says because he walks behind his parked truck, starts pacing back and forth with the phone held to his ear.

Mia. It's the same name mentioned when I first saw Holden outside the principal's office the day before school started. The same name that had my interest piqued.

He's not on the call for long, a few minutes at most, but when he returns, I can feel the shift in his mood, the change in his demeanor. Jaw tense, he waits for cars to pass before getting back on the road. I say, because silence makes me stupid, "That's kind of a sucky way to talk to your girlfriend."

"Mia's not my girlfriend," he deadpans.

Interesting. From what he's said, he's an only child, so she's not his sister, which would make her…?

"So, what is she? Your fuck buddy?"

Holden doesn't take his eyes off the road as he white knuckles the steering wheel. "Is that what Dean was to you?"

Touché. I clamp my mouth shut.

"Just leave it alone, okay?" he bites out.

We spend the rest of the ride in silence, my chest aching—a multitude of emotions swirling, coursing through my veins. I've pissed him off somehow, pressed the wrong button, and I don't know how to fix it.

That's been my life's biggest downfall: wanting to fix the unfixable.

When we get to the trailer park, Holden slows to a near stop and asks, "Which one's yours?"

"It's right at the back, but I can get out here."

He lets out a long, drawn-out breath. "Just show me where."

I guide him to my trailer, where my car sits useless in the allocated parking space. "Thanks for the ride," I say, already pushing the door open.

I need to get out of this truck.

Out of my head.

I need to go into my house, my solitude, where I can be alone and be myself, where there's no one around to judge me for dressing the wrong way or saying the wrong things.

"Look," Holden says, and I freeze with the door wide open and my back to him. "I know we have this bullshit banter going on, and it's whatever, but Mia—she's off-limits."

I don't look at him when I say, "Got it." And then I practically run out of the car and into my house. Where the only person around is the most judgmental one I know: myself.

CHAPTER
SEVEN

HOLDEN

"**D**ammit!" Jamie hisses, pulling her hands away from the blackberry bush. She looks down at the fresh scrape on her wrist caused by the thorns. It's the third time she's done the exact same thing in the space of five minutes.

When she got in my truck after school, dressed in her usual clothes, I asked her where she planned on changing. She said she didn't. So, dressed in a pale pink blouse, another nana skirt, and completely inappropriate shoes, she's been using garden shears to cut through the brush in Esme's yard.

Meanwhile, knowing what to expect, I'm in work boots, a long-sleeved khaki shirt, and gloves.

After her second hiss of the afternoon, I offered her my shirt.

She declined.

After the fourth, I offered her my gloves.

She declined that, too.

And now her hands are scratched to shit and she's glaring at the blackberries as if it's their fault. Maybe it's mine. Maybe I should've prepared her.

"At least take the fucking gloves," I offer again, exasperated.

"No." It's been an entire week since we last spoke. Even the morning locker interactions have been void of conversation. I don't *think* it's on purpose. I just haven't had anything to say. Plus, I'm usually *always* late to class, and being on time, being *present*, was part of the promise I'd made to Mom, and I'm nothing if not a man of my word. "Take my shirt then."

"No."

I drop my hands and face her. "Why the fuck are you so stubborn?"

"Why the fuck do you care?"

"Because I have to work next to Whiney Wilma all afternoon."

Her eyes thin, directed at me. "This is a big yard, Holden. Go stand somewhere else."

"You're being a bitch, *Jameson*. Take the fucking gloves."

"No!"

I drop my shears and rip off my gloves, then take her free hand and start forcefully putting them on her. Surprisingly, she doesn't fight me. I even manage to get the second one on before she speaks up, but what she says surprises me. "I'm sorry."

"For being so difficult?" I deadpan, releasing her hand and shifting my eyes to hers.

She's already watching me, those hazel eyes bright against the afternoon sun. Biting her bottom lip, she keeps my gaze hostage for a second, two, before dipping her head, her voice low when she says, "No. For what I said in your car last week."

I rear back, just an inch, and try to recall what the hell she's talking about.

"About your... your *Mia*," she mumbles.

"*What?*" I don't mean to say it out loud, but it comes out anyway. "I'd totally forgotten about that," I mumble. And now I feel shitty because if she's spent the entire week stewing over this... I don't know. It doesn't feel right.

To be honest, I'd been so consumed with other things going on in my life, in my head, that the few times Jamie's somehow popped into my mind, it'd been easy to push thoughts of her aside, to disregard them as nothing more than curiosity.

She lifts her chin slightly and looks right at me, and I notice her height for the first time. She's short. Short enough that I'd have to bend my knees to kiss her. And *where the fuck did that thought come from*? "So, you're not mad at me?" she asks, and I shove the idea of kissing her way, way down.

At least until later.

When I'm alone.

Maybe.

I still don't know what happened with her and Dean—my *friend*—and even without that aspect, Jamie annoys the shit out of me. She's too fucking blunt and obnoxious as hell, and…

And kind of cute—in that unassuming, pathetic, cliché-high-school-movie kind of way.

"Holden?" She's still looking at me, waiting.

"No, I'm not mad," I say, taking a *big* step back and away from *danger, danger, danger.*

"Oh, okay." She turns to the bush and starts cutting away. I do the same. Minutes pass, neither of us saying a word. But my eyes—my stupid, deceiving eyes—keep moving to her.

Peering at her.

Like a creep.

She breaks the silence. "It's just that you haven't spoken to me all week, so…"

Huh. I square my shoulders, pretending to focus on the task in front of me instead of the thoughts running circles in my mind. "You been keeping tabs on me, Taylor?"

"Taylor?"

I glance sideways at her. "That's your last name, right?"

She nods, a slight smile breaking through as she drops a clipping to the ground between us. "You been keeping tabs on me, *Eastwood*?"

I shrug. "Do you want me to?"

Swear, her cheeks redden. "Not even for a second."

––––––

When the hour's up, we walk to my truck together while she removes the gloves and hands them back. "I found a bus route so—"

I stop beside the passenger door, rolling my eyes at her. "Shut up. Get in."

She clearly hesitates, moving from one foot to the other, her eyes everywhere but on me. We spoke very little after her apology, so I don't know what's on her mind. If I'm being honest, I don't know what I'm thinking either. All I know is that I'm confused—about a lot of things. Mainly about the girl standing in front of me with her nose wrinkled, no doubt trying to come up with a reason to say no. Or say yes. "It's *so* out of the way."

I sigh. Out loud. *Games.* These are her games, her terms, round and round, and I don't have the patience for it, so I repeat, "Shut up. Get in."

She gets in the truck.

So do I.

And the second I'm in, my stomach *growls.*

Jamie turns to me, her eyes wide. "What the fuck was that?"

I mock pout, putting a hand to my stomach. "Listen, Taylor. I'm a growing boy. I have eight full meals a day."

"Of course, you do," she muses. "You're such a jock."

"How so?"

"Calling me by my last name is *such* a jock move."

I pat the top of her head, chuckling when she pushes my hand away. "And you're such a little weirdo."

She puffs out a breath. "My name's Jameson, by the way."

I purse my lips. "Yeah, I don't like it."

"Good." She giggles. "Because it's not yours. And *Taylor* is so impersonal."

"You want me to get up close and personal with you, *Taylor*?" I'm on autopilot, flirting as I do with every other girl in existence. The difference? Most girls don't hit back the way Jamie does. I sit, and I wait for a retort because I'm already preparing my next words.

She doesn't retaliate. Instead, she surprises me again and says, "At least let me feed you… to pay you back for the gloves and driving me home."

I start the engine. "I'm not going to turn down a free meal."

"Good," she says, settling into her seat.

"Besides, we should feed you, too." I reverse out of the driveway and wait until I'm on the road before adding, "This is about the time they serve dinner at the retirement home, right?"

She laughs once. "How long until the old lady jokes run their course?"

"Soon," I admit. "I'm running out of material." I glance sideways for a response, but she just sits there, her hands on her lap, staring out of the windshield and *smiling*. "Where to, Miss Daisy?"

"I know a place near me."

"This is a truck stop, Taylor," I groan, pulling into a parking spot.

"Don't be so judgmental."

"Oh, nice…. coming from Judge Judith."

Her exaggerated eye roll has me holding back a smile. "Just trust me."

Regardless of what the truck stop looks like from the outside, the inside is decent. Cherry-red stools line the counter, and the same-colored booths take up the windows. It reminds me of the diner back home, the only place to get a decent burger within an hour's drive.

There are only a handful of other patrons here, and most of them don't even look up when we walk toward a corner booth. Jamie slides in one side, and I slide in the other and pick up the menu. I'm starving, and I want to eat every single item listed. "What's good here?"

"Everything," Jamie's quick to answer. She doesn't look at the menu. Instead, she tugs a few paper napkins from the dispenser and dumps them in her messenger bag. "Get whatever you want."

"I want *all* of it."

"Then order all of it."

JAY MCLEAN

"Okay, miss moneybags," I say with a chuckle.

She nods, distracted by pulling out another napkin. "Seriously, go ahead." This one doesn't go in her bag. Instead, she unfolds it completely and spreads it out on the table.

"You come here a lot?" I ask, and she nods as she searches through her bag. A moment later, she's pulling out a fine marker and uncapping it with her teeth. Pen to paper, she starts to draw on the napkin—black ink blotting, spreading. I'm so enthralled in the intricate lines she's creating; I'm barely focused on her words when she says, "I work here."

I don't respond because it's not important. What she's drawing—it's fascinating, and I can't tear my eyes away. Too soon, the server—a woman in her thirties with dyed black hair and strawberry-blonde roots—interrupts us. "Hey, Jamie."

Jamie looks up, scrunching the napkin in her fist and setting it aside. I'm bummed that I didn't even have time to make out what it was before she ruined it. "Hi, Carol."

"Is this your new boyfriend?" Carol asks, motioning to me.

"No," Jamie's quick to answer. "We're working on a school project together."

Carol smiles, her eyes shifting between the two of us before finally settling back on Jamie. "He's cute."

"He's right there, Carol. He can hear you," Jamie deadpans.

"Oh, hush." Carol taps my shoulder. "He already knows he's cute."

"I do," I agree. "Though I prefer hot. Sexy. Dynamite in the sack."

Jamie *blushes*. Ah, so this is her hot button. No amount of filthy words and insults can cover up the fact that the thought of me and sex makes her... something. Or maybe she's embarrassed that I just said all that at her place of work. Yeah, that's most likely it. I should probably rein it in. Or at least *try*.

Try—it seems like it's all I've been doing lately.

"What do you want?" Jamie asks, and for a moment, I think she's just busted me staring at her. Analyzing her. But no, she's asking about the food.

54

I drop the menu. "You order for me. You know what's good."

Jamie orders the standard burger, fries, onion rings, and vanilla shake each, and once Carol leaves, I reach across the table and pull her hand toward me. "Hey, what the hell?"

Ignoring her, I turn her hand over, inspecting the scrapes now starting to scab. "It messed you up good, huh?"

"It'll heal," she mumbles, pulling her hand back and hiding it beneath the table. I don't miss the way her cheeks bloomed pink at my touch, and now I'm wondering if they were that same way when I slid the gloves over her hands earlier. I wish I'd paid more attention.

Her gaze drops to the now balled-up napkin sitting between us, and I watch as her shoulders shift as if she was about to raise her hand to collect it. She doesn't. Instead, she pulls out another napkin and starts the process again. Unfolding. Spreading out. Before she can put pen to paper, my phone vibrates, and I rush to see who's calling, my lungs emptying with relief when I see it's not Mia or her idiot dad.

"It's Dean," I tell Jamie. Then hit answer and say, "Hey, man. What's up?"

"I was just checking in. How did it go?"

I watch Jamie watching me. "It was fine."

"Cool. Did you want to meet up, grab something to eat?"

"I uh…" I don't know if Jamie can hear Dean's end of the conversation, so I don't know why I'm looking at her, waiting for a reaction —an approval of some sort to say that it's okay if I tell him we're together, doing something we don't *have* to be doing… but then I figure, *fuck it*. Whatever they have going on is their problem. Not mine. "I'm actually with Jamie right now. We just ordered."

Silence greets me while Jamie gives no visible reaction.

"You good?" I say into the phone.

"Yeah, man. I'll see you tomorrow."

He hangs up before I can respond, so I drop my phone on the table and say, because I'm sick of all the secrets, "So, Dean."

Jamie's lips press tight before her shoulders drop. Man, she must've been tense the moment I mentioned his name. "He hasn't told you, has he?"

"Told me what, exactly?"

Her mouth opens, shuts, again and again. "Can I ask you something first?"

I nod, settle into my seat.

"You know Bethany, right?" Well, that was unexpected.

"I mean, we're not close, but yeah, I know her."

"Is she *nice*?" This girl is *full* of surprises. And admittedly, I'd kind of suspected what went on. The breakup, followed by Dean and Jamie's reaction to each other, and then the secrets that followed… it wasn't hard to put two and two together. But now she's asking about Bethany, and I have to wonder what role she's played through it all. Dean—he's not the kind of guy to cheat just for cheating's sake. He's had *plenty* of opportunities, especially when I've been around, and not once has he even stoked the flames.

So, it comes down to two things: lies and deceit. And I don't want to add to the lies, so I give her the truth. "Yeah, she is," I admit, watching her reaction closely. "I mean, she's a girl with zero drama who just happens to be the most popular girl at school and the head cheerleader—not that any of that matters. But, she started and championed an anti-bullying campaign that's now enforced in multiple schools, so…" I trail off, feeling a slight twinge of pity when I see the way Jamie nods slowly as if she knows all this already. I add, just so I don't have to end there, "Truthfully, she's a little too straight-edge for me, but hey, I wasn't the one dating her."

"So… she's perfect," Jamie mumbles. "Awesome." She flops back in the seat, her shoulders slumped. And then she looks up, her sad, solemn eyes on mine. "I didn't know about her," she says, and now I'm all ears. "I wouldn't have started anything if I did. And I'm not naïve enough not to realize how it must look from the outside." She chews the corner of her lip, adding, "It was never just sex, at least not for me." I don't know why my stomach turns at that last piece of information, but it does. "I guess I just want you to know that I'm not that person. I would never knowingly do something that would hurt someone else." She pauses a beat. "Especially not to someone like Bethany." Half turning, she focuses out the window. She doesn't say anything else, and I'm too busy trying to piece it all together.

"It doesn't make sense," I mumble, more to myself than anyone else.

Slowly, she faces me, and it's clear she's on the verge of tears. "What doesn't?"

"Why isn't it all over school? You'd think Bethany would've told her friends, and they'd tell everyone else."

Jamie blinks once. Twice. "Isn't it obvious?"

I shake my head. "No."

"Because... it would be different if he cheated on her with someone worthy, you know? I'm trailer trash who washes dishes at a truck stop." She laughs, but it's filled with so much sadness it creates a sudden, forceful ache in my chest. I stare at her, right into her eyes, and I can see all the broken fragments of a girl who refuses to see her worth. I've stared into similar eyes my entire life: my mom and Mia. "I can't even imagine her shame," she says, her words uneven. I don't look away, and neither does she, not even when I can see her discomfort set in. "I mean, just look at her... and look at me."

"*I am.*" And then I clear my throat, steady my voice, filling it with enough clarity, so she never has to question what I say next. "And there's not a single piece of me that sees you the way you see yourself."

CHAPTER
EIGHT

HOLDEN

When I got home last night, I stripped out of my clothes, and—for the first time in my entire life—I emptied my pockets.

My mom would be proud.

After we ate, Jamie excused herself to the restroom, and I took the opportunity to collect the balled-up napkins she'd turned into *art*.

The first one she drew was a closeup of the blackberry bushes we'd tended to that afternoon. It was of a single branch with leaves, berries, flowers, and even the thorns. It was, and I don't use this word lightly, *beautiful*.

I don't know how she did it in such a short time or from memory alone, but it deserved to be hung somewhere, displayed and appreciated—not balled-up and trashed.

The second one was just sharp lines with no conclusive image, but she obviously created it from whatever she was feeling emotionally: Anger. Hurt. Despair. *Shame*.

It made me question what she felt when she drew the blackberries.

I laid them both out and slid them in my desk drawer.

Why?

I don't know.

And I refuse to question it.

"So, you went out to dinner?" Dean asks, running on the track beside me during after-school practice. Every opportunity he's had to ask about Jamie, or specifically, me *and* Jamie, he's used it. It's been question after question, and it's pissing me off. Obviously, I don't have a lot to say, just like him prior to yesterday. I never pushed him for more, and I wish he'd give me the same in return.

"It wasn't dinner. It was just... we finished the work, and I was hungry, and she offered to buy me a meal for driving her home."

He almost trips over his own feet. "You drove her *home?*"

I nod, too busy trying to keep oxygen in my lungs to respond verbally.

"I'm surprised she let you see where she lives."

"Why? Because it's in a trailer park?" If he answers yes, I might have to re-evaluate our friendship. As much of an asshole as I can be, even I wouldn't stoop that low. Or maybe that'll be my excuse, because honestly? I'm finding it really fucking hard to look at him without wanting to knock out his teeth, and I don't know if I'd be doing it for Jamie or Bethany or just because he was such a dick to them both. But, I have to remind myself that who he fucks is his business, not mine. And besides, he's never once criticized my—as Jamie puts it—*dick activity.*

"No," he answers through a strained exhale. "Because she's weird about people knowing she lives alone."

My steps falter. "She does?"

"Yeah," he breathes out, turning his head toward me. "You didn't know?"

Obviously not. "It never came up."

"So you didn't, like, go *into* her house?" I know exactly where he's going with this, and I get it. My history with girls is prolific and... temporary, at best.

I don't tell him that he has nothing to worry about because I am me, and Jamie has that one thing that attracts me to most girls—a vagina—but, considering what he did to her, I say, looking directly at him, "What's it to you if I did?"

CHAPTER
NINE

HOLDEN

Jamie stares at me, and I stare right back.

I've concluded that this is how things will work between us until one of us eventually dies. For now, she's better at The Staring Game than I am, so I break first. "What do you mean you don't have suitable attire?"

"I mean…" she says in that annoying *You Idiot* tone she seems to save just for me. "My closet consists of the type of clothes I'm currently wearing." And then she repeats, because she thinks I'm thick, "I don't have suitable attire."

"You don't have *jeans*?" I almost scoff. "Everyone has fucking jeans, Janice."

We're sitting in my truck after school, headed to Esme's house, and she's dressed in her grandma clothes. She did, however, bring gloves. *Rubber* gloves. What the fuck is she thinking?

Sighing dramatically, hands on her lap, she shifts her stare from me to the windshield. And for some dumb reason, I feel like I can actually breathe. "I have one pair of jeans, and I wear them to work, and since I work five to six nights a week, I don't want to ruin them.

Plus, they smell like food mixed with fryer oil and soap." My nose scrunches at the thought, and I don't hide it in time before her eyes move to me. When she notices, she looks away again, and then her voice lowers, wobbles when she adds, "I'll buy jeans for next week, okay? Let's just go."

It dawns on me—a little slower than it should have—that it isn't about the clothes or the gloves. The girl lives on her own, pays everything for herself, and works five to six nights a fucking week. She can't *afford* clothes. And I just brought attention to that. She has every right to use that tone with me because hell, I am an idiot.

Without another word, I put my truck in drive and tell her, "We're going to make a quick detour."

She doesn't respond.

I don't look at her, too afraid of what I'll see.

We make it halfway home when she finally speaks. "Where are we going?"

"My house."

Seconds of silence pass before she asks, "Why?"

I still can't look at her. "I'm going to get you some clothes."

"Your clothes won't fit—"

"My mom will find something."

"Your *mom?*" she practically shouts.

I nod, then peek over at her. She's already reaching into her bag and pulling out that same marker from last week. Then she lifts her skirt just enough to reveal the skin above her knee, where there are already swirls of ink—flowers, mainly, from what I can tell.

Probably too late, I ask, "Is that okay?"

"Uh-huh," she replies, and then she's off, creating more art she plans to get rid of.

My mom lost her job over the summer, which means she's home *all* the time. I miss the days when I could bring girls home after school, do my thing, then have them leave before Mom entered the front door. I'm not naïve enough to believe she didn't know what was happening. The twice-a-week opening of my bedroom door, spraying air freshener throughout the room while simultaneously glaring at me, proves that. Along with her random "I hope you're being careful, Holden" comments.

If we're comparing apples to apples, I'm *almost* at the age when she got pregnant, so as far as her fears go? Justified. Just so we're clear. I'm *very* careful.

By the time we get to the house, Jamie's lifted her skirt halfway up her thigh, and almost every inch of exposed flesh is covered in lines so intricate I want to snap a picture of it so that I can study it later. I don't, obviously, because there's a special place in society for that level of creep, and it's called *prison*. She looks up when my truck stops, her breaths shallow, eyeing the house and the immaculate yard. Her eyes are wide, panicked, and I ask, "You good?"

A quick puff of air leaves her lips before her eyes meet mine. "Is it weird that I'm nervous?"

I shrug.

"It's just—I know you and I… we're not anything. But with Dean, I never met his parents… *clearly*."

I offer a half-hearted smile that I hope comes out reassuring. "You're rambling, Regina. It's fine. Besides, you've kind of met my mom already—outside the principal's office. She's not like other moms. You'll be fine." I start to get out, but she tugs on my arm, bringing me closer.

"Holden, look at me."

I sigh, doing as she asks.

"Do I have dirt on my face?"

"What? No. You look fine."

She scrubs the non-existent dirt off her face. "You didn't even look!"

I want to laugh, but I contain it. "I did."

"Holden, I know you think this is funny."

"You're being a little ridiculous, yeah."

Her eyes drift shut. Stay that way. Angling her chin to the side, she says, almost in a whisper, "Just… look. Please."

So I do. And for the first time, I notice the slight freckles across her cheeks. And then her nose. I notice her fucking *nose*. Because it's little and it's cute, and the tip has a little faded summer-sun peel, and then I notice the other parts of her, like her lips, plump and more red than pink. She has little curls just around her hairline, and she's tanned—naturally—not from hours and hours in the sun, but likely from her bloodline.

"Anything?" she asks, her eyes fluttering open, unfocused, on mine.

Hazel eyes on green, I shake my head, clearing the fog she's created. "You're fine, Taylor."

I start to get out, and again, she stops me. "Do I smell?"

Turning my entire body toward her, I ask, "You want me to *smell* you now?"

She nods but doesn't speak, and I try to read her, try to see if she's just messing with me, but there isn't a single piece of her that's even close to kidding. "Just here," she says, tapping at her collarbone.

I roll my eyes and lean forward, settling my nose in the crook of her neck. And then I breathe her in, and it's the same scent from the first time she was in my truck. Citrus and flowers, only now it's heightened, and I don't know if it's because we're this close—so close, I can feel the heat radiating off her, or because my eyes are shut, and the only thing I can seem to focus on is the rapid beating of my heart.

"So?" she asks, and I don't do what I know I should.

I don't pull back, don't move away. I inhale. Again. "You smell…" *Like my childhood.* Like memories of better days out on an endless green field, when my parents were still together, and my best friend was still my best friend, and we'd laugh and play and didn't have a single care in the world.

"I *smell*?"

I push down the knot in my throat before snapping my eyes open and rearing back. "You smell fine, Florence. Let's go."

• • •

"Is that you, you little shit? Shouldn't you be doing that club thing?" Mom calls from somewhere not visible from one step inside the house.

"I'm not alone!" I shout, holding the door open for Jamie.

"Hi, Dean!"

"It's not Dean!" I respond, closing the door after Jamie. "It's a girl!"

"Well, shit," Mom mumbles, and a chair scrapes, doors open and close, and by the time I go through the living room and toward the kitchen table, Mom's nowhere to be seen.

"Where'd you go?"

"Getting dressed! I'll be out in a second."

"Nudist family?" Jamie quips, and I openly gag at the thought.

"Shut up." I don't tell her that what she could've walked into is the new normal: Mom sitting at the table, working on a puzzle in the same robe she's in almost twenty-four seven. She barely leaves the house, not even to look for a job. And I don't push her. I can't. Because I understand that it isn't forever. Right now, she's just... stuck on being broken.

"Who does puzzles?" Jamie asks, motioning to the table.

"Mom," I answer, walking over to it. "And me, sometimes. It's like, our thing."

"That's... cute."

I don't respond, too focused on the single piece missing from a completed area. I flick my finger through the piled-up pieces and find the right one, putting it in its place.

"I hate when you do that," Mom says, and I look up at her standing in the kitchen doorway, now dressed in shorts and a t-shirt, hair brushed to one side.

I can't help but smile at the sight of her. "Mom, this is Jamie. Jamie, my mom, Tammy," I say, pointing between them.

"It's a pleasure to meet you, ma'am," Jamie says, sounding almost shy.

"Tammy is fine," Mom responds, stepping toward us. "What are you guys doing here?"

Grasping Jamie's shoulders, I push her toward Mom. "She needs clothes."

"What's wrong with the ones she has on?"

"Besides the obvious?" I state. "Grandma's clothes are covered in mothballs."

Mom sighs before scolding, "Don't be a dick, Holden."

Jamie snorts. "I just assumed it was his default setting."

CHAPTER
TEN

JAMIE

They say that social awareness kicks in between the ages of eight and ten. For me, it was two days after my eighth birthday. I only remember this because two days prior, my mother had managed to sneak in a whispered "Happy Birthday, baby" along with a kiss on my forehead. There was no cake, no party, nothing to celebrate the fact that I'd somehow made it that far.

That was the day it was confirmed, though I'd sensed earlier than that something was… *different* about me. If it wasn't the heated whispers from behind open palms from adults, then it was the constant teasing and isolation from other kids.

Looking back, I wished I'd asked *why*. What was it about me that had them doing those things? But I knew, deep down, why I never asked—for the same reasons I never asked Mom about my birth dad. I knew the truth would hurt me, and it did.

———

I was in second grade when I found myself in a random room at my school. The principal was there. So was the school nurse and my teacher, Miss Holland. They were huddled in one corner while a woman I'd never seen before sat in the chair next to mine. There was a single sheet of paper on the table in front of me, plain white, with an outline of a cartoon character I'd seen on the TV the few Saturday mornings I was permitted to watch.

I remember looking down at the paper, fearful of why I was there. Why everyone was there, and I could only come up with one reason.

Earlier that day, I'd been doing the same thing: looking down at a sheet of paper. Only that one was a math worksheet. The worksheet was stained, smudged with dirt, and it took me a moment to realize that the dirt was coming from me. My hands, specifically. Grime coated almost every inch. Darkness pooled on my fingers, especially around and under my fingernails.

I'd looked up and around me, seeing my classmates all busy doing the same work. They sat together on tables made for four, and I sat on my own.

I always sat on my own.

I'd raised my hand, waited for Miss Holland to look up from helping another student. I remember clearing my throat, using my voice for the first time that day. "Miss Holland," I'd said, and I waited for her to make her way to me. I didn't say anything more, I just showed her my hands and then my worksheet.

She'd looked down at me; her lips pulled down in a frown. The same way the strange lady—who I later worked out was a social worker—looked at me. "What color do you think you want to go with, Jameson?" the social worker, who introduced herself as Sophia, asked.

I looked down at the cartoon character, then the plastic cup filled with colored pencils. I didn't have colored pencils at home. When Mom locked me in the closet under the stairs, she only gave me blank pages and black pens—pens with so little ink the lines I'd create would end up fading before I could even finish the drawings.

I flipped the page over and picked out a gray pencil from the cup. And then I drew my own picture. Used my own imagination.

I drew mountains and waterfalls and sunsets and birds free to roam the vast, endless skies.

"It's beautiful," Sophia said. "Have you been somewhere like this before?"

I felt a tightness in my chest as I drew the birds' wings, but I didn't respond. I didn't tell her that the scenery wasn't the focus. I'd just created the backdrop so the birds had something beautiful to look at, somewhere to call home.

I wanted to be the birds.

I wanted to fly.

Far away from everything in the world that kept me grounded.

I drew, and I drew, and I drew some more, and soon enough, the lead was gone from the pencil, and so I picked another color as close to black as possible.

The entire time, Sophia continued to ask questions—questions that were left unanswered.

It wasn't until the she stood up and moved toward my teacher that I stopped focusing on the drawing—or at least pretended to.

My ears filled with their hushed tones and whispered words, and my pulse beat to the only rhythm it knew: fear. Thunder pulsed in my rib cage, echoing off the emptiness inside me. Isolated. And then the Principal spoke, looking directly at Miss Holland, "Neglect is a form of abuse, Alice."

At eight years and two days, I learned two things:

one: Mrs. Holland's first name was Alice, and Alice would be the new cause of Beaker's hatred toward me.

And two: I would forever see myself through the eyes of others.

CHAPTER
ELEVEN

HOLDEN

Turns out, Jamie offered to buy me an early dinner the first time we went to the truck stop because she didn't have to buy anything. Yeah, the food was free, and when I found that out, I made her take me again.

So, that's where we are now, sitting in the same booth as last week, playing what might possibly be my most favorite game ever: The Staring Game.

My phone vibrates on the tabletop, and she flinches just a tad. I hold back my smirk because I know she's about to lose the game in three… two… "Answer your fucking phone."

"No."

"What if it's an emergency?"

"It's not."

"How do you know?"

Because my parents and Mia have specific ringtones. "I just do."

There's no affect in our tones as we sit statue-still, playing The Staring Game. "What if it's important?"

I raise a single eyebrow. "Define important?"

"More important than sitting here staring at me," she answers after a beat.

I laugh once. "Well, when you say it like that..." I still don't look at my phone. Not even when it stops ringing, starts again.

"I'm going to answer it," she says, and it comes out as a threat.

I chuckle under my breath. "Go ahead." Did I mention that I'm really enjoying this game? Because I am. And I don't know if it's because I'm able to scrutinize every one of her features openly, *brazenly*. Or if it's because I like the way she's doing the same. Or, maybe I just really fucking *love* the way she challenges me.

Her focus dips to my phone, then right back up. "It's Emily," she informs, her mouth clamping shut a moment later.

I narrow my eyes at her. "What?"

She shrugs.

"You're holding back, Taylor..."

"Well," she says, leaning forward, elbows on the table, "last time I made an assumption about a girl, you didn't speak to me for a week."

"False," I respond. "At least not intentionally."

She nods. "So... girlfriend?"

I shake my head, continue to ignore the vibrating phone between us.

"Friends with benefits?"

"Minus the friends."

Her lips purse, nose scrunched. "Fuck buddy?"

I nod.

"Are you supposed to be meeting her tonight for a... session?"

Another nod.

Jamie *smirks*, answers the call, and says, "Holden's busy." Then she hangs up, drops the phone to the table, and smiles as though she's just done the naughtiest thing in the world. It's kind of... adorable.

"How does that even work?" she asks, then lowers her voice to a whisper. "A fuck buddy?" Her cheeks bloom pink, and she must realize it because she lowers her head—putting an end to The Staring Game.

"I have rules," I answer.

Her eyes meet mine again. "Rules?" she laughs out, rolling her eyes. "Oh, this'll be good. What are your rules, Master Boner?"

A chuckle forms deep in my chest, in my gut, and I can't hold it back in time. "The rules are simple," I start, counting off each one on my finger. "*I* don't stay the night. *They* don't expect anything more than sex. And *we* don't catch feelings."

She seems to turn this over in her mind for a few seconds before asking, "So… what's the point?"

"The point is *sex*, Doris. Sex is fun. And who doesn't like to have fun?"

"I guess." She shrugs, her nose wrinkling with her response. "I don't know that I'd enjoy it as much without the feelings, you know?"

"But your feelings got screwed right along with your body, so…" I regret it the second the words are out of my mouth, and even more so when she doesn't bother to hide her reaction. Her features fall, eyes hardening, and it's like the moment you realize you've misplaced a piece of a puzzle and everything is wrong, wrong, wrong.

"Sorry," I mumble. I fucked up. Bad.

"It's fine," she says, but her walls are up again, and I didn't even know—until right this moment—that I could differentiate the two vastly contrasting versions of her. After clearing her throat, she looks at me, but not directly. She can't look me in the eyes anymore, and it pisses me off. Not because of her reaction, but because of mine. As someone who creates and lives by rules to make sure I don't hurt anyone, I've hurt *her* of all people, and she doesn't deserve it. "So, your rules…" The bullshit banter is gone, so are the games, the challenges, and now we're making small talk. *Great.* "Girls are okay with it?"

I push down the discomfort forming in my stomach. "As long as I'm honest from the beginning, yeah," I respond, then sit taller because if we're going to make *small talk*, I may as well make it substantial. "Look, girls like sex just as much as guys do, and not everyone wants to fall in love and be in a relationship, so it's just about finding those same people."

"And why not feelings?" And this might be the reason I'm more pissed than I should be. She's obviously not cracking my fucking head open trying to understand *me*. To get to know *me*. She's trying to figure out why Dean was a dick to her.

And sensing that, knowing that, I give her the truth, no matter how much it might hurt her: "Because having *feelings* is a double-edged sword. It's good, and it's bad, and at seventeen, I can't ever promise that I won't give you the bad." And that bad can change the course of your life forever.

I'm proof.

So is Mia.

Jamie bobs her head slowly, but I can tell she still doesn't get it. She doesn't have to. My rules. My life.

After a full minute of neither of us saying a word, I ask, trying to crawl out of the uncomfortable silence, "So, I assume you're not working tonight?"

She's digging through her bag, and a part of me hopes she's going to pull out the marker, but she comes up empty-handed. "No, it's my one night off."

The food is taking its sweet time getting to us, and I don't know how much longer I can sit here. "And you're stuck with me," I murmur.

She offers a smile that reaches her eyes. "You're not *so* bad."

I can't stop looking at her, trying to figure her out. *What's inside that pretty little head of yours, Jameson Taylor?* "How old are you?"

"That's random," she says through a giggle. "I'm seventeen. Why?"

"You're not eighteen?"

"I'm pretty sure I know how old I am."

I pick at a worn spot on the table. "It's just Dean—he mentioned you live alone, so I assumed…"

"Dean talks to you about me?" I *hate* the hint of excitement in her voice. Not because I'm jealous of her and Dean, because why the fuck would I be? It's just... at some point, she has to realize that Dean did a fucking number on her, and the sooner she accepts it, the better off she'll be.

"He just said that one thing. Before that, he refused to say anything."

Nodding, she clamps her bottom lip between her teeth, turning the more-red-than-pink flesh white.

"It must be hard," I add, "having to work so much, plus go to school, all so you can support yourself. I mean, I don't know how I'd survive without my parents. My mom still buys my clothes."

She doesn't respond, and I don't push her. A moment later, our food arrives, and I dive right in, grateful that I have something else to focus on. It has to be at least a few minutes before she answers, "It was just my mom and me."

I look up, surprised, the burger halfway to my mouth.

"When we knew she was close to death but still 'of sound mind,' we filed the emancipation papers."

I drop the burger. "Damn, I'm sorry." And it's only then I realize she hasn't even touched her meal. She's probably been watching me the entire time.

"It's cool. People die all the time."

After grabbing a napkin, I wipe at my mouth before saying, "Yeah, but that doesn't mean..." I break off on a sigh because what the fuck do I know about her situation?

"Look, it's not a big deal," she says, picking up a fry and dipping it in ketchup. "I've been on my own for a long time, even before she died. So..."

She doesn't eat the fry, just drops it on the plate and pushes the whole thing toward me. Then she pulls out a napkin, starts unfolding it, and laying it out in front of her. She's done with talking, and that's fine. I'd rather watch her draw anyway.

"Does your mom have a favorite flower?" she asks, pulling out a marker from her bag.

"Hydrangeas."

"Hydrangeas," she repeats, her lips pursing as she eyes the ceiling, thinking, thinking. And then she blinks, and without another word, it's *go time*. She puts pen to paper, and I swear, it's even more fascinating than the first time.

Captivated, I make a note of the way she holds the pen, the way the muscles in her wrist shift with every movement. The way the multiple mood rings she always wears change color, reflecting off the overhead lights. The way she stops, her nose scrunching when she feels like she's made a mistake. And I watch her hands move so fluidly, so expertly, that it makes me question *exactly* how good those hands of hers are at other things.

"I like hydrangeas," she murmurs, and I don't know if she's talking to me or just talking out loud. "There are approximately seventy-five species in the world, mainly in Korea, China and Japan."

"How do you know that?" I ask.

Her hand freezes, and she looks up. "Huh?"

"I grew up on a nursery. Dad put me to work from the moment I could walk, and since my mom loved them, we'd always have stockpiles of them. And even *I* don't know that random piece of information, so... how do you?"

She shrugs as if it's no big deal. "Books."

"You read books about *flowers*?"

Another shrug before getting lost in her art again. "It was all Gina had."

I don't even bother asking who Gina is. "And you memorized facts about hydrangeas?"

"Not *just* hydrangeas," she says.

"Let me get this straight," I ask, watching as she perfects the shape of the leaves. "You memorized facts about a bunch of flowers that you learned from books because it was all Gina had?"

"Yep," she says, then taps the end of her marker to her temple. "It helps to calm the storm in here."

My breath halts, and I realize now... I have no fucking clue who

78

the girl sitting in front of me is. And worse? I highly doubt Dean did either.

She's like… a riddle.

A paradox.

An incomplete picture.

It's as if she only gives people fragments of herself.

Pieces.

I can't help but smile.

Jameson Taylor is like a puzzle.

And I've always liked puzzles.

Searching for the right piece to fit perfectly in just the right place… it's time-consuming and challenging, but it brings a kind of order to the chaos, and if you put in the effort, the end result is always rewarding. And that's why I do it: for the reward.

And now… sitting opposite Jamie, watching her, I feel like I need to somehow piece her together.

I crack a smile at the thought of my newfound hobby.

Jamie does not.

Instead, she looks up, glares across the table at me. "What's with your face?"

"Nothing."

She hands me the napkin as she stands, pulling the strap of her bag across her torso. "Can you give this to your mom—to say thank you for the clothes?"

"Sure."

I don't meet up with the other girl. I don't give my mom the picture either. I put it in the drawer, along with the other two. Now I have the first three pieces of the puzzle. I just need one more to have all four corners. And then everything else will fall into place.

CHAPTER
TWELVE

JAMIE

The day after the social worker visit, I no longer questioned why I had no friends, why no one sat beside me on the bus, why no other kids even talked to me. It was just as that realization struck—as I was standing a few feet away from the other kids waiting for the bus, looking down at my worn sneakers with my toes poking through the tops—that a gentle hand landed on my shoulder. I looked up at the older woman beside me, from her brown leather shoes to her gray stockings and the plaid skirt past her knees. She wore a blouse, crisp and blindingly white, not a single stain.

She was the complete opposite of everything I was.

Everything I knew.

The woman's gray eyes crinkled at the corners when she smiled down at me. "It will get easier," she said. "I promise."

I shoved my hands deep in the pockets of my coat to hide them. I'd spent all night trying to rid the dirt—the evidence of my so-called abuse. After a phone call from school, Beaker had thrown a wire brush at my head and stood over me while I scrubbed and scrubbed until my cuticles bled and the tears that fell mixed with the crimson staining the water.

When I got off the bus that afternoon, the elderly woman was there again, waiting. "Do you remember me from this morning?" she asked, and I nodded in response. "Can I walk you home?"

I nodded again, and we fell in step, side by side.

"What's your name, sweetheart?"

I glanced up at her. "Jamie," I said. And because I had no idea what was happening or why she was there, I asked her, "Are you my grandma?"

"No, darling." She shook her head, her eyes sad as she took my hand in hers. "But I can be your *Gina*."

CHAPTER
THIRTEEN

HOLDEN

I'm in a mood, and I'm not even attempting to hide it. I'm throwing shit around, cursing under my breath. You know, just being a general asshole. Even Esme's surprise of having her pool fixed and usable, along with her offer of allowing us to use it didn't bring a hint of a smile to my face.

I drop the wheelbarrow I'd been hauling around, maybe a little too carelessly, and it topples over to one side, dumping its contents all over the ground we'd just cleared. "Fuck."

"You're an idiot."

Oh, and I also have to deal with Whiney Wilma and her wise-ass comments. The last thing I need right now is to be in possession of sharp objects, burning alive under the sweltering sun while listening to Jamie tell me how useless I am.

When I don't respond, she asks, "Did your mom like the drawing?"

It's been a whole week since I've seen Jamie in more than just passing, and this is the first conversation we've had that doesn't involve me grunting in frustration and her sighing for the same reason. "Yeah, she liked it a lot," I lie. My mom didn't even see the drawing. It's still sitting in my drawer, waiting for the next piece of the puzzle.

"I started doing a proper one on cotton paper with watercolors, but then I wasn't sure what species she liked best, so…" she trails off, dumping a handful of pulled weeds into the wheelbarrow. "So I didn't know what colors to use, and it's probably stupid anyway, like who the hell am I? Thinking my crappy two-minute doodles are worthy of gift-giving?"

I glance over at her, and unlike the many other times I've done the same, I don't catch her watching me. She's staring off into the distance, chest rising and falling to a steady rhythm. She seems lost, and I don't know how long she's been like this because I've been too fucking consumed in my own superficial misery that I've barely looked twice at her.

"Jamie," I say, and then I stutter a breath when her eyes meet mine. It's strange. When I'm not with her, I barely think of her. But when she is around, and she's this close, she consumes every thought, every breath, every heartbeat. "You should finish it," I tell her. "I'm sure she'd love it." And by she I mean *me*. *I* would love it. "I'm sorry I'm being such a dick."

Her eyebrows rise. "Wow, an apology?" She's smiling a half-smile, but it's enough to pick away at the hardened pieces of me she hasn't yet seen. Until today. After a shrug, she adds, "It's okay. I figure you're just going through something."

"And you're not curious what it is?" We're both on our feet now, facing each other. And The Staring Game doesn't feel like such a game anymore.

"If you want to tell me, you will. When have you ever held back before?" That's true. "But I'm here… if you need to vent or dump your emotional baggage on someone."

"I don't know that your shoulders are strong enough to carry that weight."

"You'd be surprised," she muses, and I have absolutely no doubt she's right.

"We had our first practice game last Friday."

She nods as if she already knows what's coming. "I heard."

"How much did you hear?"

With a grimace, she replies, "I don't know shit about football, but your name's been thrown around, and people seem to be pissed, so…"

"It's not about the fucking game." I sigh, motioning toward a bench in the shade where we keep our water bottles. I lead her there and sit, then wait for her to do the same. "I choked in the last five seconds and lost the game, but I feel like that's all that's been happening with me lately."

"Losing games?" she asks, half turning her body to mine.

I shake my head. "Choking in the last five seconds."

She doesn't respond. And how could she? "None of what I'm saying makes sense. It *barely* makes sense to me, and I'm the one living the lies, putting on the face, the facade, when all I want to do is crawl into the same hole everyone else around me seems to have done. And some days, I just want to fucking break down and beat the shit out of everything, but I can't because it's not *who I am*. And then there's the pressure to be what everyone expects of me. To be a good son, which yeah, I am, but I don't know how much longer I can watch my mom struggle to get out of bed every morning and not shake her and say *I exist too*, because she's so caught up in what happened with my best friend, Mia. And Mia…. our entire lives, I've been her rock, her constant, and when it counted, I failed her. And now Mom wants me to actually work hard in school so I can go to college and get a degree, all because she couldn't because she was too busy growing a fetus. I don't even want to go to college. I don't know what I want to do, what I want to *be*, and it's fucking bullshit that I have to decide right fucking now. Add all that to the fact that my parents can't even *afford…*" I take a breath. "I just—I need… I need…"

"I know what you need," Jamie cuts in, and *holy shit*, I wasn't even aware that I'd said all that, *out loud*, and unleashed all my *feelings*, and to Jamie of all people. Great, now she has way more material on me than I do on her, which means she has the upper hand in this game. It's like I let her peek at my fucking hand, and now she can use it to annihilate me.

"What?" I ask. God only knows what the hell's going to come out of her mouth next.

"A hug."

A burst of laughter emits from deep in my chest. "A *hug*?"

She moves to stand in front of me and motions with her hands for me to do the same. With a heavy inhale and an even heavier exhale, I groan when I get up, raising my arms and rolling my eyes like the petulant child I am. "Fine. Hug me, but it won't help."

"You don't know that," she insists, raising her arms just enough to slide around my waist.

"I'm quashing your expectations now, so you don't get all butt hurt over it."

"Shut up," she says, then adds as she moves in close, pressing her chest to my abs, "Keep your hands in all the safe places." She shifts closer again, leaving nothing between us—no space, no air, no questions, and… no *games*.

Her hands flatten on my back, her cheek pressed against my pecs, and she's closer than she's ever been.

Without thinking, I hold her to me, rest my chin on top of her head. My nostrils fill with her now-familiar scent, and I close my eyes, keep them that way.

"Your heart's pounding," she says, pulling away.

"Wait." It comes out before I can stop it, and I don't know… maybe she has some wicked good superpower, or maybe she just gives good hugs. "Your hugs hit different," I tell her, my eyes snapping open, going wide, because what the fuck? *Your hugs hit different?* Who says that?

"They do?" She rears back so she can look up at me. With her arms still around me, her soft fingers splay across my hard back.

"Yeah," I admit. "I mean, to be fair, it's the first time I've hugged a girl without imagining them naked, so…"

She pulls away, *all* the way away, and I stupidly miss her touch.

And her smell. *Jesus.* "And you're not imagining *me* naked?" She almost sounds disappointed.

"No," I answer truthfully. "Do you *want* me to?"

She shrugs. "Every girl wants to feel attractive, I guess. Even to a manwhore like you."

"You are attractive," I assure.

"Oh, great. A pity compliment. That's where we are now?" she says through a giggle.

"No." I'm shaking my head, laughing with her. "You are, in like..." Shit. How the fuck do I say this? "This kind of..."

"Oh my god, stop. I'm not your type. I get it."

"Honestly, no. You're not."

Her smile falters, just for a second. "Thank God for that, right?" she mumbles, turning to get back to work.

I grasp onto her shirt to stop her. "Wait. That came out wrong."

She faces me, her smile genuine. "Holden, honestly, it's fine. I won't be losing sleep over—"

"What I should've said is that imagining a girl naked is the first and pretty much only thing I do when I'm even touching a girl, but you're... different." Too late, I rush out, "In a good way! And no, you're not my *usual* type because you're not *easy*. And I don't just mean sex, I mean, in general. You're complex and unpredictable and...." I take a breath. Then another. "And I *like* you because you challenge me."

And I like the way you look at me.

The way your eyes hold mine.

The way you can read me without forcing me to be an open book.

After seconds of silently staring at me, she finally says, "Thank you."

And I reply, "You're welcome."

"Nice save, by the way." She starts back toward where we'd been working, and, over her shoulder, she adds, "Should've done that on Friday night. Maybe if you were always that quick on your feet, you wouldn't have choked so badly."

My eyes narrow, aimed at her retreating back. "You're mean."

"No," she says, facing me with a smirk that has every single muscle in my body loosening, my lungs expanding, and my smile widening. "I'm *challenging* you."

I laugh. "Game on, Grandma."

"Kids!" Esme calls out, opening the back door, "someone's here to see you!"

JAMIE

At the sight of Dean standing next to Esme, my breath falters, and it's loud enough that Holden notices. He also notices the way I step closer to him as if *he's* somehow going to protect me from the raging storm I'm suddenly caught in. "You good?" he asks low enough that only I can hear him.

With a nod, I try to shake off the nervous energy causing goose bumps across my flesh. It's different having to deal with Dean at school. Multiple exits make it easy to avoid him, spit a few heated words in his direction, and then carry on with my day as if Dean Griffith doesn't exist. At least physically. But in my mind, he's there, and those thoughts of him are a constant gray cloud looming over me, watching me, *judging* me.

"What's up?" Holden calls out, somehow blocking Dean from my view completely. I pretend to focus on the work I'd been doing while simultaneously trying to level my breathing.

"One of the other teams needs someone with a truck, so I'm letting you loose," Dean answers, and he's closer now, only feet away.

"You *have* a truck," Holden retorts.

Dean makes a hissing sound. "Yeah, the other team is Bethany, and she sure as hell doesn't want me there."

My jaw tenses, while Holden says, "I fail to see how that's my problem." There's a bite in his tone, and I don't quite understand where it's coming from.

"Look, my dad's there waiting to help you lift some furniture, so…" So, Holden has no out, no real reason not to go.

"You couldn't have called with this? Sent a text?" Holden sounds *outraged.* "You didn't have to show up here."

Dean's quiet for so long my curiosity gets the better of me, and I look over my shoulder at him. He's already watching me; his lips turned down at the sides. "I figured Jamie would need a ride home."

I start to protest, but Holden beats me to it. "Jamie's coming with me."

"You have a two-seater, and Bethany will need to go with you to sign off on some shit," Dean replies. He seems to have an answer for everything. "I suppose Jamie and Bethany could share a seat?"

"No," I cut in, my eyes pleading with Holden. "You can go. I'll be fine."

Holden lowers his head, shaking it. "This is bullshit, Dean. Obviously, she doesn't want to ride with you."

"When did you suddenly become an expert on what she wants?" he accuses.

"When *you* paired us together, or did you forget about that?"

"Shut the fuck up, Holden," Dean sneers.

My head spins, trying to catch up with their back and forth.

"Between *us*?" Holden almost shouts. "The fact you're here proves otherwise."

"Dude, what the hell are you doing?"

"You didn't want her, but you don't want anyone else to have her, right?" He scoffs. "I'm taking her with me," Holden says, adamant. "She can stay in my truck, and Bethany can drive herself."

Dean is *pissed.* "What do you think I'm going to do to her? She'll be fine."

I finally find my voice. "*She* is standing right here." That shuts them both up, and it gives me the quiet I need to figure out that Dean had paired me with Holden on *purpose* because he didn't want me with anyone else. But Holden? Granted, they're friends, and even though I'm new to the school, it didn't take me long to work out Holden's reputation when it comes to girls—and Dean *wanted* me with him because…

Because he was so positive Holden wouldn't want me.

89

Just like he didn't want me.

I face Holden. "I'll be fine," I tell him, trying to keep my voice steady. The last thing I want is for him to ruin his friendship with Dean over something as insignificant as me. And I can handle Dean. I've handled much, much worse.

"Are you sure?" Holden asks.

And Dean murmurs, "Jesus Christ."

I nod, keeping my gaze on Holden, who sighs as he removes his gloves. "Let's go clean up."

"Her time's not up," Dean interjects.

Holden *growls.* "I'm not having her out here working alone—or with *you.* She doesn't know what tools to use or *how* to use them."

That's… kind of true. I've shown that I'm a fast learner, but I still need his guidance. I don't think I realized until right this moment how much attention Holden's paid to the details of our interactions.

"Come on," he says, tugging on my sleeve and practically dragging me toward the house, leaving Dean behind. We make it to the laundry room, where he shuts the door after us and turns on the faucet, filling the room with the sound of water hitting cast iron.

Without a word, Holden takes one of my hands in both of his and slowly removes my gloves. It's such a contrast to the first time he put them on me. Back then, he'd been rough, annoyed with my stubbornness to accept his help, and now—now his touch is gentle, intimate almost. His demeanor, however, is the opposite. I glance up at him through my lashes, notice the tightness in his jaw, the straight line formed on his lips, and the angry slashes marring his brow. He's so close; I can feel his body heat radiating from him, the warmth of it floating across my flesh, making my heart pound to an irregular beat.

"You don't have to go with him," he says, his voice low as his eyes meet mine.

"I don't mind."

Shaking his head, he takes a tiny step back. "And I don't mind fighting your battles for you, but—"

"Is that what you're doing?"

"I don't know what I'm doing," he says with a sigh, and I can feel his anger through his inflection. "But your reaction to him was fucking *visceral*, Jamie, and I don't like the fact that you're about to be trapped in his car with no way out." He digs into his pocket and pulls out his phone, tapping it a few times before handing it to me. "Put your number in there." It's an order, and I comply, then hand it back to him.

"I'm going to text you, so you have mine, and if at any stage you feel even the slightest bit uncomfortable, I want you to call me. I'll drop whatever—"

I kiss him.

On my toes, hands flat on his stomach…

My mouth is on his…

And I'm kissing him.

And then I'm not.

"I'm sorry," I rush out, shoving him out of the way to get to the sink. I scrub my hands, my mind, my *heart* clean of all the tarnished pieces of me. I shouldn't have let my emotions drive me, but he was standing there, only inches away, and he was *protecting* me. And while I'd spent my entire life being protected, it was always *during* the vicious storm. Never before and never after.

"Jamie," he says, and I don't look up.

"I'm sorry," I repeat.

"Jamie," he says again, reaching around me to switch off the water. I stare at my hands and nowhere else.

Large fingers curl around my waist, and he turns me to him.

I shut my eyes tight, too afraid to see his face.

Even when he's the one kissing me.

CHAPTER
FOURTEEN

JAMIE

I wait until the warning bell goes off before going to my locker the following day, which I'm aware is entirely *lame*. But the truth is, I'm scared.

I don't want to face Holden.

Or Dean.

Yesterday, just as Holden placed his mouth on mine, the laundry door opened, and Dean was there. He saw what he saw, but he said nothing as he watched us pull apart. And he remained silent the entire drive to my house.

I've been trying to convince myself that I don't care about any of it.

Only I do.

I'm grateful that the locker bay is mostly empty when I arrive, and I rush to throw in my bag and grab what books I need. When I slam the locker shut, I jump back a step, my hand to my heart at the sight of Holden leaning casually against his. "Question," he says, and he's smiling the kind of smile that, no doubt, makes girls stupid. I *may* be one of those girls. It's yet to be determined.

"You're going to be late to class," I tell him.

He shrugs. "What's with the mood rings?"

"*What?*" I almost laugh at how ridiculous the interaction is. Yesterday, his tongue was just parting my lips when Dean interrupted. And now… now he's asking about my jewelry? I look down at my hands, at the four large rings on my fingers, just so I don't have to look at him. Because looking at him reminds me of the way his body felt against mine, first with the hug, and then with the kiss. He was so solid against me, and last night, I went to bed thinking about it. About *him*. About how strong he is… and how that strength had the power to destroy me.

"Is it so you can warn people about what mood you're about to grace them with?" he cracks, pulling me back to reality. "Because you might need to walk around with a giant neon sign to explain what the colors mean."

"I don't think it would help," I tell him, letting my shoulders relax in his presence. I splay my fingers out between us. "See? They're all different colors, anyway."

His eyebrows dip as he inspects them. "So, what's the point?"

I let out a breath, the sudden anguish tainting the smile I'd worn only seconds ago. "I wish I knew."

———

"All right, I'm off," I say through the most dramatic yawn in the history of yawns. It's 11:30 p.m., a half-hour since my shift should've ended.

"Thanks for hanging back," Zeke says, handing me a twenty for the extra time. Zeke owns the truck stop diner named after him and is always super generous when it comes to paying me—and feeding me.

It was almost four years ago that Mom and I randomly popped in for a bottomless coffee that we both inhaled like junkies into our bloodstream. Caffeine, at that point, had become Mom's new addiction—a new bad habit to replace the ones she was trying to kick.

94

We'd been driving around for weeks by then, and we had no real destination in mind. We slept in the car whenever we needed to rest and drove when Mom got restless. Whimsically, we referred to that time in our lives as a Girl's Trip.

In reality, we were running away.

Our first visit here, we hung around for five hours before Zeke asked us if we needed help with anything else. Those were his exact words. *Help*. And I could tell by the look in his eyes that he knew we were desperate for *something*. We just didn't know what. He offered us both jobs, Mom on the floor and me in the back, and so we stayed and found a cozy little trailer nearby that we soon called home. The job didn't last long for my mom. Just like all the other potentially good things in her life, Mom's "bad habit" found a way to ruin it. In the end, once she was gone, I kept my job, and Zeke, so he says, kept me in his prayers.

It seemed that during the few months Mom was able to work here, Zeke had found a soft spot for the woman he affectionally called *Darl*, a play on her real name.

When she died, I caught Zeke by the dumpsters out back and asked him if he ever felt the urge to ask my mom out on a date. From what I knew about Zeke, he'd never been married, never even been in a serious relationship. The diner was his baby, and he spent almost every second of every day there. He stood taller when I asked, his ever-present ball cap on backward, covering his dark hair. After adjusting the sleeves of his flannel shirt, he shook his head, a puff of cigarette smoke emitting from his lips, and said, "Nah, your ma's a sweet lady, but she's one you admire from afar."

"Why not close up?" I'd asked him.

He smiled, but it was so, *so* sad, and I'll never forget what he said next. "Because when you look too closely at anything, you always see the cracks. And your mother was nothing but imperfections."

I hated him at that moment.

And I'd forgiven him the next.

Because he was right, and it made me wonder how people saw me.

While I got my name from my father, I'd gotten all my looks from my mother. But there was one thing that differentiated us. She was shattered into pieces from years and years of abuse, and I... I was just beginning to crack from the weight of the world on my shoulders.

"Do me a favor?" Zeke says now, motioning to the kitchen exit. "Take out the trash before you go?"

"You got it, boss." Hands occupied holding multiple trash bags, I shove the door open with my back. The cool night air fills my lungs the second I step outside, and I make it two steps toward the dumpsters before I freeze in my tracks. I guess of everyone from my past that could show up in a dark alley to accost me, Dean's the lesser of two evils. I'm not even surprised he's here, at the exact place we met all those months ago. He'd pulled in behind the truck stop to empty his bladder, and I'd literally busted him with his dick out. I could tell he was embarrassed, and it was, by far, the least embarrassing thing I could've caught anyone lurking back here doing, so I cracked a joke. "Bathroom's for paying customers only."

He laughed and replied, "Looks like I'll be getting a coffee to go."

He got a coffee, but he didn't go. And even though I was working in the back, he waited for my shift to be over, and then he asked for my number.

And the rest, as they say, is history.

But now? Now... I'm annoyed. And that annoyance comes out of me in a disbelieving laugh.

"What's wrong?" Dean asks, hands shoved in his pockets as he makes his way over to me. Behind him, I can see his truck parked, headlights on low, engine still running.

"Nothing. It's just the last thing Zeke said to me was to take out the trash," I tell him, moving to the dumpsters. "Who knew the trash was already waiting for me out here."

He takes the bags from me and effortlessly throws them into the dumpster. "I always did like your smart mouth, Jamie."

"Really?" I cross my arms, shielding myself from him. "Pretty sure you liked all the *other* things I did with my mouth, but okay."

"Does Holden like it, too?"

"I don't know." I turn around, walk away. "Why don't you ask him?"

"Jamie!" he calls out, grabbing my elbow and spinning me to him. "Are you and he...?"

I raise a single eyebrow.

"Holden isn't right for you," he says, followed by a groan because he knows how hypocritical he sounds right now. "Just be careful, okay?"

I scoff so loud it echoes through the surrounding darkness. "You got some big ass balls to be saying that to me." I mock contemplation. "But then again, I've seen your balls, and they're nothing to write home about."

Even with the little light around us, I can see his jaw working. "When did you become so..." he trails off, his eyes narrowing.

"Jaded?" I ask. "Cynical? Pessimistic? Contemptuous? Pick a word, Dean. Any word!"

"Cruel," he answers after a beat, shaking his head. "You weren't like this when we were together."

"You just answered your own damn question," I mumble, spinning on my heels again. My phone alerts me to a text, the sound slicing through the silence. I'm momentarily surprised because my phone never goes off anymore. I've kept it solely for the alarm. When I slip it out of my back pocket and check the notification, I see that it's a text from Holden.

"It's him, isn't it?" Dean asks, voice low. He almost sounds *hurt*. As if he has the right.

I don't respond. I just keep walking.

"At least let me give you a ride home, okay?" he urges.

I can hear his footsteps nearing. "No."

"Why not?"

I'm so done with these games. So over this bullshit. I turn around so quickly, I almost knock into him. "Do you know that you've never once said sorry to me?" I hate the way the evidence of my heartbreak comes out in the wavering of my words.

"I *tried*, Jamie! When you showed up at school, I tried to talk to you, and you wouldn't even hear me out."

"School?" I ask, dipping my head forward so my ear's closer to him, because what the fuck am I even hearing right now? "High school, right? Not the college you told me you went to."

His eyes drift shut and snap open a moment later. "I didn't want…" he trails off.

I laugh—bitter and full of disdain. "You didn't want me involved in your *actual* life, so you fed me lies. Lies upon lies upon fucking lies. Like when you told me you loved me? Was that a lie?"

"No," he's quick to answer.

I almost believe him.

Almost.

"You had three weeks! From the moment we broke up until I saw you at school. Three weeks, Dean! And you never once—"

"I couldn't," he cuts in. "I was too ashamed over what I'd done to you."

I shake my head, fighting back the liquid heat burning behind my eyes. "Shame? You don't get to have that emotion. In this scenario, I *own* shame!"

His lips press tight, a mannerism I'm all too familiar with. He's thinking of the right thing to say or do next, but nothing will ever be enough. *Nothing.* "I'm sorry."

"No, you're not! You're just sorry you got caught."

"I *am* sorry," he repeats, stepping closer and tentatively reaching for me.

I take a step back.

After a defeated sigh, he says, "I wasn't lying when I told you I love you, Jamie. I do." He takes a breath. "Please, just give me another chance."

"I DID!" I scream. And then I lose it. Completely. I break apart in front of the only person in the world I allowed to see my cracks, see every damaged piece of me. "I gave you a chance!" I shout. "Even after *your* girlfriend came knocking on *my* door, looking for *her* boyfriend, I gave you a fucking chance! And I told you, Dean! I told you to choose. Her or me. And who did you choose?" His silence does nothing to placate my anger, and so I shove him. *Hard.* "Who did you choose?" I cry, pushing him again.

"We both know what happened," he grinds out, trying to keep his balance.

"Say it!" I demand. "I want to hear you say the words!"

"Why?" He sounds as exhausted as I feel.

I tell him the truth. Every pathetic, heartbreaking piece of it. "So I can stop fucking loving you!"

It's strange—how a few simple words screamed into the void can give clarity to the haziness I'd been living in.

Dean broke my heart. A heart he *knew* was barely beating. And it wasn't just about our so-called feelings for each other. It was about *me* —about my inability to trust, to care, to *love*. He knew all the parts of me I'd never breathed a word to anyone else before. And he urged me to confide in him, to reveal all my secrets, my shame, my torment… and then he took all those things from me, along with my fragile heart, and he severed them into

tiny,

irreparable

pieces.

"Say it," I beg, my voice barely audible over the pounding in my eardrums. "Please."

He gives me what I want. What I need. "I chose her."

CHAPTER
FIFTEEN

JAMIE

W hen my mother died, there was no funeral.
No big goodbye.
No shock.

No tears.

One minute she was there, and the next, she was gone.

It was 3 a.m.

I don't know why I wait until the same time to check the message from Holden. After my run-in with Dean, I'd come home, and I did something I rarely allow myself to do: I cried. And I'm not sure what I was crying for or about. I just... felt like I needed to cry. So I did. There were tears and snot and a lot of sobbing into the paper napkins I steal from work. It was a *whole* experience. One I don't plan on repeating anytime soon.

And now, reading Holden's text, I kind of wish I hadn't read it at all.

Holden: *So... what's with the mood rings?*

I take a while to come up with a response—one with enough truth that it can be defined as a solid answer. After I hit send, I crawl into bed, and I let the day's exhaustion consume me. I fall into a deep sleep and dream about stupid mood rings.

The day after Mom died, I found the box beneath the sink with the card addressed to me. There were no words to accompany the card—just my name. The box was filled with dozens of the mood rings I'd grown up watching her wear, alternating between them every few days, sometimes every few hours. They were all cheap, the type that stained your fingers green.

My mom had loved the movie *My Girl*, and the rings were an homage to that love. It was kind of sad, in a way, because if she thought about, *really* thought about it, Vada's stupid mood ring was the reason Thomas J went into that forest in the first place, and we all know what happened to him.

But she had loved those rings, treasured them. Because they were the only things she owned that was hers and hers alone, and so she protected them.

Almost as much as she protected me.

———

There are still remnants of her existence in the place I tried so hard to make our home. Her bed was the first thing I got rid of, followed by her clothes and then everything else. One by one, I took them all to the field behind the trailer park, ignoring the looks of the other residents.

And then I set every single piece of her memory ablaze.

It wasn't until that very moment, as the heat from the flames floated across my cheeks that I realized I was officially an orphan.

And then I smiled. Not because she was dead. But because for the first time in years, I was no longer my mother's keeper.

CHAPTER
SIXTEEN

HOLDEN

Jamie: They were my mom's. They're the only pieces of her I want to hold on to.

The reply to my text came through just after 3 a.m., and it was the first thing I looked for when I woke up.

I try to make sense of it through my morning brain fog, but I can't. And so I read the words, over and over, and every time I do, they lose more and more meaning.

The truth is, I don't even know where to put that piece of the puzzle.

It feels like it doesn't belong.

Superficially, Dean and I are the same as always. On a deeper level, I can tell that he's feeling some type of way toward me. I just don't know what that way is. And now, sitting opposite him in one of our teammate's back yard, I can tell he wants to say something. Even the fire pit burning between us is nothing compared to the amount of heat I'm getting from his glare alone. Tonight he can be found doing only one of two things:

one: downing enough alcohol to kill a small horse.

Or two: avoiding Bethany at all costs.

It's been a shitshow of a Friday night, and since I'm not drinking because I have to be up at the ass crack of dawn to drive Mom to the airport, I, too, have been in my feelings.

Confusion mainly, mixed with a little apprehension. Both things completely unrelated to Dean. Or maybe not. I haven't quite mentally deep-dived into the events of my and Jamie's *barely* kiss. Overthinking it would be pointless and ignoring it would make it seem like I didn't want it to happen.

I did.

I *do*.

And the more I think about her—which, lately, seems to be frequent—the more I want to do it again.

"I'm out," I tell whoever is listening. It doesn't seem like anyone is because no one reacts. I get to my feet; my hand already shoved deep in my pocket to pull out my keys. I make it all the way to my truck parked out on the street when Dean calls out, "Eastwood!"

I freeze with my fingers on the door handle and heave out a sigh. The last thing I want is to deal with whatever he needs to get off his chest. I could leave. Just get in the car and drive away and pretend like I didn't hear him. But that would be pathetic. And kind of ridiculous. And so I square my shoulders before turning around and facing reality. "What's up?"

He waits until he's standing right the fuck in front of me to say, "Have you heard from her?"

He's cradling a bottle of beer to his chest as he attempts to keep the glare in place, but his bleary eyes make it hard for me to take him seriously. "Who?"

"Don't play dumb."

I almost laugh. *Almost.*

"She wasn't at school today, and she isn't responding to my texts."

"She's her own person," I tell him. "If she doesn't want to talk to you, then she doesn't have to."

Lowering the beer to his side, he asks, almost sounding defeated, "What's the deal with you two?"

Now I actually *do* play dumb. "What do you mean?"

Dean's single laugh floats between us, and it's so full of sarcasm, I want to knock the sound out of his mouth with my fist.

"Look," he says, his lids heavy when he looks up at me. "I don't know how well you've gotten to know her—physically or otherwise —but I *know* know her. And trust me, man..." He pauses a beat. "She's way too much for you to handle."

My eye twitches as my fists ball at my sides. He must notice because he takes a step back. "Who the fuck are you to tell me what I can and can't handle?"

He scoffs, bitter, and raises his chin in defiance. "She's gotten to you, hasn't she?"

"No." The lie falls effortlessly from my lips. "Not even a little."

"Holden, is that you?" Mom calls out the second I step foot in the house.

"No, it's Santa Claus!"

"Smartass."

I shut the door behind me. "Where are you?"

"Bedroom!"

I make my way over, pausing at the doorway when I see her packing a small suitcase.

"I thought you were at a party tonight," she says, her gaze flicking to mine quickly before focusing back on her task.

"I was," I respond. "It was lame." Then I slump down on the edge of her bed next to a pile of her clothes. She's only going for a few days, so I don't know why she needs all this. I look up at her, and for the first time in what seems like forever, I catch her smiling. "I didn't want to stay out too late since I'm driving you to the airport."

Her hands pause mid-fold, eyes trailing to mine. "I didn't tell you?" she starts, and I can hear the hesitation in her voice. "Joseph organized for a car to pick me up."

I hold back an eye roll, fight back the anger brewing deep, deep, deep inside me. "Of course, he did," I murmur.

"Holden." It's a single word—my name—but when she says it like this, it carries the weight of a thousand meanings.

What do you mean, Holden?

You're being unreasonable, Holden.

It's not what you think, Holden.

She throws the dress she'd been folding into the suitcase and sits down beside me, her entire body turned to mine.

"It's not like that, *Holden*," she says, but her smile says otherwise.

Joseph is Mia's dad, my mom's ex, aka, the man I *hate*. "I don't like the guy," I state, even though she already knows this.

Mom sighs. "That's all in the past."

"Is it, though?" I ask, facing her completely. "Because he's paying for your flights and rides to the airport, and—"

"It's all for Mia," she cuts in. "What do you want me to do?"

"Not fall for his bullshit." I'm quick to answer. But I know it's too late. I was there the moment they saw each other for the first time in seventeen years. I saw the spark in their eyes, heard the gasps catch in their throats. It was like they saw a ghost. Which is—in a way— exactly what Joseph is. A ghost from her past... set out to haunt her for all of eternity.

Eighteen years ago, he bailed on her, and a year after that, he did the same thing to his newborn daughter. And he's going to do it again, and I can't fucking comprehend why my mom can't see that, why she thinks this motherfucker walks on water.

I drop my gaze to the worn carpet. "You're smiling, Ma, and I haven't seen you smile in a long time, and I know it's not the excitement to see Mia because there's nothing *good* about what she's going through right now, so... just..." I take a breath, trying to settle my thoughts. I know that, in reality, my mom can do whatever she wants. But there's no fucking way I'm just going to sit by and watch her ruin her life. "Just be careful, Ma."

Mom's quiet for so long, an unease settles at the pit of my stomach, turning, twisting. I gather my strength and glance over at her.

Tears well in her eyes, and I'm quick to look away. "Ma!"

She sniffs once. "When the hell did you grow up, kid?" And then she sobs, and I rush to my feet, start for the door.

"Ma, you know I don't do crying girls," I whine.

"Holden!" she calls out, and I freeze in her doorway but refuse to turn around. I *really* don't do crying girls. "I don't have a lot to show for the life I've lived," she says. "But I have you. And I'm proud of myself for raising you. For creating a man who loves as hard as you do, and protects the ones he loves with everything inside him." Her single exhale fills the room, fills my lungs with some much-needed clarity. "I've made some pretty shitty choices in life, and I'll probably make even shittier ones in the future. Just... promise you'll never stop loving me the way you do?"

My shoulders drop as I suck in a breath, then force myself to face her. Moving closer, I ignore the redness of her nose, the tremble of her lips. I look past the tears soaking her cheeks, and I kiss her there, just once. "I promise," I tell her. And then, because I don't do *deep* just as much as I don't do *crying*, I shove her suitcase off the bed, emptying its contents to the floor. I start for the door again. "Go to bed. You have to be up early."

Mom's single sound of laughter feels like a missing piece to a puzzle. The problem? I have no idea what the complete image will be.

CHAPTER
SEVENTEEN

JAMIE

I don't have a lot in my trailer. Most of the furniture was already here when we moved in. There's a couch that once doubled as my bed, a coffee table, and a TV that we found in the same field where I burned all memories of my mother.

My bed is the only things that's new. The only thing in my life that I bought just for me. When we moved in, the walls were covered in horrid wallpaper. It took Mom and me three weeks to peel it off and replace it in blindingly white paint. We had some leftover, so I painted whatever furniture I could the same white as the walls. My mom said it looked like a room in a psych ward, but I didn't care. I like the white. White reveals all the dirt and the dust and all the other things I've spent years trying to cleanse from my existence.

Saturday mornings, I do just that: rid my world of impurities, and my body of shame. I dust every piece of furniture, wipe down every surface, clean every inch of flooring, and then wash every piece of clothing I own. I iron out every crease, polish every button.

And I continue to ignore that ache in my chest when thoughts of Gina make their way through my mind, my heart.

. . .

The *Zeke's Diner* paper bag sits on my lap, the warmth of it coating my thighs. I grip it tighter when we go over a bump in the road, my head knocking against the bus window. It takes twice as long to get to my destination than what I'm used to, so by the time I get off at the stop, I have to gear myself up for the one-mile walk under the scorching sun.

When I finally make it to the house, every single inch of me is covered in sweat. I don't even want to know how I look. Or smell. And I should've really called before I came because now that I'm here, standing at the front door, I realize that not everyone spends their Saturdays stuck in the house until they're forced to leave.

Sighing, I raise my fist, knock twice. It takes only seconds for the door to open. Esme's eyes are wide, her smile as warm as the sun currently burning me alive. "This is such a lovely surprise," she says in greeting, ushering me inside the house. The air conditioner pricks at my flesh, does wonders for my lungs as I take in a sharp inhale. Esme adds, "Did you plan this?"

I face her once the door is closed and shake my head. "I just thought I'd come by for a visit." It's only a half-truth. After completing my Saturday morning routine, I sat on the couch, staring at the blank television, lonely and afraid. And before I allowed a single tear to escape, I got up, got dressed, and headed to the one place I could think that would take away both those things.

I used to go to Gina's.

And now I'm here.

I lift the bag from Zeke's. "I brought some cakes and desserts from my work," I say, hating the slight wobble that comes with my words. "I thought we could sit and... chat?"

"Well," she says, rubbing her hands together, "it's almost lunchtime, so why don't I make us some sandwiches first."

After a nod, I follow her toward the kitchen. "You should get Holden," she says over her shoulder.

I wave off the idea with a flick of my wrist. "Oh, I'm sure he's busy," I tell her, at the same time she says, "He's out in my Wesley's workshop."

Holden is exactly where Esme said he'd be, standing in front of Wesley's workbench with three large containers set out in front of him, each one containing some form of clear liquid. In workout shorts and a loose gray tank that shows off his large arms and solid chest, he looks like… like it shouldn't matter how he looks.

Still unaware of my existence, he inspects the shears in his hands, rusted beyond repair, before dumping it in one container and moving to the next tool, and I realize I'm staring. *Shit.* Finally finding my voice, I manage a "Hey."

His focus snaps to me standing in the doorway, sweating twice as much as I was on the walk here. I hadn't expected to see him, and it's the last thing I want.

Maybe.

"Hey," he says, his eyes trailing me from head to toe, and it's only now I realize that I'm not dressed the way he usually sees me. I swipe my palms along my simple summer dress, just as he says, "What are you doing here?"

"I just came to visit for a little." He nods at that, then goes back to the tools, and I shift on my feet, telling him, "Esme's making lunch. She asked me to get you."

It's *awkward*. For me, at least. I don't know how he feels, but going by the way he drops the tools, silently moves toward me, and then *around* me, I suspect he feels the same.

All we did was share a *moment*; I remind myself. A single, insignificant moment, and then I made it worse by revealing a cryptic piece of my past—*pathetic*—and now he's here and seeing me might be the last thing *he* wants.

Maybe.

If he wants to act as if it never happened, then good.

Great, even.

"So you just came here to *visit*," Holden says skeptically, peering over his shoulder at me. He slows his steps, waiting for me to catch up with him.

I offer a shrug. "I brought some cakes and—"

"Did you bring that lemon—" My nod cuts him off. "Did you know I was going to be here?"

"No. What *are* you doing here?"

He shrugs, holding the back door open for me. "I came to fix some tools we'll need to... wait—you really didn't know I was here?"

"Not a clue," I say, releasing a disbelieving snort before I can stop it. "As if I'd come because of you."

He smirks, leans in closer. And I really should've known what was coming before he even opens his mouth. "Give it time, Trudy. We've *barely* even kissed."

CHAPTER
EIGHTEEN

JAMIE

Holden won't stop staring, and I... can't stop staring back. But there's something different in the way he's looking at me. Gone is the emptiness that once lived in his eyes, now replaced with heat so intense I can feel the warmth of it pumping through my veins.

I wish Esme were here as a buffer, but I'm shit out of luck. She had a friend from church drop by unannounced and ask if she wanted to go to bingo. Holden and I were so happy and proud that Esme had found the courage to put herself out there and make friends that we rushed to get her ready and practically pushed her out the door of her own house. After we waved her goodbye from her front porch, Holden helped me clean the kitchen, and I helped him lock up the workshop—tasks that took all of ten minutes—and now we're here, standing poolside, staring at each other, completely wordless.

I know we should talk about what happened. It's the mature thing to do... I can't keep avoiding, and he's obviously done with pretending. But I don't *want* to. In fact, I'd rather stick forks through my eyeballs. "Well, see ya!" I finally break the stare and start marching toward the side gate. I make it two steps before Holden grasps my messenger bag by the strap, tugging it loose from my shoulder until it falls to the ground. I look up, eyebrows bunched. "What the fu—" That's all I can get out before his arms are around my waist, and I'm flying through the air, *squealing*, arms and legs flailing until I'm surrounded by nothing but cool water.

My feet hit the bottom of the pool, and I almost kick off and come to the surface. But then I hear him laughing—*like a jackass*—and now I'm pissed. So, I make a show of coming up for air, waving my arms some more. "Holden!" I gasp, slapping the water's surface with open palms. "I can't swim!" I duck under the water again, flapping my limbs around aimlessly. I'm still beneath the surface when he curses, and I smile when I see how swiftly he kicks off his shoes, removes his tank top, and empties his pockets before diving in.

I come up for air, and now I'm the one laughing—also *like a jackass* —especially when his head pops up, eyes searching. "That's what you get!" I laugh out, splashing water in his face.

His eyes narrow… right before that wicked smirk of his makes an appearance. "You better run, Regina."

A restrained squeal erupts from my throat, and I turn toward the pool edge, and start swimming for it. But I forgot Holden is an *athlete*, and I've barely ever been in a pool. He catches up to me effortlessly, his hands going to my waist again. He spins me in his arms until we're chest to chest, his eyes right on mine. Flecks of emerald spark against the raging sun, and he walks us to the pool wall. With one arm snaked around my middle, he rests the other on the smooth brick border, and says, "Hi." And then he smiles—and that smile is a spark, a flicker of light on the darkness inside me.

I both love and loathe it.

I *cannot* be crushing on Holden Eastwood. That would be ludicrous. And dangerous. And *fun*. I push that last thought aside, my voice barely audible when I say, "Hi." And then my treacherous little hands find their way up to his bare shoulders.

Losers.

He's so hard beneath my touch, so solid, so strong.

"Hey…" He moves closer again, his lips kicking up before he says, "Remember when you kissed—"

My eyes snap shut, and I'm so quick to lower my entire body, head and all, under the water just so he doesn't see the evidence of my embarrassment staining my cheeks. It's one thing to be somewhat attracted to Holden. It's another for him to *know it.* Oh, the games he could play.

Even through the sounds of the water rushing around me and my pulse pounding in my eardrums, I can hear his stupid chuckle. And, because I don't feel like dying today and need this ridiculous thing called *oxygen* to survive, I come up for air and face reality.

And reality is a boy currently shaking droplets of water from his hair, causing it to fly in all directions. After scooping water in his hands, he runs them both through his hair, leaving lines of liquid gold in his wake. "You didn't let me finish." He laughs out, his hand finding my waist again. "You apologized right after. Why?" I must imagine the hurt that flickers across his features. "Do you regret it?"

I should push him away.

I should adjust the way the bottom of my dress rides up my torso.

I do neither.

Eyes wide, like *this should be obvious,* I tell him, "Because you literally just got done telling me I wasn't your type, and then I practically accosted you in—"

"*Accosted?*" He shakes his head, eyes dropping to my cleavage.

"Perv!" I release his shoulders so I can push him away, but he's a solid wall. A statue. "Do you have the time?" I ask, changing the subject. "I need to work today, so…"

He drops his hand from my waist when he rears back, and I'm suddenly cold. Not just from the water but from his lack of touch. "What time do you have to leave?" he asks, adjusting the fancy watch on his wrist.

"The bus comes at three."

He taps his watch a few times, then says, "I'll give you a ride."

"You don't have to—" I start, but he cuts me off.

"You work too much." He sighs, shifting closer. "Don't you ever just want to be a kid?"

God, what I wouldn't give… "I don't know," I tell him honestly. I've thought about what I'd reveal to him, should our conversations ever get deeper than they have, and I still haven't come up with an answer. "I've never really been a kid." It's more than I expected to give him, and I hope it's enough. For now, at least.

His head tilts to the side, eyes assessing. "What do you mean?"

My gaze drops to the little space between us. "You know what?" I say. "You're right. I *do* want to be a kid, at least until I have to go to work." And because I don't have the courage to face him, I move away, floating on my back toward the other end of the pool. He follows, of course, walking swiftly beside me. "Question," he states, and I settle with my head against the wall, hands gripping the edge of the pool. Legs kicked out in front of me, I squint to fight off the sun beaming down on me. He asks, "How does the whole emancipation thing work?"

I peer over at him and give him a half-hearted shrug. "You just have to explain your situation—dying mom and no other family, in my case—and then you have to prove that you're financially able to take care of yourself and not rely on government handouts."

"That's it?" he asks, and I nod. "And you can do that? I mean, prove you can support yourself?"

I nod again.

"So… you've saved up enough money from working at the diner…" He sounds skeptical. I would be, too.

"Not really," I tell him. "But Zeke vouched for me, said I'd always have a job if I needed it."

"You wash dishes, right?" he asks

My eyebrows bunch as I glare at him, confused as to where the hell he's going with this.

He's still standing beside me, his gaze switching from my legs to my face, skipping all the parts in between. "Wouldn't you make more money being a server? You'd at least get tips that way."

I snort, drop my feet to the pool floor and hold my dress down beside my thighs. "Why are you so obsessed with my finances?"

He laughs once, moving an inch closer. "I'm not, Nora. It's just that you work so many hours, and it doesn't give you a lot of time to do anything *fun*."

Fun? There's that word again. I raise my eyebrows. "I'd hate to think of what your definition of fun is."

He steps closer again. "What if I invited you to watch my football game?"

"Why the hell would you want *me* there?" I scoff.

He rolls his eyes. "Fine. What if I invited you to a party or something?"

My nose scrunches at the thought.

He chuckles, low and slow. "Or what about a *date*?"

Now I'm the one laughing, loud and unrestrained.

He pokes at my side. "What's so funny?"

"You?" I say, pointing at his chest. "Taking a girl on a *date*?"

"I date," he states, matter-of-factly.

Well, color me shocked. "You do?"

"Yeah, if I like a girl, then we *date*, Deloris."

"Ah, so the sexcapades are just for the times in-between."

He's watching me, staring again. "Pretty much, yeah."

There's one thing about Holden that I'm utterly jealous of: his ability to not give a shit about what people think of him. I find it fascinating. And admirable. "Huh."

"So?"

I glance sideways, then back at him. "So... what?" I hesitate to ask.

His exaggerated eye roll makes me giggle. "What if I asked you on a date? Could you get time off work?"

I sigh, give in to the truth—even though it'll hurt me. "You don't want to date me, Holden."

Clearly perplexed, he stands right in front of me, his hands finding my waist again. "Why not?"

Because I'm so many levels of fucked-up, he can't even begin to comprehend. I don't tell him that. *Obviously.*

At my non-response, he says, "You know Dean said something similar." My gaze drops, and he bends his knees, ducking, so I have no choice but to see him. "He said that I wouldn't be able to *handle* you."

I hate the weakness in my voice when I tell him, "He knows you better than I do, so maybe he's right."

"Hmm," he says. Then adds, "And he knows *you* better than I do, right?"

"I guess."

Holden shakes his head, then cracks the tiniest of smiles. "Hey, remember when you kissed me?"

I roll my eyes, a short laugh bubbling out of me. "We're back to this again?"

"I'm pretty sure I said that I *liked* you because you were complicated."

"Yeah, right before you said that you like the way I challenge you." I find the courage to look up at him, right into his eyes. "Is that what I am to you—a challenge you have to win?"

"God, you're annoying," he almost *growls*, his arms tightening around me, leaving nothing between us. "Why are you like this?"

This time, my laughter comes from pure nerves. "I wish I knew."

"Well, knock that shit off." And before I can stop him, his hands are gripping my thighs, forcing them apart so he can settle between them.

I instinctively wrap my legs around his torso while he presses into me, and I can *feel* the effects I'm having on him, feel his hardness bear down on my center. My entire body flushes with heat, my eyes drifting shut at the contact.

Without actually kissing me, Holden presses his lips to my shoulder, then up my neck until his mouth's at my ear. "Whenever you're ready to beg me to bend you over that workbench and *bone* you, just let me know."

"Shut up," I laugh out.

His shoulders shake with his chuckle as he holds me tighter.

"Hey, Holden?" I say because I can't seem to *shut up*, either.

Lips on my jaw—so, so close, he croaks out a "Yeah?"

"You're hugging me."

He runs his nose along mine, lips skimming my mouth, his heated breaths falling shallow against my face. "I'm well-aware."

I tug on his hair, pulling him back until his eyes settle on mine. And then I smirk. "Are you thinking about me naked yet?"

He laughs under his breath, his mouth on the crook of my neck again. I run my hands through his hair, eliciting a moan from deep in his throat. I *feel* the sound in areas I'm too ashamed to admit. "Actually," he states, moving from my neck to my ear. And then his fingers dig into my thighs as he says, "I'm wondering what these thighs would feel like pressed against my ears while I slowly lick the entire length of your pussy." He pulls back, eyes half-hooded. And then he blinks.

Once.

Twice.

And just like that, the moment's gone.

Holden drops my legs, and I drop the idea of what *fun* could mean. He looks at his watch just as the alarm goes off. "But we don't have time right now, so…"

He hops out of the pool and then offers me his hand. Once upright and poolside, he keeps me close, eyes holding mine, searching, right before he asks, "Did the shit with Dean make you afraid to try again?" He shakes his head quickly. "Not necessarily with me, but just in general?"

The single act of shrugging reveals my truth.

He sighs. "He broke your heart, didn't he?"

"Yes," I admit. "He kind of annihilated it."

Holden sucks in air through his teeth but keeps his eyes on mine. "You know they say time heals a broken heart…"

"They say that, huh?"

He releases me to make a show of cracking his knuckles. "Time can heal broken arms and legs, too, Jamie." His lips form the slightest hint of a smile. "You just say the word and I'll finish that motherfucker for you."

CHAPTER
NINETEEN

HOLDEN

Jamie doesn't say a word on the drive back to her house. She does, however, draw. With a black pen pressed to her thigh, she makes magic with her fingers. I almost veer off the road multiple times because I'm too fucking focused on her, and she's too focused on her task that she doesn't even realize we're at her house until I practically slam on the brakes.

Driving was a distraction, and the sooner I stopped, the more I could watch her. But now we're here, and she's pushing her dress down, throwing the pen back in her bag, and it would be crazy of me to beg her to keep going, right?

Before I can contemplate it, she's opening the passenger door and turning to me. "Did you want to come in?"

Only if you keep drawing. Clearly, I need to get out of the part of my brain that she seems to have overpowered.

I get out of the truck and meet her at the front door, where I watch her slide in the key, turn it, yank at the handle, kick at the bottom, and then finally push that fucker open.

The inside of her house is... white. And immaculate. And

completely clutter-free. Not at all what I had pictured the few times I let my mind go there. There's a small living room with a couch, a white coffee table, and a TV on a bookshelf—also white. The kitchen's on the left, and to the side is a hallway, which I assume leads to the bedroom and bathroom. The space is compact, but it's more than enough for one person. I wonder for a moment how it felt when her mom was around.

The house gets blanketed in darkness when Jamie closes the door behind us, then flicks on the light switch. Nothing happens. "Oh, no," Jamie says, flicking the switch on and off a few times. "I swear I paid the bill," she murmurs, and my stomach sinks as I watch her use the flashlight on her phone to go to the kitchen. She pulls out a folder from a cabinet, and I go to part the curtains. No light comes through because a piece of cardboard covers the entire window.

The cardboard, too, is white.

"Too many creeps around," she mumbles, and she's too distracted by whatever she's doing; she doesn't seem to notice the visceral reaction I have to that one statement. "I knew I paid it," she almost yells, and then she just stands there, in the dark, her figure only half illuminated by the light of her phone.

"Maybe it's a mistake," I offer. I don't really know how this shit works. The only times I've even looked at a bill was when I went through Dad's finances at the farm to make sure he could make it through another season.

"It's never happened before," she says, and I wish I could go to her, comfort her somehow, but I've never really been *that* guy. At least, not with anyone besides Mia. Dean is that guy. But Dean is also a dick, so... "Shit..." She grabs her keys from the kitchen counter and marches back toward me, grabbing me by my arm, before leading me to her front door. She turns and yanks on the doorknob three times before it finally swings open, and *Dean* should've fixed the fucking door for her.

By the time we get outside, her nails are digging into my forearm, but she's so clearly pissed, I'm afraid to even mention it. "Stop me from killing him," she says over her shoulder, stomping through the trailer park and past a group of trailers way beyond their life expectancy.

"Killing who?" I ask, wincing when her fingernails dig deeper. I can't even imagine how we must look. Me at 6'4" and her at *tiny*— dragging my gigantic ass across the dry, dirt ground. She stops at a trailer at the front of the park and slams her fist on the door. "Calm down," I tell her, and if looks could kill… she just knocked me out with a single glare. And also maybe gave me a half-chub because Angry Jamie is insanely hot. I'll be sure to tell her. Later. When my life or the life of whoever is on the other side of that door isn't in question.

A guy in his mid-thirties answers, dressed in boxer shorts and what I'm sure was once a white tank top. "'Sup, Jamie?" he says. "Got rid of that preppy asshole, I see." His gaze drops to her tits, and I take a step forward.

"You shut off my power, Jayden?" Jamie sneers.

Jayden shrugs, pulls a cigarette from behind his ear, and sparks it. Through a ribbon of smoke, he says, "And water."

"Why?"

"You were short on your rent."

"It was twenty dollars!"

"Still short."

I pull out my wallet and hand him a fifty. "Here, turn it back on."

"Holden!" Jamie yells, but the guy's already taken it from me.

"Can't," he says. "Maintenance is out until Monday morning. I'll make sure he gets to it first thing." He slams the door in our faces.

Jamie turns to me, that glare in place, arms crossed over her decent rack. "You just gave him fifty dollars."

"I know."

"Don't fucking do that again, Holden!" She's *beyond* pissed, and now she's storming back to her house, dirt flying with each one of her stomps. "I don't need you or anyone else saving me."

I tell her, "It's just money. You'll pay me back."

She spins on her heels so fast I almost knock into her. "That's not the point!"

Oh, God, she's about to cry. I cannot see her cry. I clear my throat, stand taller. "You're very pretty." *What the fuck is wrong with me?*

"What?"

"I mean, you're insanely hot when you're mad like this... but... but you're pretty always." *Shoot me. In the head. Right now.* "I just thought you should know..." *Jesus Christ. Stop talking. Stop talking. Stop talking!*

Big hazel eyes, blink, blink, blink. Again and again. Until the tears are gone. *Thank God.* "Well... thank you."

I shrug, my muscles loosening with relief. "You're welcome."

She starts walking again, this time with more reasonable steps. "I mean it, though, don't do that again."

"Okay," I say.

"And I'll pay you back."

"Okay," I repeat.

Back at her house, she walks through the darkness, down the hallway, and into her bedroom, and I follow because... to be honest, I'm still sporting that half-chub, and her dress is still damp, clinging to parts of her I've thought about way too much since she kissed me, and I kissed her back.

She uses her phone as a source of light while she goes through her drawers, and I take a moment to look around the room, using my phone for light. Like the furniture out in the living room, the bed is white, wrought iron with brass toppers on the corners. It's so lush and fancy and seems so out of place; it makes me question who she *really* is. If you take away the reality of her situation, is this the kind of stuff she'd like to surround herself with? The sheets, too, are white, and I sit on the edge of the bed, run my hands across the soft material. There's a small dresser with a mirror—guess what color—and on the dresser is the only thing in the room that isn't white. It's a small box, most likely for jewelry, made of dark wood, with a carving of a single flower. A dahlia if I'm not mistaken.

She drops her clothes on the bed beside me, the black garments a complete contrast to *everything* else. "I have to get dressed," she states, standing in front of me.

"Who's stopping you?" I challenge, but she's clearly not in the mood. I sigh, thinking about my next words for all of a millisecond. "I'm about to do something insanely creepy here, and I'm going to need you to let me. And in return, I'll let you hold it against me for the rest of my life."

Her eyebrows shoot up. "The rest of your life?"

I nod, then settle my hands behind her thighs, bringing her between my legs.

"Holden," she warns.

"Relax, Jamie," I mumble, eyes on hers as I bring my hand to the front of her leg, just under her dress. "If I was going to finger fuck you or taste between your legs, I'd have done it at the pool."

"You're so crass," she states, but there's not even a hint of disgust in her tone.

"Yeah, and you're not the slightest bit mad about it, are you?" I lift her dress, slowly, so slowly, loving the way her muscles tense beneath my touch, the way her breaths become short, ragged. Her forearms land on my shoulders, and I dip my head forward, just under her breasts, and I breathe her in: *sunshine and solace.*

"Creep," she whispers, and she has no idea.

I grab my phone, open the camera app, and take a picture of her thigh, of her art. Of her masterpiece. She's drawn the profile of a girl's face, a girl so similar to herself. Large flowers with matching leaves cover the back part of her head, where her hair should be, both in front and behind the figure, and it's… "It's beautiful, Jamie." I pull back, release her completely, and try to maintain some form of composure. I don't know what it is about this girl and her art that has me so drawn to them both. I clear my throat, push aside all those thoughts. "You're taking art, right?"

"Yes," she says, stepping back. She stares down at her hands—such dainty, gifted little things.

"Is that what you plan on doing? Like at college, or career-wise?"

Shifting from one foot to the other, her words are quiet when she says, "Not really. I draw as an escape and sometimes as a necessity." Her nose scrunches, shifting the freckles on her cheeks. "But it's not

125

really a passion or something I want to do for the rest of my life. Besides, I don't know if I'm good enough."

"Jamie." I make sure her eyes are on mine when I tell her, "If you never believe a single word I speak ever again, believe me when I tell you that you *are* good enough." She stares at me with blank confusion. "I mean it," I say, getting animated. "I've never once looked at a piece of art and felt *anything*… and when you do it, it's like… like…" How the fuck do I even describe what it's like to need to rush home from school just so I can open my desk drawer and peek at her work? "It's like feeling everything all at once…"

… And then nothing at all.

CHAPTER
TWENTY

JAMIE

"Do me a favor?" Zeke calls out, standing in front of the grill gripping a spatula.

"I already got it!" I reply, closing the trash bag and collecting the two that are already there.

"See you tomorrow?"

Like I'd be anywhere else. "Of course."

The moment I step out of the diner, I'm blinded by headlights aimed directly at the door. I block it by raising the bags in my hands and keep walking toward the dumpster. "Jamie!"

I instantly recognize the voice because it's one I've spent the past six hours replaying in my head. I lower the bags, and Holden comes into view, dropping from the hood of his truck. "You stalking me now?"

"Only in your fantasies, Taylor," he says, slowly approaching me.

"How long have you been waiting here?" In a way, I'd expected him to be here. I'd spent my entire shift thinking about all the ways I'd tell him how I feel about him trying to fix my problems. I put it all down to words and organized those words in an order that would make sense. In my head, I went through this entire conversation numerous times, and now that he's here, standing right in front of me, I can't seem to find a single one to say to him. "I'm scared" wouldn't work because then I'd have to explain that fear. And while my fear is simple, the reasons behind it are not. I never want to get to a point in my life where I have to rely on someone to fix me. To *save* me. My mom gave Beaker that power, and in return, he abused that power as much as he abused her, physically and emotionally.

"Like, five minutes. I called the diner. Zeke told me what time you finish. Nice guy." He takes a breath. "And I'm picking you up," he says as if it's the most obvious thing in the world. He takes the bags from me and throws them in the dumpster, then just stands there with a goofy grin splitting his face in two. "And then I'm taking you back to my place."

I'm quick to shake my head. "The hell you are."

His smile drops. "You're kidding, right?"

"Not even a little."

"You honestly think I'm going to let you stay in your house with no power or water when you distinctly told me that there are—and I quote—*too many creeps around?*"

Shit. I did say that. But still—it doesn't explain why he's here, and maybe I'm reading it wrong, or reading too much into his kindness, but... *ugh*. With a heavy sigh, I reach into my pocket and pull out the fifty Zeke had given me as an advance. I slam it on his chest, wait for him to take it before dropping my hand. "You can't do this, Holden."

He scoffs, eyes narrowed and right on mine. "Do what *exactly*?"

"You can't just show up all Captain-Save-The-Day," I sneer, stepping around him, ready to start my walk home.

"I can't be *nice*?" he shouts at my back.

"Nope!" I yell over my shoulder. "Not with me!"

"Why not?"

I'm angry. And frustrated. Not at him, or because of him, but for so many other fucked-up reasons. And those reasons are either dead or creating another illegal concoction of high-end drugs in his basement laboratory. Neither my mom nor Beaker exists in my life anymore.

But Holden does.

And Holden's here.

And so I take that anger and frustration out on him. I spin on my heels and face him. "I don't need you to save me, Holden!"

"So, you've said," he says, his voice low, a complete contrast to mine. He takes a wary step forward, and then another.

I pull away, my pulse pounding in my ears.

"What the fuck is your problem, Jamie? I'm just trying to help."

"I don't want your help!" I take a moment to breathe, push back the tears of defeat threatening to fall. "I don't know how many ways I can tell you that until you get it through your head." His eyes narrow, lips parting, ready to say something, but I don't let him. "I'm not that girl, and—"

"What girl?"

"—stop looking at me like that!"

"Like what?" Now he's pissed—his balled-up fists and tight jaw proof.

"Like you pity me!"

"Oh my god," he murmurs, hand rising to grip at his nape.

I flinch at the movement—an instant reaction. Luckily, his eyes are closed, and he doesn't notice the split second of fear that locked up every muscle, blurred all my senses. Holden seems to take a moment to himself, one he uses to settle whatever thoughts are racing through his mind. His hand lowers at the same time his eyes open, and his chest rises with his single, sharp inhale. He says, "You don't get to control how I look at you, Jamie. And if I look at you like I pity you, it's because I do. You're a fucking orphan who's spent the past few years of her life watching her mother die, and now you have the weight of your entire existence on your shoulders. You have no real life. No real friends. No real *future*."

"Fuck you!" I spit. "You know nothing about me!"

"Why the fuck do you think I'm here!" he shouts, his words echoing through the stillness around us. The sounds of our heavy breaths resonate between us while he stares down at me, and I stare back, but *nothing* is a game between us anymore.

Nothing.

I hold my ground, my arms stiff at my sides. "Why *are* you here?"

I don't know how much time passes before he makes the first move, inching toward me. Panic kicks at my flesh from the inside, and I say, "Holden, I…" I want to say so many things, reveal so many truths, but then his hand is on my jaw, fingertips digging into my nape, and he's pulling me toward him. His mouth crashes down on mine, and it's not at all what I expected to feel when Holden Eastwood *actually* kisses me. And when his tongue slides against the seam of my lips, begging for entry, I give into the conflict. To the fear. To the inevitable. Up on my toes, I tilt my head, swipe my tongue along his. I moan the exact moment he does, our breaths merging, sounds rolling into one. He pulls away first, leaving me dazed and breathless. With his forehead resting against mine, his exhale warms every inch of me. "I'm here because I can't seem to keep the fuck away from you."

CHAPTER
TWENTY-ONE

JAMIE

grip tightly to a marker while Holden drives us to his house. Unfortunately, I'm wearing jeans so I can't use my thigh, and no matter how frantically I search, I seem to have gone through all the napkins in my bag. I don't know why I didn't think to bring a sketchbook when Holden drove me back to my place to pack for the next couple of nights. Yes. *Nights*. Plural. Because—as Holden said—it's either that or he's sleeping in his truck. The bed, to be exact, and to prove his point, he showed me the sleeping bag thrown in there, along with enough snacks to last a lifetime.

Holden asks, "You good, Gladys?"

I'm the furthest thing from *good*. "Stupid napkins," I murmur, sitting upright. I kick at my bag for no real reason.

"You seem… agitated," he points out.

I suck in a breath, let it out in a *whoosh*. "Your mom's cool with me staying, right?"

He makes a hissing sound that instantly doubles my nerves. "Yeah, full disclosure: my mom's back in North Carolina for a few days, so—"

"Holden!"

"Relax," he says, stretching out his back. "I asked permission like a good little boy, and she said she'd be disappointed if I didn't drag your ass there."

"So, you told her about my situation?" I cringe at the thought.

"Yes, and shut up about it. Also, she made me stay on a video call with her while I made up the spare bed, even though I told her we'd probably end up staining it, anyway."

"Holden!" I gasp, backhanding his chest.

He simply chuckles. "I'm kidding." Then he reaches across to his glove box, opens it, and throws a handful of napkins at my head.

I squeal with relief and don't hesitate, not even for a second. I uncap the marker with my teeth and draw a single straight line. Blank ink swims across the paper, bleeds through the dips unseen by the naked eye. I draw another line, this one shorter. "Give me a flower to draw," I order.

He contemplates for a moment. "Dahlias."

I freeze mid-movement, gaze flicking to his. There's no possible way he could know. "Another one."

He eyes me suspiciously, but only says, "Tulips."

"Tulips," I repeat and take a moment to think. I picture the ones Gina would pull from her garden and place into thin vases and then the ones in all the books I'd seen. When I'm ready, I start with a single petal. "Tulip bulbs can be substituted for onions when cooking."

He chuckles. "You're such a little weirdo, Taylor."

———

I'm sure It's probably rude to be taking as long a shower as I am, but holy shit. It's been so long since I've had a shower with actual water pressure where that water stays warm for over two minutes, and I never want to leave. Never. "I'm never getting out!" I shout. I have no idea where Holden is or if he can even hear me. When we got to his house, the first thing I asked for was a shower. I needed to get the grease and grime and bacon smell off me asap.

An eternity later, I force myself to switch off the water, whispering sweet adorations and words of future longing to the shower head. Then I slowly part the shower curtains, just in case Holden's crept into the room without me knowing. He hasn't. I dry off as quickly as I can, get dressed just as fast, and then I just stand there, my toes curling, pressing into the tiles. If I thought I was anxious in the car, it's nothing compared to how I'm feeling now. Which is pathetic, really, because up until four days ago, being around Holden made me feel… indifferent.

Strange what a couple of kisses given in the heat of the moment can create.

Because now there's this tension. And expectation. And Holden's and my expectations are, I'm positive, vastly different.

I groan, more at myself than anyone else, because I sure talk a lot of game for someone scared shitless to deal with the inevitable. Slowly, I face his bedroom door, my feet barely lifting off the floor as I make my way toward his room.

I don't knock.

I should've.

Because he's at his desk, slamming the drawer shut and turning to me with wide eyes, and is he… *blushing*? I never thought I'd see the day. Clearly, I've just busted him doing something he knows he shouldn't be doing, and that thought has me grinning like a fool. "What you got there?" I tease, swaying from side to side.

His features level. "Nothing." And then he clears his throat, stands in front of the drawer, hands gripping the handle.

My giggle pours out of me like the loosening of a valve. Slowly at first, and then all at once. I move toward him, my shoulders hunched, tapping my fingertips together. "Is it treeeasure?" I can't stop laughing, and really, it's not that funny, but catching him like this has me *giddy*. It's like I've won a game I didn't even know we were playing.

"Jamie," he deadpans, and the tone in his voice has me cutting my bullshit real quick. I look up at him, see that same heat in his eyes from earlier today, and I remember that I'm standing in front of him in my sleep clothes—an oversized shirt and underwear, and *nothing* else. My damp hair's loose, and a droplet of water streaks down my temple. Or maybe I'm suddenly sweating. I can't tell. "I didn't realize…" His voice breaks, and he clears it, twisting a strand of my hair between his fingers. "I didn't know your hair was this long."

"I always wear it up," I whisper. *Yeah, because that's relevant.* But I don't know what to say or how to act when he's looking at me the way he is—as if he wants to devour me whole. Or bend me over his desk and *bone* me. I swallow, thick, and say, "So… no raging orgy to attend this fine Saturday night?"

I regret it the second the words are out of my mouth because he's reaching for his phone, his lips twisted as he holds back a smile. "I hadn't planned it." He holds up his phone between us. "Want me to call some friends?"

I smack the phone out of his grasp. "I'd rather shove barbed wire in each one of my holes."

His chuckle is deep, affecting me in ways I don't want to admit. "No barbed wire here, but I'm sure my dick will make a stellar replacement."

I start to roll my eyes, but he tugs on the front of my shirt, bringing me forward until I'm standing between his legs. Arms loosely around me, he asks, "Are you tired?"

"Not really. I'm always wired after a shift."

"So…" he smiles to one side. "What do you want to do?"

I flatten my hands on his solid chest and rise to my toes. Mouth right to his ear, I whisper, "Whatever you're thinking…" I trail off, flicking his ear with my tongue, and smile when he groans, his arms tightening around me. "*Not* that."

He pushes me away. "Remind me again why my dick's so fucking hard for you?"

"I didn't know it was," I say with a giggle.

He grasps my shoulders, pushing me back a step, and motions down to the bulge in his shorts. I'm successful at my lack of response when he shoves his hand down there to adjust himself. "You're mean."

I shrug. "It's a defense mechanism."

He watches me as if trying to read between the lines. It's not that complicated. You get burned enough times; you stop trying to find warmth in other places, other *people*.

"You want to get high?" he asks, and I shake my head, start looking around his room. "You want to drink? I think I have a bottle of—"

"Pass," I cut in. *Hard pass.*

He motions toward the television. "Want to play Call of Duty?"

I grimace. "I suck at PacMan on the arcade game at the diner."

Holden chuckles. "I can probably find some paper if you want to draw…"

"You're sweet," I say, at the same time I find exactly what I've been looking for. Ever since he brought me here the first time, I've wanted to do a puzzle. I found some phone apps that simulate it, but I'm sure it's nothing like the real thing. I point toward the bookshelf where boxes of puzzles sit side by side, asking, "Can I?"

His smile is ridiculous. "Yeah?" He releases me completely. "Take your pick."

CHAPTER
TWENTY-TWO

HOLDEN

Two minutes later, we're sitting on the floor, my back to my bed while Jamie sits to the side. I mash at a PlayStation controller, and Jamie stares down at hundreds of tiny cardboard pieces, her brow furrowed in confusion. Shoulders slumped, she heaves out a sigh. "I don't even know where to start," she mumbles.

"You've never done a puzzle before?"

Shaking her head, she answers, "Not a real one."

I drop the controller on my lap and tell her, "The beginning's the easiest part." Flicking the pieces around with my finger, I add, "You just need to find all the edges and corners, and then everything else will come together."

It doesn't take me long to find three corner pieces, and I move them toward her. She picks up each one, compares them to the box's image, and places them roughly where they need to go. "You're really good at this, huh?"

I shrug, focus on the television again. "I grew up doing them. Probably like you with drawing, right?" I glance at her, but she doesn't respond, too focused on the puzzle. "I put pen to paper, and nothing happens. I can do the good ol' generic dick and balls, but that's basically it."

She smiles, letting me know she's listening, and that smile gets wider when she finds the fourth and final corner piece. "What was it like for you? Growing up, I mean. You said you grew up on a nursery?"

"Uh-huh." The TV's on mute, and I'm mid-match, but all I'm doing is smashing buttons. I could've died twenty times by now, and I wouldn't have noticed because I can't seem to take my eyes off her. She's wearing a t-shirt way too big for her, and it makes me question where she got it. I don't recall ever seeing Dean wearing it, but it's not like I would've paid attention. It bothers me. And I really shouldn't be feeling any type of way about her wearing some other guy's clothes. But... I'm an only child, and I'm not good at sharing. Not that Jamie's mine, but... I don't know.

To be completely honest, I'm out of my element here. Sure, I'm used to having girls in my room, in my bed, but there was always a game plan. There's a middle, a beginning, and an end, but with Jamie—I have no idea what to expect, and maybe that's what draws me to her. What excites me about the prospect of possibly having her.

"Holden?" she asks, pulling me from my thoughts. "What was it like?"

"It was..." I take a moment to think about it. "Honestly, it was the best. When I was living there, I hated it. I used to promise Mia that I'd get us out of that shithole as soon as I could, but now that I look back on it, I wish I could go back there. Not so much to that place specifically, but to that time and place, you know?" I pause a moment, reliving the best memories of my life. "Like, we lived on hundreds and hundreds of acres, and we'd spend all day just play-ing, not a single care in the world. There was no pressure to be or do anything but be kids, and that—that's what I miss the most. And my dad, obviously."

"Do you still talk to him?"

"My dad?" I ask, and she nods, eyes still focused on the task in front of her. "Every day."

"And Mia?"

"I try. Multiple times a day," I say through a sigh. "But she's not really in the headspace to be talking to my dumb ass."

Jamie glances up, then right back down, placing an edge piece in a separate pile. Her lips part and snaps shut a second later, and I can tell she's holding back. "What's on your mind, Mildred?"

Shaking her head, she looks up, stares right into my eyes for one second. Two. It's barely a whisper when she says, "I'd have given anything to have a friend like you growing up."

And maybe it's that nanosecond of a high from her maybe-compliment that has me admitting, "You kind of smell like home to me." *Yep*. That came out just as creepy out loud as it did in my head.

She snorts with her abrupt laugh. "You know what I smell like?"

I sit up straighter. "Have you forgotten that time when you sat in my car and forced me to *sniff* you?"

After a groan, she mumbles, "I purposely blocked it out of my mind. Thanks for the reminder."

"What the hell was that about, anyway?"

Jamie goes back to the puzzle, flicking pieces around with her index finger. "You ever have that kid in elementary school who was always dirty and stinky and—"

"I was home-schooled, so no," I cut in.

"Oh." Her eyebrows knit, inspecting a single puzzle piece laid flat on her palm. "Well, that was me. I was kind of neglected as a kid and constantly teased or talked about, so I guess being clean or whatever —it's my way of overcoming some fucked-up psychological child-hood trauma." She says all this without ever looking up, without taking a breath, and I have no idea if she realizes what all she's just revealed. I try to picture a younger version of Jamie precisely the way she described, and for the life of me, I can't fucking do it.

For me—being dirty and smelly was part of growing up the way I did. All that outdoor play meant being coated in mud and sweat, but those things came from laughter and joy and… I can't even process

139

being raised any other way. And maybe that's on me. Maybe I've lived in a bubble my entire life, or maybe I'm just way too self-absorbed that I hadn't realized until right at this moment that the world is as messed up as it is.

I get some things are inevitable and out of our control. Like death, for example. But my greatest fear growing up was simply that —*growing up*.

It's *still* my biggest fear.

I don't know what to say or how to react, and so I do the worst thing possible: I do nothing at all.

Seconds pass, or it could be minutes, and then Jamie exhales, the single sound filling the room. Her eyes are already mid-roll when she glances up, letting out a groan. "Right," I say, forcing myself to look away. "Don't look at you like I pity you."

"No. That's not it." She shakes her head. "It's just… I tell you not to feel sorry for me, but then I give you the fuel to add to the fire. And now you have no choice but to carry the weight of my burdens, and it's not fair to you."

I heave out a sigh, my eyes unintentionally trailing back to hers like they always seem to do. "It's not really fair to you, either, Jamie."

Her eyes stay on mine for a long moment, and then she forces an exhale, her eyebrows dipping. "It kind of bugs me that you're not at all what I expected."

Cracking a smile, I say, "That's because you judged me way too early."

"I think it was all that big dick energy you harvest." Her nose scrunches in feigned disgust, and I can't help but laugh.

"You sure talk a lot about my dick for a girl who's never experienced it." I stare at her, one eyebrow cocked.

It's a challenge.

She knows it.

I know it.

"Let me guess," she says, slowly getting to her feet. "You're going to suggest that we somehow rectify that." There's no inflection in her tone as she says this, glancing at the bedroom door. I assume she's about to leave the room, the house. Instead, she walks toward me, stopping with one foot planted on either side of my legs.

Looking up at her, I throw the controller across the room and reach up for her at the same time she settles on my lap. We're close, but with her arms held up between us, her hands on my chest, and her eyes right on mine—she's created the distance she seems to so badly need. I settle my palms on her bare thighs, keep them there.

"Holden?" she starts, hands shifting from my chest to my shoulders, then up to the back of my head, where her fingers splay, lace through the hair there. My eyes drift shut, a strangled moan forming in my throat before I can stop it. "Do you have a God complex?"

I shake my head. "Not that I'm aware of."

She tugs on my hair, forcing my eyes open. Then she scoots forward, just an inch, and my hands drift higher, higher.

"So you're not just drawn to me because—"

"No." I don't even know what she's talking about anymore. I can't think straight when she's this fucking close. Physically. Mentally. No other girl affects me the way she does, and it's been this way for days now, ever since we kissed. It was instant—these fucking *feelings*. And pathetic, really. But no matter how much I tried to deny it, or how hard I tried to fight it, she was always there, on the forefront of my mind, wreaking havoc on all other thoughts, all other senses. It's why I went to Esme's this morning—to clear my head. Or maybe to somehow feel closer to her. Who the fuck knows anymore? "I'm not playing these fucking games with you, Jamie." Her eyes widen. Just a tad. "I like you because I fucking do, and I want you because, honestly, I don't think I have a choice." Her hands are on my jaw now, thumbs stroking. I tilt my head, kiss the inside of her palm as if it's something we've done a thousand times before. "And you have no idea what it does to me when you touch me like this."

Eyes locked, she moves closer again until her front's pressed to mine. She's so warm against me, so small. So *fragile*. "You know what I like about you?" she asks, pressing down on my already hard cock. The heat from between her legs floats across my flesh, and I'm so fucking done with waiting. I press my lips to her neck, parting them just enough to suck lightly at the skin there, and she moans, her hands in my hair again, fingers curled. "I like that you say exactly what's on your mind. You're like an open book."

"I have nothing to hide," I murmur against her jaw, nearing where I want to be.

Need to be.

"I'm kind of the opposite," she says, and I fight back a smile as I pull away.

"Nah, I'll crack you open." I thrust up. Just once. Just so she can feel exactly what she does to me. "Starting with your spine..." I cock an eyebrow, smirking. "When I bend you over on all fours and press you down on the mattress." And then I tighten my hold around her waist, keeping her there, right before I dramatically—and *rabidly*—hump the air.

She giggles into my chest—breathy—and I want to dive deep in the sound, bathe myself in it. Face pressed to my chest, she says, "You're such an idiot."

"Thanks." I bust out a laugh, then drawl, "My mama says it's part of my charm." And then I shift the hair away from her eyes so I can see her clearer. "Honestly, I just like trying to make you laugh. It's kind of my new favorite hobby." And, because I'm not really into self-torture, I kiss her.

I kiss her like I've wanted to for days—without urgency, without motive. I kiss her because I want to. And she kisses me back, our tongues meeting, moving slowly. I sigh, like a fucking *girl*, because I had no idea how tense I was until my muscles relaxed beneath her touch.

She tilts her head back, breaking the kiss and giving me access to her neck. My fingers dig into her thighs while I kiss her collarbone, licking between sniffs like a creep—because that's what Jamie's turned me into. A stalker-type creep who locks away pieces of a girl in his desk drawer.

"Tell me your stupid rules again," Jamie pants, and she's grinding against me, her hips moving in slow circles.

I take a second to work out what she means. "The rules don't apply to you," I manage to say, grabbing her ass—*hard*—forcing her to stop moving.

"Why not?" She actually has the audacity to sound peeved.

"Because they just don't." I try to kiss her again, but she pulls away.

"What if I want them to?"

"Will you shut up," I say through a chuckle. "God, you're frustrating."

She laughs at that. "And yet, you still want to fuck me."

"Oh, I want to do a hell of a lot more than just fuck you, Jamie."

Her eyebrows rise. "Well, what are you waiting for?" she says, pulling back to grasp my jaw. "Show me your *dick activity*."

A guffaw builds in my chest, emits before I can stop it. "You're so fucking wild." I kiss her, just once, then settle my hands on her waist, under her shirt. "And I like you... a lot."

I don't know if she hears me, because she's too busy reaching for the drawer of my nightstand. "Have you got condoms?"

I reach up, tug down on her arm. "I'm not ready for that yet," I say and wait for her eyes to meet mine. They're only there a second before she looks down at the space between us, where my cock stands at full attention, and obviously, *yes*, I'm physically ready, but mentally? "I want to take my time with you," I admit, pushing off the bed and standing up, taking her with me. Her legs wrap around my torso, arms clinging to my neck. I move around the room, switching off the light, turning off the TV, and flicking the lamp on before pulling her limbs off me one by one, all so I can dump her unceremoniously on the bed. She lands with an *oomph*; her dark hair splayed on the light gray of my pillow. "Besides," I say, crawling between her legs. "I'm convinced you're batshit crazy, so who the fuck knows if you'll ever let me do this again." I remove my t-shirt before dipping my head, shifting the bottom of her top just enough that I can kiss the inch of exposed skin. Her stomach muscles shift beneath my lips, her hands finding the back of my head again. I bite down on the band of her underwear: navy, lacy, with a tiny little bow right in the middle. Then I glance up at her. "Thank God you don't wear granny panties because that's a whole other fetish I'm not prepared for."

She laughs—the exact reaction I wanted. "What is *wrong* with you?"

"So many things," I reply. And before I know what's happening, Jamie's removing her top, and I'm dragging her underwear down her legs. She lies back down, completely bare, laid out just for me.

"Holden," she whispers, and I can see the sudden insecurity flicker in her eyes. She starts to reach up, to cover the parts of her she's blessed me with.

"Stop." I grasp her wrists. "You're just... so much more than I expected." It doesn't even make sense. Not to me. And definitely not to her, because she's fisting the blankets now, trying to cover herself. "Stop," I say again. "You're beautiful, Jameson." And there's that fucking word again. "Your body's insane. Knock that shit off." Shoving my hand down my shorts, I try to ease the throbbing building in my cock. "I just need a minute, or I'll be giving you a pearl necklace to suit all your clothes."

Her eyebrows bunch. "I don't even know what that means."

"It means I'm going to blow my fucking load all over those perfect tits."

"Oh," she says, and then I'm parting her slit with a single finger. "Oooh." She's already so wet. So warm. So ready for me. I lick my lips, reaching up to flick my thumb across her nipple. Her thighs jerk in response, her head thrashing to the side. And I can't fucking wait any longer. I flick my tongue along the entire length of her, just like I'd fantasized.

It's just one lick.

A tease.

A taste.

"Jesus, Holden," she moans, and she's everything I thought she'd be and nothing at all like I'd imagined.

Just like her art.

Jameson Taylor is a masterpiece, and I'm in way, way over my head.

I lick her again and again, the room filling with her moans with each flick of my tongue. Then I slide a finger inside her, smile against her clit when she curses under her breath, her fingers digging into my scalp. I settle in, ready to watch her come undone beneath me, but then light shines upon us at the same time tires squeal, and then voices. Lots of them. All male. All familiar to my ears. "Fuck." I reluctantly pull away, my jaw tight as I sit up. "Don't fucking move," I tell her.

Her hands shift to cover her most intimate parts while I stand, move to the bedroom window where she's already looking. More voices—laughter—then some dickhead yelling, "Let's fucking goooo!"

"Holden?" Jamie asks, and I glance at her just in time to see her drag the covers over her. "What's going on?"

I already know what I'll be seeing when I part the blinds. I can sense it. I do it anyway. On my front lawn, illuminated by the taillights of Billy Butler's truck, is the absolute last fucking thing Jamie and I need right now. Shoulders slumped, I press my thumb and forefinger to the bridge of my nose and turn toward the naked girl waiting in my bed. "It's Dean."

CHAPTER
TWENTY-THREE

JAMIE

loved her, man. And I fucked up." Dean's words are slurred as he moves toward Holden's bedroom. Or, more accurately, is dragged toward it. The only reason he's upright is because Holden's keeping him that way, carrying his dumb ass the way athletes heave injured players off the court or field or whatever they're on.

According to Holden, his so-called friends from the football team rolled Dean off the back of one of the guy's trucks and then sped off. Holden saw the tail end of it—Dean's landing—and the worst part? It wasn't the first time this has happened. When I questioned why... just *why*... he simply said, "You've met his dad, right?" And I understood.

Kind of.

He told me all this in the few seconds it took for him to slip his t-shirt back on, adjust his hard-on in his shorts, and leave to make his second rescue for the night, mumbling something about blue balls and cock blocks.

Dean's still talking about Bethany, and I don't know why I care, why I feel the need to witness this sudden shitshow. Standing in the doorway of Holden's room, I lean against the frame, ignoring the sinking in my gut at Dean's drunken words. Holden catches my stare and throws me a smirk, right before he brings two fingers to his mouth, separates them, and starts flicking his tongue between them.

I snort-laugh. I can't help it. And Dean—he looks up at the sound, his bleary eyes narrowed. "Jamie," he whispers. "What are you…" He's at the doorway now, trailing his gaze from me, dressed in the same way he's often seen me, to the unmade bed behind me, where Holden and I were about to— "I'm going to be sick," he groans. And then he does just that. Right where he stands, he pukes directly onto the carpeted hallway.

"Motherfucker," Holden spits, releasing Dean.

Dean falls forward, and because I'm built on shitty life choices and self-sabotage, I grab Dean around the waist, keep him steady, and lead him toward the bathroom.

"How the fuck am I supposed to clean this shit up?" Holden yells.

In front of the toilet, I help Dean onto his knees and squat down beside him. And then I just look at him. Look at the big brown eyes that held my happiness for weeks. Months. They're glossy now, stained with red. Face pale, every inch coated in sweat. "I'm so sorry, Jamie," he croaks, his voice cracking with emotion. "I never meant to hurt you."

My hands twitch, momentarily wanting nothing more than to reach up, brush his hair away from his eyes the way I'd done after he'd whispered words of forever right into my neck. Instead, I cross my arms, keep them safe. Keep *me* safe. "You'll feel better once it's all out."

He responds by throwing up in the toilet bowl, again and again, his entire body convulsing with the urges. I get to my feet, look down on him. For someone who swore black and blue that they didn't consume alcohol, Dean sure is suffering the aftermath of said consumption.

I wish I could say that I'm surprised, but I'm *seriously* not. If life has taught me anything, it's that people lie for a plethora of reasons. And those lies become so viscerally inked beneath our flesh, like black tar heroin swarming through our bloodline, dark and destructive, ruining us from the inside out.

"Seriously, how do I clean that shit up?" Holden moans, now leaning against the doorway of the bathroom. He runs a hand down his face, eyes to the ceiling. "My mom's going to be *pissed.*"

"I got it," I tell him, moving around him. Over my shoulder, I add, "Just watch him. Make sure he doesn't choke on his own vomit." I leave them in the room, my past colliding with my present, and then I do the one thing I know I was born to do: I bury the burden of bad habits.

It takes a half-hour to clean up the mess Dean had gifted us with, and when I'm done, I go back to the bathroom. Holden's on his phone, leaning against the bathtub while Dean lies in a fetal position by his feet. When I was wiping his vomit from the carpet, I heard Dean puke a few more times, and each one came with Holden's own gagging sounds.

Holden glances up at me, his nose scrunched. "Your boy puked all over his clothes," he tells me, lightly kicking his passed-out friend.

"*Your* boy," I reply. Then add through a sigh, "He was never really mine."

With a huff, Holden stands. "Now, what do we do?"

I step over Dean to get to the sink and wash my hands. "I should probably get him in the shower."

"So..." He shoves his phone in his pocket; his eyes narrowed, jaw working when he says, "You're going to see him naked?"

Our eyes lock through the mirror in front of me, and I can see the indecision there. I stop myself from overthinking it, from creating something out of nothing. "Why?" I break the stare and look down at my hands, focus on scrubbing them clean. "You jealous?"

Warmth coats my back as he curls his arm around my middle,

pulling me against him. He drops a kiss on my shoulder and waits until I look up before asking, "Do I have a reason to be?"

I turn in his arms, flatten my wet hands on his chest. "Not even a little bit."

Lips kicked up at the corners, he tightens his hold, lowers his mouth to mine. They've barely touched when Dean's groan forces us to pull apart. "Dude, I'm so fucked."

"No shit, Sherlock," Holden cracks, his eyes never leaving mine.

I peer down at Dean as he says, eyes closed and lips barely moving, "I keep thinking Jamie's here, but, like, why would she be?"

Holden starts to speak, but I cover his mouth, stopping him. Whatever Dean has to say in his drunken state, I want to hear it. "That would be the worst..." he mumbles. "Her seeing me like this."

Pulling back, Holden gently grasps my wrist, lowers it between us. "Why's that?"

My lungs begin to shrink, my heart hammering against my chest. I try to push Holden away, try to get out of his hold. He doesn't let me. And so I do the only thing I can think to do: I lower my head so he doesn't see the tears I'm fighting to restrain.

I cannot break down.

Not now.

Not in front of both of them.

"Her mom was a drunk," Dean says, and they're such simple words that create such immense pain. "It's what killed her."

CHAPTER
TWENTY-FOUR

JAMIE

don't even hear Holden approaching until he flops down beside me. I'm in his living room, on his couch, sitting in the semi-darkness with a pen and notepad I'd found on his kitchen counter.

I have no idea how long I've been here.

At some point, I heard the shower switch on, and everything after that is a blur.

Usually, when I feel this way—as if the entire earth is collapsing beneath my feet—I clean. I clean until there's nothing left but memories too ingrained to erase.

But... this isn't my house, and besides, there's nothing physical about the filth I was momentarily forced to drown in.

I realize I'm *almost* crying, and *almost* is as real as I'll allow myself. Tears would be woeful, really, because nothing Dean said is news to me. My mother *was* a drunk. And it *is* what ultimately killed her.

"Are you okay?" Holden asks, and even though he's right next to me, he seems so far away. So distant.

"I'm fine," I lie. *My ex-boyfriend just unintentionally bared my entire fucking soul to you. That's all.*

Minutes pass, and I can feel him watching me, but he doesn't say a word. I stare ahead; my mind consumed with all the things I wish I could say. I'd spent so much of my life forced into silence, and now that I have the freedom to speak, I can't seem to find my voice.

"What's going on, Jameson?" He rarely calls me Jameson, and I really shouldn't know that, considering how little time we've spent together. I feel him shift and then a *click* as he flicks on a lamp on the side table. The light creates a soft glow throughout the room, but it feels like it's a spotlight on all my secrets.

I lower my head, focus on the notepad on my lap. There's nothing but black ink and deep, harsh scratches marring layers of pages.

Holden must follow my gaze because he heaves out a sigh. It's not the "beauty" that he's used to seeing.

But I'm used to it.

I *am* it.

Or *was*.

"She wasn't a bad person," I blurt out.

"Who?"

Finally finding the courage to face him, I say, my heart in my throat, "My mom."

Another sigh, and then he's taking the notepad from me and ripping off the first few pages. He discards my ugly emotions by throwing them over his shoulder, and then he drops the notepad back on my lap. It's a blank canvas. A fresh start. "I never said she was."

I keep my eyes on his. "You don't have to say it out loud for the thought to exist."

"Who gives a shit what I think?" Dropping his head forward, he pinches the bridge of his nose, his eyes shut tight. It's only now I realize he'd just spent however long manhandling a drunk Dean in the shower and most likely getting him to bed, and now he's here—having to deal with my bullshit. He must be exhausted. "You told me that you draw as an escape, sometimes as a necessity." He pauses a beat, eyes meeting mine. "Did your mom drink for the same reason?"

Without pause, without hesitation, I breathe out a, "Yes."

He nods as if he already knows where this is going. "Were you there?"

"For her drinking?" I ask.

Shaking his head, he replies, "No. For the things she was trying to break free from."

Break free?

Of all the things my mother tried and failed at, *breaking free* wasn't one of them. Still, I answer, "Yes."

Holden's reaction is as instant as it is visceral. Eyes closed, he balls his fists, his chest rising with an inhale that seems to calm the sudden storm. When he opens his eyes again, they lock right on mine. I try to look away, but I can't. I can't seem to stop looking at him. Like a moth to a flame. Or a gnat to garbage—not that Holden is trash... it's just... I don't know what the fuck either of us are thinking. Or doing.

Or *feeling*.

Before I can get a word out, his arm is sliding beneath my thighs, and he's scooping me up and settling me sideways on his lap. He holds me to him, my cheek to his chest until there's nothing between us.

No space.

No air.

Only a million reckless, fleeting emotions.

"I need to say two things," he says. "One, I'm sorry about your mom. And you—having to be witness to it. No kid should ever have to be around that." His lips press to my temple, soft and warm, coating me with an emotion I'm too afraid to discern. "You know, I grew up in a town with fewer than two hundred people. My mom— she got pregnant with me at seventeen. It was the most scandalous thing to happen in that bible-thumping town for decades. They ostracized her the second the rumors started." He must see the confusion set in my features when his gaze slides to mine, because he adds, "What I'm getting at is that before I could even talk, my mom instilled in me one simple rule for life: when it comes to judgment from others—*fuck everyone*."

153

I let out a giggle, but it's one that filters out with all my withheld emotions, and I don't know if I'm truly laughing or crying.

"Dean's an idiot for saying what he did," he says. "He had no right to reveal your secrets and to put your mom in a box like that… as if that was her life, The End. That's bullshit." He taps my leg. "And you—assuming I thought she was a bad person, or a bad *mother*—which I don't, just FYI—but even if I did, so fucking what? That's on me, and you have absolutely no obligation to justify other people's perceptions of you."

I take in his words, one by one, until each of them sinks in—deep in the parts of me I keep hidden from the world. Gina once told me that nothing is forever. That the way I'd been treated, and the way people saw me—it wouldn't last. I was eight years old, sitting in a stranger's bathtub, a stranger who'd soon become my only friend. The water was murky, stained with my stigma and up to my neck, and I'd looked up at her, liquid agony clinging to my lashes, and I couldn't understand why she was saying what she was.

My mom had always told me that *this* was the life that was *chosen* for us, and there was no way out of it.

Gina had given me an out, and in a way, I believe *she* was the only thing in the world "chosen" for me.

And now Holden's here, doing the same, and it's not that I believe he was put on this earth for me and me alone, like Gina was, and maybe Holden and I aren't destined to be Best Friends Forever, but we could be something… for *now*.

And maybe that's all I need.

A Holden *for now*.

I take his hand in mine and link our fingers. It's a bold move, one I wasn't expecting to make, but here we are.

"Besides, what the fuck are you going to do?" he says, pulling me from my thoughts. "Tell everyone who judges you that they're wrong?" He scoffs. "No. You walk with your head held high, and you—"

"*Fuck everyone*," I cut in.

He barks out a laugh, squeezing my hand as he turns to me.

"Well, maybe not that part. I mean, eventually I'd like for you to fuck *just* me, but…"

My laughter starts low, contained, until I can't keep it in anymore. My head throws back with the force, my stomach aching, tears welling in my eyes, and Holden *stares*, watching me go through all the million

fleeting,

reckless

emotions.

And maybe I had it wrong.

Maybe Holden Eastwood isn't the flame to my moth.

Maybe he's the moon.

The light.

Guiding me out of my darkness.

CHAPTER
TWENTY-FIVE

JAMIE

Sitting opposite me at Holden's kitchen table, my locker neighbors look between each other and me, again and again. I spent the night in the spare bedroom, alone, and Holden slept on the floor of his room so he could monitor Dean. I have no idea what happened between them last night, but something seems different. *Off*.

They're both on their third bowls of cereal for the morning, and I've barely touched my toast. "Sourpatch Kids" by Brice Vine plays softly through the Bluetooth speakers on the kitchen counter, and Dean mumbles, "Bro, it's like this song was written about you."

Holden nods, agreeing. And to say things are awkward, at least for me, would be an understatement.

The song ends, and another begins, and it's... it's "Hopelessly Devoted" from the *Grease* soundtrack. Two seconds in and Dean busts out a laugh, spitting milk back into his bowl, remnants of it trickling down his chin. Holden's laugh starts low, a chuckle of sorts, before he joins his idiot friend in what I can only describe as *howling*.

I stare at them, my eyebrows drawn, and as soon as the chorus kicks in, Holden turns the volume *all the way* up, and now they're both on their feet, shouting the lyrics between fits of laughter, and what the fuck is actually happening right now? I don't know what dimension of real life I'm currently living, but I want out. "You guys are so weird," I murmur, biting into my toast.

Dean must hear it, because he has the nerve to say, "Dance with me anyway."

I should throw his cereal all over his face. Or just throw the entire bowl directly at his head. It's a shame I don't do either. Instead, I get up, and move toward Holden's bathroom while they continue to yell, *"Hopelessly devoooooted to you…"*

————

Holden plays that same stupid song the entire drive to my work, occasionally chuckling to himself for reasons I'm sure only he and Dean know. I don't ask. In fact, I don't speak at all.

"I'll pick you up at 11?" Holden asks, parking just outside the rear door of the diner. When I got out of the shower this morning, Dean was no longer there. I have no idea where he went, and Holden hasn't mentioned him once.

"Yeah. Thanks." I start to get out but his hand on my arm stops me.

"Kiss me," he says, and it's not an order, but it's not really a request either. I fight back a smile and lean across the cab, kiss him on the cheek.

He rolls his eyes. "If I wanted a kiss like that, I'd go visit my grandma." A retort stays trapped in my mind when his hand slides to my nape, fingers digging in as he pulls me toward him. His lips are already parted when they crash down on mine, and I lose my breath when he's like this. When he needs as much as he wants, gives as much as he takes. He moans, the single sound echoing through my mind, my body. He chuckles as he pulls away. "Tonight," he says, squeezing my thigh as he presses a single kiss to my forehead. And then he smiles that dirty, wicked smile of his. "The things I plan to do to you…"

———

Holden's already waiting for me when my shift ends. Sitting on the bed of the truck, he looks up as I approach, but doesn't move to get down. "Hey," he says, and it's too dark to make out his expression.

"Hey, I wasn't sure if you'd be here," I reply, gripping the straps of my backpack. "I tried calling." He didn't answer, obviously, but since I'm not really into waiting alone in dark alleys, I wanted to be sure.

"Yeah, sorry," he says, and he's still hasn't moved. Eyes dropping to his lap, he adds, "I spent the day with Dean. I didn't have my phone on me."

"Oh," I reply, stopping in front of him. And the more I watch him, the stronger that same feeling I had this morning courses through me. Something is different. Something is *off*. "Everything okay?"

He looks up, eyes on mine, and I can instantly see the discomfort there. The *regret*. "You know he was talking about you, right?"

"What?" I breathe out, standing taller.

"When we came into the house," Holden says, "he said '*I loved her man, and I fucked up…*'" He pauses a beat. "He was talking about you, Jamie."

Nerves prick at my flesh from the inside, and I can feel the tightening in my chest. Feel it harden. Feel the defensive walls rebuild there, brick by brick, piece by piece.

Holden clears his throat, his shoulders squaring when he says, "I've kind of been a dick to him ever since I found out what he did to you, and to be honest, I don't like the way I've treated him."

I take a slow step back, already knowing where he's going with this. And to think that less than twenty-four hours ago I'd fallen asleep *smiling*, actually excited for what the next day might bring. *Foolish*. "It's fine, Holden. It's not—"

"Dean's my best friend here," he cuts in.

"I know."

"He's my *only* friend, really."

I shake my head. I really don't need to hear any more. "Holden, you don't need to explain—"

"It's just that… he's never once judged me when it comes to the shit I've done with girls, and I think it's only fair I do the same." He says all this, his eyes right on mine, words rushed as if he just *had* to throw them out there before he could take them all back.

After moments of silence, I raise my chin, push back the unexpected heartache and try to keep my voice steady when I tell him, "Honestly, it's whatever." And it was so stupid of me to think it was anything more.

I turn to leave, grimacing when I hear him jump down off the truck, his feet landing with a thud.

"Jamie!" he calls out. "I still want you to stay at my house."

I stop in my tracks, give myself a moment to breathe.

To process.

To think.

And then I turn to the boy who only minutes earlier had me looking forward to this exact moment—being face-to-face with him. "Um…" I swallow the knot in my throat. "I called today because I got a hold of the maintenance guy. I gave him my sob story, and he went and turned everything back on, so… you really didn't have to come here."

"Oh." Holden stares at me, his head tilted, trying to work out if I'm bullshitting. "Well, that's good," he says, nodding.

I nod back.

He motions to his truck. "At least let me give you a ride home."

I wish he'd just go. "You know, it's a nice night out. I'd prefer to walk."

"It's late, Jamie. And this area—"

"Is where I *live*," I cut in. "Besides, I've done it hundreds of times before." I unzip the side pocket of my backpack and pull out the can of pepper spray Zeke had brought me. "See?" I say, holding it up between us. "I'm good."

"I don't feel comfortable—"

"Please," I grind out, and I'm way too close to losing it. The last thing I want is for him to witness it. I exhale slowly, try to keep my emotions in check. My voice cracks when I beg, "Just let me go, Holden."

"Jamie..." He looks away. He can't stand to see me like this as much as I can't stand that I'm *feeling* like this.

If I don't take control of the situation, things are going to spiral. And fast. "I don't want your pity, okay? We're good." I shrug. "I just... I want to walk home, and I want to wash this filth off me, and I want to sleep..." And not wake up for days. "So if you care about me, even a little, you'll let me do that."

"I *do* care about you."

"I know," I say, and there's no lie in my statement. Whatever Holden and I are, or *were*, I know, deep down, that he harbors some sort of protectiveness over me. I smile through my sadness, telling him, "I'll see you at school."

It's the last thing either of us says, and then I'm walking, the pepper spray gripped tight in my grasp. I ignore the racing of my heart every time headlights appear beside me or every time I hear irregular noises behind me. And I ignore the familiar ache in my chest, the one of longing, of loss. By the time I slide the key in my front door, my cheeks are wet, stained with the remnants of all my withheld fears. I'm on autopilot when I step inside, flick on the light switch.

Nothing happens.

Because people lie for a plethora of reasons.

And I am one of them.

CHAPTER
TWENTY-SIX

HOLDEN

I'd grown up in such a small town, and even when we ventured out, we didn't go far. My grandparents moved to Tennessee from North Carolina a few years before we did, and so I'd visited them for short periods during the summer. Even so, visiting them isn't the same as actually experiencing regular high school. It was a culture shock. The school. The people. The girls. The *parties*. I was only two weeks into my freshman year when I came home drunk and maybe a little high, and as cool and forgiving as my mom can be— she wasn't having it. She threw threats my way, mainly to ship my ass back home—which was a huge *fuck no* for me. So, we negotiated the first of many punishments to come. I was grounded for a month and all technology privileges were revoked during that time. It was hell, and I wasn't quiet about how much I hated it. Not only to my mom, but to anyone who would listen. And to make things worse, she'd come up with a list of "fun" mother-son activities for me to endure during that time.

One of those activities was that every Saturday night, she would introduce me to her favorite movies that consisted of, but were not limited to, *Bridget Jones's Diary, The Wedding Singer, The fucking Note-book, Titanic, and 500 Days of Summer* (which wasn't too bad). On the third weekend of my grounding, just as she was about to hit play on *Grease*, there was a knock on the door. It was Dean. He convinced my mom that in no way did the terms of my grounding state that I couldn't have friends over. My mom conceded, and let him stay on the premise that he, too, join in on the movie night.

So, Dean and I sat side by side on the couch and watched Sandy make shitty life choices just so Danny would accept her around his dickhead friends. When it was over, Dean had made such an impression on Mom that she allowed him to spend the night. We lay top-to-toe in my bed, and I was almost asleep when I heard him humming that fucking song. And then I started singing it, too. And then we were both singing it. *Screaming* it. The next moment we were in fits of laughter, dancing around the room, the song playing loudly through the speakers, while we held invisible microphones to our mouths.

At some point, my mom opened the door, saw what we were doing, and slowly retreated out of the room.

It was at that point I realized that Dean—he could've been doing anything else with anyone else, but he was there for *me*. And the rest, as they say, is history.

———

"Mom hired a tutor to help me write my college essay," Dean says, shaking his head as we make our way to the lockers.

It's Tuesday morning, we've just finished the morning's weights session, and my hair's still damp from the shower. A bead of water trails down my neck, and I slap it away. "That's what we're doing now? College essays?"

"It's senior year, dude," he says, slapping my back. "Time to grow the fuck up."

"I'd rather not," I mumble. Just the thought of it makes my skin crawl. Our steps slow when we see Jamie's open locker. I didn't see her at school yesterday, and I know Dean didn't because he asked about her. I could only guess why she didn't show up, but I didn't want to share my thoughts, especially with him.

Dean sighs. "Remind me again how bad I was."

"I would, but I'm not into torturing people I can tolerate." To be honest, I'm not sure which of us is more afraid to face the potential wrath of Jamie, and I wish I knew her better so I could prepare myself for what's to come. We get to our lockers at the same time Jamie shuts hers, and I find myself in the middle.

Physically.

Metaphorically.

"Hey," she says, but she's not talking to me.

Stepping around me, Dean replies, "Hey." And then he just stands there, silently, like an idiot. Exactly the way I am.

"So…" Jamie rocks on her heels, her eyebrows drawn as she looks up at Dean. She's in a dress today, past her knees, light pink with white floral print and lace around the neckline. A braided leather belt exposes the curve of her waist, and as unattractive as it seems at first glance, it suits her to perfection. "How are you feeling?"

Dean grips the back of his neck, eyes downcast as he says, "Extremely embarrassed. And remorseful, and—"

"Yeah, no…" she cuts in. "I don't give a shit how you feel *emotionally.* I meant physically."

"Right," Dean deadpans. "Yeah, I'm okay… thanks to you, I guess."

"Well, you know me," she almost sings. "I've got that shit in the bag with all my experience."

Dean cringes, hissing a breath.

"How did you word it exactly?" She's putting him in his place for the shit he said, and so she should. Her teeth show with her exaggerated smile as she slaps his arm. "That's right. My mom was a drunk, and it's what *killed* her." She turns to me, all expression wiped. "I left a bunch of stuff at your house."

"I'll take you there after school to get it."

"You can't just bring it tomorrow? It's all on the bed in the spare room."

Hands shoved deep in my pockets, I nod and lower my gaze, because I've never felt as small as I do at this moment. "Yeah, I can do that."

"Thank you," she says, and the way she says it... the genuine gratefulness in her tone has me looking up and right into her eyes. "And thank you for opening up your home to me when I needed it." She reaches into her locker again, pulls out a bunch of hydrangeas. Handing them to me, she says, "For your mom... for letting me stay." Her voice breaks at the end, her emotions cracking under the weight of her words. "Can you please let her know that I truly appreciate it?"

All I can do is nod because the sudden ache in my chest prevents any other response. The fucked-up thing is, I know why it hurts to see her like this.

Or why it hurts to see her at all.

I just don't know how to admit it... to myself or to anyone else.

———

The spare bed is made, the sheets immaculate, not a single crease. Even her bag that she'd packed is overly neat. The zipper's open, and I can see her clothes in there, folded methodically in a pile as if they've never been touched. Her messenger bag is here, too, the one she uses for school, and I should've realized she might need this stuff prior to her asking for it back. I would've brought it with me on Sunday when I picked her up from work, but I didn't know she wouldn't come back with me. Foolish, now that I think about it, because why the hell would she?

The flap of the messenger bag is open, and the corner of a sketch-book peeks out at me, teasing me with all the things it could reveal.

I shouldn't look through it.

I *wouldn't*.

With a heavy sigh, I sit down on the edge of the bed and drop my head in my hands. Not surprisingly, I haven't slept well the last couple of nights, my mind too consumed with thoughts of a girl too broken to repair. Not that I want to "fix" her. Not that I even could. But maybe she was right. Maybe I do have some messed-up God complex because I hate the way we left things.

My need overpowers my conscience, and blindly—*miserably*—I reach for the sketchbook and flip it open. The first page is a sketch of Esme, and I smile. Jamie's captured Esme's entire personality in her eyes alone, the sadness mixed with hope, and then her face—a face that bears the lines of age and grief and life and heartbreak. I study the sketch for far too long before moving to the next page. It's another older lady, one I've never seen before. The only reason I can assume to know who it might be is the string necklace she's wearing with beaded letters that spell out her name: *Gina*. I'd heard Jamie mention her name before, but I never asked her who she is to her, and now I regret it because I might never get the chance.

The following sketch is… a complete contrast to the first two. It's a giant dick and balls, wearing a backward cap and a goofy-ass grin, and look, I'm not one to jump to conclusions, but I'm pretty sure it's a picture of me. Of how she sees me. And I imagine her in her house, on her couch, sketching this up, laughing to herself because it's fucking ridiculous, and I find myself doing the same—the ache in my chest somewhat easing because, at some point when I wasn't around, she was thinking about me. Even if it was in this way, she was still thinking about me, and that has to mean something.

An idiotic smile still in place, I start to flip to the next image, but something slips from between the pages and lands by my feet. It's a folded sheet of paper from the same book, and I'm so quick to pick it up and reveal its content, I don't have time to prepare for what I'm about to see.

It's a sketch of a compass in the center of an anatomic heart, but the heart is misshapen, wrapped tightly in vines as if it's about to explode. Beneath the drawing are two simple words—words that instantly wipe my smile and replace it with a downpour of regret and desperation: *Forever lost.*

"Holden!" I'd been in such a trance, staring at the drawing for who knows how long, that I didn't even hear the front door open. I knew Mom was coming home today. I expected her arrival. I should probably get up to greet her, but I can't seem to move. "Aww! Did you get me flowers?"

My eyes drift shut, and I can't for the life of me find my voice. The second I got home, I placed the hydrangeas in a vase and set it in the middle of the kitchen table.

"Holden?" Mom calls out again.

"In here!" I finally speak, then listen to her footsteps near. I wait until she comes into view before saying, "Jamie. The flowers. As a thank you." I can't even put together a complete sentence.

"That's sweet," Mom says quietly, her eyes doing that thing where she seems to take in everything with a single glance. "Is this all hers?"

"Yeah." I'm still sitting on the bed, my elbows on my knees, holding onto paper anguish.

"Her house is all fixed?" Mom asks, sitting down next to me.

I nod.

She shoves my side with hers. "You okay, kiddo?"

"Yeah." I clear my throat, blink hard to regain some form of normalcy. "Yeah, I'm fine." I look over at her. "How was it? How's Mia?"

"She's… not well, but she will be…" Her shoulders drop. "I don't know how much my being there helped."

"I'm sure it did, Ma. She loves you, so…"

Mom's nod is slow, her gaze dropping to the sketch I can't seem to let go of. "What's that?"

"It's uh…" *It's everything all at once.* And then… "It's nothing at all."

CHAPTER
TWENTY-SEVEN

JAMIE

*S*uckage.

It's the only way I can describe the anticipation leading up to this very moment: being alone with Holden.

And sure, I could have come up with some generic illness that would sideline my attendance for the day, but what would be the point? There would still be next Wednesday, and the following Wednesday, and all the sucky Wednesdays after.

I haven't done the research, but I'm ninety-nine percent sure that there isn't a disease in the world that pops up every seven days and hangs around for twenty-four hours before disappearing.

Besides, I'd still have to see him at school, most mornings at our lockers, and I really wish I hadn't listened to the stupid counselor in the emancipation program because regular high school blows. I've considered leaving, just dropping out and getting my diploma via homeschooling, but there's no way I'm going to let some guy, or two of them, be the reason I fail to achieve the only substantial thing I've set out to do with my life.

. . .

One night, after cleaning up my mom's vomit mixed with blood off the kitchen linoleum, I sat down on the floor beside her bed with a sketchpad and marker and attempted to draw. I closed my eyes and tried to envision being anywhere but there. Nothing came to me. When I closed my eyes, all I could see was the emptiness that lived and breathed and grew inside me. I remember looking up at her, seeing the sweat form across her forehead and the dark circles around her sunken eyes. Her face had changed over the years. The cuts and bruises that were once prominent had healed over time, replaced with the scars of addiction. It was at that moment, looking at my mother, I knew we were close to the end.

We only had weeks left together.

Months if we were lucky.

Without even a hint of a prognosis, I could sense it.

I tried to wake her, just so I could tell her that I loved her. That no matter what I thought of her in the state she was in, I'd still *miss* her. That I wish I could've gotten to know her—who she was as a person before her life and her love and her need and her want took hold of her and squeezed and squeezed until all life left her eyes. Her body. Her *fight*.

I wanted to ask her so many questions. I wanted to know what she was like at my age. What she aspired to be. What impossible dreams she kept tucked away, hidden from the world. I wanted to know who her first kiss was and what... what the hell happened in her life to tear it all apart.

But more than any of that, I wanted to ask her what she wanted *me* to be. What dreams she had for *me*. Because I sure as fuck didn't have any for myself besides making sure she didn't die.

She never woke up that night.

By the time she came to, the sun had already been up for hours, and I'd created my own list of dreams and aspirations. As pathetic as it is, on top of that list was to graduate and move on with my life—a life without her. It was more a challenge than an ambition, but I felt like if I could just do this one thing once she was gone, then at least I'd give her a reason to be proud.

I would be proud.

Over the next couple of days, I went through all the stages of grieving as if she was already dead: denial, anger, bargaining, depression, and acceptance. And then I found myself back to the beginning: denial.

I went through all the paperwork her doctors had given her, the same ones I found in her purse when I was thirteen. The ones that led to my begging her to escape the wrath of Satan's hold.

I read over the pages one by one, every word, every footnote, and I came to terms with what I already knew: there was no denying her final breath. And so I quickly moved on to the next stage: anger.

I think I've been stuck there ever since.

"You good, Gladys?" Holden asks. We're sitting in his truck, in Esme's driveway, while he eyes the numerous bags by my feet, as well as on my lap. There are the ones I left at his house, along with my replacement school bag, plus one filled with the "suitable attire" his mom had let me borrow—they're washed and ironed now, ready to be returned. The less connection I have to the boy beside me, the better off I'll be.

If it weren't for all the extra baggage I'd be lugging around, I would've caught the bus home.

I force a smile. "Ready when you are."

It's the most we've spoken all day. Even when we were working in Esme's yard, Holden found a way to give directions without actually talking. I don't know if he's simply mirroring my mood or if he's in a mood of his own. Either way, it doesn't matter. I have nothing to say, and he has nothing I want to hear.

When we finally make it to my house, Holden speaks for the first time. "Do you need a hand carrying—"

"Nope," I cut in, already halfway out of his truck. "I'll see you at school."

I hate that he still cares enough about me to wait until I'm inside before slowly pulling away.

But worse, I hate that I notice it… that I *like* it.

• • •

Gina used to say that there isn't a problem in the entire world that couldn't be solved with a long, hot bath. Unfortunately, my trailer doesn't have a bath, only a shower, and so that's what I do. I set the temperature to scorching, and I stand under the stream, let the water crash down on my shoulders, and I try to breathe through the constant pain of existence. I ignore the liquid heat that falls from my lashes, and act as if it's coming from the showerhead.

I try to imagine the feeling of soft, beige carpet beneath my legs, the warmth of the fireplace heating my flesh. I try to remember the smell of books, the scent wafting up with every flip of the page. For a moment, just one, I can feel her with me—Gina—her gentle hands combing through my hair and her shaky, aging fingers wiping away my tears. Sometimes, I wish I was back there, the only place in the world I felt cared for. But that would mean going back in time—a time when I was safe… but my mother lived a life of destruction.

I sniff once, standing taller as I push the thought aside, angry with myself for even thinking it.

When the hot water runs out, I reluctantly switch off the shower. Just as I reach for a towel, I hear the knocking on the door.

Not knocking.

Banging.

Fear closes my airways, fills my bloodline with panic. *Dread.* Before I know what's happening, I'm standing behind my door, wrapped in a towel, with a loaded gun held tightly in my grasp.

The banging continues, only now it comes with a familiar voice. "Jamie!"

I push out an exhale—relief mixed with anger—and open the door. "What the hell, Holden!"

"What took you so fucking…" His words die in the air when he notices my lack of clothing first, and then the gun. His eyes meet mine, confused. Worried. "Why do you…"

I turn on my heels, stomp toward the bedroom. Over my shoulder, I snap, "Why are you knocking on my door like you're the goddamn police!" Or a violent, jaded ex-boyfriend looking for his punching bag.

"That's how you want to answer the door if cops come?" I hear him close the door, lock it, and then his footsteps following behind.

After replacing the gun in the drawer of my nightstand, I turn to him. "Why are you here?"

"Why are you answering the door with what I assume is a loaded weapon?"

I flop down on the bed, the adrenaline still coursing through my veins, causing my knees to bounce, my hands to shake, my pulse to pound in my eardrums.

I hate that he's here, that he's witnessing this, and so I try to hide it. I get up, move past him standing in the doorway, and grab a towel from the bathroom. After sitting back down, I busy my hands with drying my hair. "What do you want, Holden?" I ask, trying to level my breathing. The last time I felt this amount of fear was when I caught Jayden, the "property manager," in my house when I'd been out. He said he was checking the gas lines. I bought a chain lock the next day.

"I just... I don't like the way we are right now," Holden answers.

I laugh once, bitter. "What exactly do you want from me?"

"I don't know, Jamie, but the silence is killing me, and you're being weird, and I don't know how to take it, and..."

I struggle to find some calm in the chaos of my mind. "And?"

He doesn't answer, and so I look up to see him watching me. His eyes are on my bare legs at first, and then they trail up, past my waist, to my chest, barely covered by my towel. His throat moves with his swallow as his gaze slowly shifts up to my eyes, and I notice the familiar spark. The heat. The *need.*

I can sense his discomfort building, the veins in his neck popping with the need to move, to do *something.* The muscles in his forearms flex as he balls his fists, his broad chest rising and falling with each harsh, shallow breath.

Too bad that seeing him like this only intensifies my anger.

He still hasn't said a word, but the more he stares, the more I realize that I have something else to focus my anger on other than my dead mom and all the bullshit emotional trauma she left me.

I give up on drying my hair, throw the towel across the room, and push out my breasts. I smile when Holden's face pinches, his hand going to the growing bulge in his shorts. And then I take it one step further. Because fuck him. "I bet it must be killing you that you can't touch me."

"What?" Eyes narrowed, he stands taller. "You think I don't have any self-control?" He steps toward me, a challenge in his eyes that sets off an inferno deep within me. One hand on the bed beside me, he leans over, but not close enough that he's touching me. Heat radiates off him when he whispers, his mouth right to my ear, "I bet you've thought about that night... can't get it out of your head... my mouth on your pussy, my tongue on your clit, my fingers deep, deep, *deep* inside you..."

He's right. "Fuck you."

He laughs, deep and husky. "I bet you're soaking wet right now just thinking about it..."

I drop my gaze to the erection tenting his shorts and fight back the urge to reach out and touch him. Just to fuck with him. Instead, I lean back so we're face-to-face, only inches apart. Head games. That's all this is. And when it comes to mental fortitude, perfectly stable Holden Eastwood has nothing on me. "I don't know..." I deadpan, begging my body not to betray the coldness of my words. "Let's see." I reach down, slowly dragging my towel higher up my thighs as I spread my legs.

Holden pushes off the bed, stands to full height again. Lips parted, he watches my every move while I watch his expression switch from defiance to raw, unfiltered lust, and I have him right where I want him. I slide a finger between my folds, moaning when the evidence of my pleasure soaks my flesh. Goose bumps prick across my skin, and I push a finger inside me. Then two. It's the most daring move I've ever made, but the way Holden stares, watching unabashedly, his heavy breaths floating between us—it only pushes me further.

"Put your feet up on the mattress and spread your legs. I want to see it all," he orders, his eyes trained right where I want them.

"Fuck you," I seethe. "Make me."

Touch me.

Want me.

Do dirty, filthy things to me.

He doesn't respond. He simply removes his shirt and then his shorts until he's standing naked in front of me, and I can't help the strangled sound that emits from deep in my throat when I see him like this. I take him in, slowly, slowly, and he's nothing but solid strength, lines and angles, curves and dips, and damn what I'd give to draw him. Exactly like this. Nothing but lights and shadows.

Grasping his cock, he slides his fist back and forth.

My pulse pounds against my chest, and I subconsciously lick my lips.

He smiles, cocking an eyebrow as he gets down on his knees. "You're just dying to have me in your mouth, aren't you, baby?"

"Baby? Fuck off." I shake my head. "And as if I'd give in to your wants." Holden moves closer again, his head between my knees, gaze locked on my fingers rubbing my clit, again and again, and I can feel my release building. His arm moves—rapid, rhythmic, jerking off to the sight of me.

I push him one step further and remove my towel, baring me to him. Then I taunt him some more, run a hand up my stomach and to my breast, touching, teasing.

His eyes follow the movement. "Fuck," he spits, his jaw set. A shiver runs through him, makes its way up his spine until his shoulders shudder.

It's such a reckless, dangerous game we're playing, and damn, if there isn't a high that comes with this level of dominance.

No wonder it's so addictive.

Drugs.

Power.

I clear my throat, wait until his eyes meet mine. "It really is a shame you'll never feel the warmth of my mouth, see my lips stretched around your cock. Licking. Stroking. *Sucking.*" I don't even know what I'm saying anymore.

All I know is that I want to break him.

Ruin him.

If only once.

If only now.

His eyes widen and he exhales, his harsh breath landing on my wet center. My eyes drift shut, imagining everything I've just teased with him. I picture the head of his cock parting my lips, the feel of his softness mixed with steel against my tongue. I imagine looking up at him, see the fire in his eyes as he watches me pleasure him.

Heat burns, courses through my veins, and I hasten my movements. I rub harder, bringing myself closer and closer to the edge. I moan out his name—a mistake… or maybe a win, because he grinds out, "Fuck this." And then his hand's on my wrist, pulling me away, replacing it with his mouth. His fingers. I jolt in response, a strangled squeal falling from my lips before I can stop it. Grabbing my ankles, he lifts my legs, places my feet on his shoulders, all while he licks me, tastes me, *devours* me, his fingers deep, deep, *deep* inside me—just like he described.

I grasp his hair, hold him to me, and grind my hips. I use him— his mouth, his body—until I explode on his tongue, pulse around his fingers. He gives me a minute to recover before he stands, hand curled around his erection while he wipes the remnants of my pleasure off his chin, his mouth. Through my post-orgasm haze, I notice the sweat coating every inch of him. "Jesus Christ, Jamie," he says through gritted teeth. "I've never needed anything as much as I need to *fuck* you right now."

"Fuck off," I say, reaching into my nightstand to grab a condom. I throw it at his chest. He doesn't even flinch, just rips the packet open with his teeth. Sliding on the rubber, he says, "I want you on top. I want to squeeze your ass and grab your tits while you ride me. I want you to use me like you just did."

"No," I tell him, and I don't even know why I say it because the moment he lies flat on my bed, I'm climbing on top of him, our hands meeting between us, guiding each other toward where we both want to be. *Need* to be.

The sounds of our drawn-out moans fill the room the moment he's inside me, stretching me, filling me. And I'm suddenly inundated with too many emotions, too many questions. I settle my hands on his chest, refusing to look at him when I say, "This doesn't change anything, Holden."

He runs his hands up my thighs, softly, slowly, and it's too gentle, too affectionate. I don't like it. "What are you talking about?"

"It's just sex," I remind him. *And myself.* "It doesn't mean anything. It never has before." I look up, right into his eyes—eyes so green I want to walk through the forest, get lost in there. A tightness forms in my chest, and I ignore what it could mean. "You made your choice," I manage to get out. "You chose loyalty over lust, so—"

"Lust?" he cuts in, sitting up, shifting himself inside me. One hand gripping my waist, he uses the other to grasp my face, bringing me closer to drop a kiss on my forehead. "This isn't fucking *lust*, Jamie..." He rolls us over until I'm on my back, and he's laying on top of me, weight held up by his forearm. He grips my leg, wraps it around his waist as he thrusts into me slowly. Then he kisses my shoulder, my neck, my jaw. "I don't know what the fuck this is," he says, "but it's sure as fuck a hell of a lot more than *lust*." And then he's kissing me, sinking into me, deeper and deeper. Not just physically, but in every other way possible. Deep into my body. Into my mind. Into my soul. He replaces my emotional pain with our physical pleasure.

And it's terrifying.

And delusional.

And destructive.

And *perfect*.

For now…

CHAPTER
TWENTY-EIGHT

HOLDEN

The Patience Game is simple: Jamie and I test each other's patience until one of us eventually cracks.

Sometimes it's a verbal spar.

Other times, we don't say a word. This version of The Patience Game is merely an extension of The Staring Game.

Jamie stands at the doorway of her room, her arms at her sides, completely naked.

As soon as I'd... *finished*, she tapped my shoulder and said, "Okay, you can leave now."

I was literally still inside her, my cock still pulsing, and there was no way I was going anywhere. Nevertheless, I mumbled a "sure" and got up. After cleaning up the aftermath of our pleasure in her bathroom, I opened the door to see her standing there, naked, and while she was doing her business in the bathroom, I crawled back into her bed.

Now, she's watching me, waiting for... I don't even know what. "Look." She finally cracks, crossing her arms. I fight back a smile at the small victory. "We both got what we wanted, so you don't need to stay."

I shrug. "I want to stay."

"Liar," she says, moving to her dresser. She pulls out a drawer and finds underwear and a tank top, slips them both on, and reluctantly crawls in beside me. She settles on her back, looking up at the ceiling. "This isn't awkward at all," she murmurs.

With a chuckle, I state, "You're *making* it awkward." I slide an arm beneath her neck and pull her toward me until her front's pressed to my side. After a long moment, she finally relents, settling her leg over mine, her arm on my torso. Her fingertips splay against my chest, warming the parts of me that crave her the most.

I stare up at the ceiling and say, "Question." I don't wait for a response before adding, "Are you taking psychology?"

"No."

"Biology?"

"No."

"Hmm… Chemistry?"

"No!" She's so over my bullshit. "What the hell, Holden?"

"I'm just trying to figure out why my dick gets harder for you the more you hate me."

She doesn't respond right away, and I'm too afraid to look at her, so I keep my eyes up. Her ceiling's made up of panels, also painted white, like the walls, and I wonder if they were like that when she moved in. Or maybe she and her mom went out and painted it to hide whatever was here before them. I'd only been here once before, and it was dark, and seeing it in the light… her home doesn't feel much like a home. It's so empty. So sterile.

"It would make things so much easier if I *could* hate you," she finally says.

I realize I'd been deep in my own thoughts the entire time; I'd almost forgotten what I'd said. I flip to my side, so we're face to face. Her eyes meet mine, lips still swollen and red from my attack. "You don't hate me?"

Shaking her head, she answers, "No."

I shouldn't ask. I do anyway. "Why not?"

After a heavy sigh, her gaze drops. "Because your heart is pure, and your intentions are good, and I can't fault you for that."

In my arms, she's exactly where I want her, where I *need* her, and I should really keep my mouth shut before it blows up in my face. "I'm sure there are plenty of other things you could fault me for."

"Oh, I'm sure," she states. "But none of those things are relevant to *me*."

———

I wake up the next morning, confused, and instantly blinded by darkness. It doesn't take long for my senses to kick in. A single inhale of sunshine and solace, and I smile at the memories of the night before.

We'd stayed in Jamie's bed for another hour after she deemed that she didn't, in fact, hate me. We talked shit, pushing each other's buttons until my stomach growled its annoyance at me. Jamie laughed at the sound, that husky laugh that almost brings me to my knees. And then she rolled her eyes, struggled to pull me out of bed by my arm, and we got dressed, walked to the diner together. I offered to drive, but she said it was a nice night out, and she'd prefer to walk, and I'd pretty much do anything she requested because that's the power she has over me.

Halfway through our meal, I asked her what her plans were for the rest of the night. She told me she usually catches up on all the homework she hasn't had time to do. So, that's what we did. We went back to her house, and she sat on the floor between the couch and the coffee table, studying, while I laid across the couch, scrolling through bullshit on my phone with headphones on. At some point, I woke up to my phone ringing. It was my mom asking if I was coming home. I'd looked over at Jamie, obviously listening in on our conversation, and I asked her, "Am I going home?"

She shrugged, but I caught her hint of a smile when I told Mom,

"I'm going to stay at Jamie's." Jamie packed up whatever she was doing and led me to her room by my hand, and then we... *slept.*

We did nothing but hold each other and sleep, and it did things to my soul that being between her legs did to me physically.

It released all the tension I didn't know I was carrying.

And as much as I want to feel that again, right this second, Jamie's not in bed with me. She's in the shower. With all the windows blocked out, I have no clue what time it is... until my alarm goes off a second later.

6:30.

I throw the covers off me, make my way to the bathroom, and enter without knocking. "Holden?"

"No," I say, slapping toothpaste on my finger. "It's the other guy you masturbated in front of last night."

The shower curtains part just so she can glare at me through the mirror. "If you tell anyone about that, I'm going to strategically slice off your balls with a chainsaw."

I chuckle. "Noted," I say, at the same time she switches off the shower. I hand her the towel while finger-brushing my teeth. And then I turn around, lean against the sink with my arms crossed, and make no attempt to hide the fact that I'm ogling her. "You really do have an insane body, Jamie."

She glances up, then right back to her towel-covered hands sliding up her leg. "Thank you."

What I'd give to be that towel. "You're welcome."

Standing to full height, she wraps the towel around her before stepping out of the shower. "I meant what I said, though. Don't tell anyone—"

"Anyone?" I cut in "Or Dean specifically? Because I'll handle Dean."

"*Handle* him?" she asks, moving past me to get to her room. "What's there to *handle?*"

I follow behind her, sit on the edge of the bed as she stands in front of the dresser. Slipping on my shorts from the night before and keeping my eyes on hers through the mirror, I say, "It'd be different if you were just some... side chick." Her brow knits, but she doesn't respond. I add, "But he *loves* you, Jamie, so like I said, I'll handle it." I don't know how, or why I'm even making this promise.

She turns to me, her gaze lowered. I know she wants to say something; she just doesn't know if she should. And so I wait. Play out The Patience Game. "Did he tell you I gave him a second chance?"

I sit taller, all ears. "What?"

Her eyes meet mine. "Yeah. Even after Bethany came knocking on my door and exposed him for the piece of shit he is, I—pathetically— still wanted him. I asked him to choose: her or me." She spins around, picks out a ghastly shit-brown cardigan, and faces me again. "So he can *tell* you that he loves me. He can even say the same to my face. But it's pretty fucking obvious who he chose, Holden."

"It's not that simple," Dean says, slamming his gym locker shut. We'd planned to do a morning weights session, and so here we are. Jamie leaves as early as she does because she catches two busses to school. We were one of the few cars here when we arrived, and she said it was perfect since she'd have the art room all to herself. I should've gone to the art room with her because now I'm having a stand-off with my *friend* over a girl he *chose* to leave behind.

"How is it not?" I scoff. I'm trying to contain my anger, but my tone defies me. I lean against the lockers; hands shoved in my pockets. "You know, Jamie thinks that Bethany hasn't told everyone because she's ashamed that you cheated on her with a girl who scrubs dishes at a truck stop and lives in a trailer..."

He doesn't respond, and when I glance up at him, the look in his eyes is answer enough.

"You guys are such fucking elitist assholes," I say, pushing off the locker. I need to get away from him before I say something I'll regret.

"Holden, stop," he grinds out, hand on my chest. "You know better than anyone what my parents are like. Image is everything to them. And to *them*, Bethany and I fit in their picture-perfect box. Could you imagine how they'd react to me bringing Jamie home?"

I *cannot* be hearing this. I slap his hand off me. "Are you fucking serious right now?"

"I'm not like you, bro," he says, his voice rising. "I don't have the freedom to live my life however I want. Everything's set in stone for me." He ticks off his expectations on his fingers. "I get college paid for, I marry the girl everyone expects me to, I work in real estate with my grandpa, and when he retires, I take over the business and live happily ever after. The end."

"Who the fuck are you right now?"

"I'm a fucking realist, Holden!"

He may be right, but still. "They're not just other people's expectations of you. They're yours, too. *Your* wants. *Your* needs. *Your* future. And you don't give a fuck who you hurt on the way."

He's quiet for a beat, and I can see the question in his eyes before he expresses it out loud, "Why are you so invested in this?"

I square my shoulders, ready myself for whatever he's going to throw at me. "Because I'm seeing her."

He laughs once, fueled by bitterness. "You mean you're *fucking* her?"

"No, Dean. I mean, I'm *seeing* her."

"Right," he says, stepping back. "So, what do you want from me? My approval?"

"I'm not asking your permission. I'm *telling* you."

He rolls his eyes, picks up his gym bag from the bench beside us. "Well, this will be good," he murmurs.

"What the hell is that supposed to mean?"

After dragging the strap over his torso, he says, "You don't even realize the disaster you're about to inflict on yourselves." He scoffs. "You guys are complete fucking opposites. She's had a messed-up life that's forced her to mature to an age you can't even fathom, and you —you're like Peter Pan—the leader of the Lost Boys—the boy who wouldn't grow up. You can't even get your shit together enough to think or even care about what you're going to do once we're done here." He steps closer until we're toe-to-toe. "So have your fun, man. But don't be surprised when she gets sick of your shit—when she wants more than just sex and a good time." He inches forward, his mouth right to my ear. "You're nothing but a rebound, *friend.*"

I shove his chest—hard—but it only makes him laugh. I'd never seen this side of him before. This resentful, cruel version of him. "How the fuck are we friends?"

Head bent, he settles his laughter enough to look up and face me. Stony eyes meet mine, hardening his words when he says, "My dad asked me to be so you would join the team."

"Fuck you."

"You're nothing to me, Eastwood," he deadpans. "You never were."

CHAPTER
TWENTY-NINE

JAMIE

He's nothing more than a lone silhouette beneath the moonlight, but I know who it is before he even looks up. Ball cap pulled low on his brow, Holden makes no attempt to move as I approach him. He's sitting on the hood of his truck in the alleyway behind the diner, and I try to recall if we'd made plans.

We hadn't.

"What are you doing here?" I ask, stopping in front of him.

He doesn't say a word as he jumps down and goes to the passenger's side. Then he opens the door, motions for me to get inside.

"Hey!" I flick the brim of his cap so I can see his face. "You suddenly gone mute on me?"

He smiles, but it's forced, and he offers a "hey" as he settles a hand on my waist. "I wanted to see you."

To be honest, I'd looked out for him at school, but I hadn't seen him. Not even at our lockers. So I sure as hell wasn't expecting to see him here, now. "You saw me this morning."

Eyes rolling, his shoulders slump as he urges me into his vehicle. "Shut up. Get in."

. . .

There are no questions when we get to my house. Holden exits the car before I do and waits for me to open the door. The second we're inside, he is *on* me—his hands, his mouth, exploring parts of me he familiarized himself with only yesterday.

He has me pressed against the door when his mouth moves down to my jaw, toward my neck, and I'm suddenly aware of the fact that I'd just finished work, and I'm probably covered in grime. "Holden, I'm so gross right now." I flatten my palms on his chest, trying to push him away. "I probably taste like bacon grease."

He laughs against my neck, but it does nothing to ease my embarrassment. "I love bacon," he states, and then he's sweeping me off my feet, our mouths locked. My legs wrap around his torso while my fingers lace through his hair, and I have no idea where his hat went.

I can feel his need through the bulge in his shorts, rubbing against my center as he walks me to the bedroom. Heat swarms through my veins when he drops me on the bed, and there isn't a hint of hesitation as he lowers my zipper, removes my jeans. His hands are rough when he grabs at my breast through my shirt, squeezing hard, and I wince, but he doesn't hear me.

He doesn't seem to notice anything: the pace of his actions, the hint of uncertainty momentarily locking up my bones. He's way too distant… too *lost*. I can see it in his eyes now, sense it in the way he touches me, the way he maneuvers me onto my stomach, and then to my hands and knees.

I watch his face as he rolls on a condom—his eyes mainly—and I wish I could see something there. See the passion, the heat, the desire. But there's nothing: nothing but an illusion of life set in the forest of his irises.

I flip onto my back before things go too far, and it's only now I realize that the motherfucker's still fully dressed. Shoes and all. "What the hell are you doing?"

"What?" He has the audacity to sound pissed and *fuck him*.

I stand up, pushing him away as I pass him, and move to the

other side of the room. I fight back my anger, my disappointment, and keep my eyes on his when I say, "Don't do this shit again, Holden."

"Do what, exactly?"

"Do *what*?" I repeat, louder than I'd expected. "You think it's okay to come here and just use my body as a vessel to empty your pent-up emotions? Fuck you!"

His gaze drops, chest deflating with his exhale. After discarding the condom in the trashcan by my dresser, he breathes out, "I have to go."

"Of course you do," I murmur, shaking my head as I watch him stalk toward the door.

He halts mid-step, eyes snapping to mine. "What does that mean?" he sighs out, his face pinching with irritation.

"You know..." I start, my gaze dropping to the rings on my fingers, "the day after my mom died, I burned all her shit in the field out back, because that's how I deal with my emotions. I *destroy* them, and then I bury them." I take a breath, attempt to stay calm, but I'm losing the battle. The fight. "And it's cool if sex is how you deal with yours. They're both fucked up, but the difference? I wasn't hurting anyone."

His eyebrows shoot up as he takes a step toward me. "I *hurt* you?"

"Not physically. No."

His shoulders visibly relax.

"But you just made me feel like trash right now," I say, reaching down to the floor to pick up my jeans. I slide them on slowly, needing the distraction, so he doesn't see the tears threatening to fall or hear the pain in my voice when I add, "Why is it so easy for you to use me and just throw me away?"

"Jamie..."

There's an ache in my chest, twisting, burning heat behind my eyes, and I can't let him see me like this. I can't give him this power over me. "I get that we did this whole thing last night, and it might be confusing to you, but I never agreed to be your *fuck buddy,* so if that's all you want—"

"It's not." He leans against the wall opposite me, head lowered as he cracks his knuckles. "I'm sorry." I focus on the largeness of his hands, the strength each of his fingers possesses. "The last thing I want is to hurt you. Physically or otherwise. And I'm sorry I made you feel that way."

My pulse rages against my chest, beating hard against my flesh. And I don't even try to hide my resentment. "Yeah, well you did, and I don't know if sorry is going to cut it."

When he doesn't respond, I slide my focus from his hands to his face. Eyes already on mine, I watch the myriad of emotions fleet across them—a mixture of conviction and uncertainty. And I know that look… know that feeling. I drown in it every time I look at him.

Motioning toward the bed, he stands taller, mumbles, "I didn't come here for… *that*."

"Then why *are* you here? Because it sure as fuck isn't to talk. You've barely said two words to—"

"Because you're the only fucking thing that makes sense to me right now!" he shouts. And then he takes a breath as he eyes the ceiling; his hands now fists at his sides. "And I wish I knew what to make of that, but I don't." He reaches up, runs a hand through his hair. "I don't know what it means, Jamie, and I don't even know why I'm telling you this because…" He trails off, his eyes meeting mine, and I wish I were doing more than just standing here, in shock, silently replaying his words in my head.

I'm the only thing that makes sense to him? What does that even mean?

"I have to go," he says again, pushing off the wall.

He's already one foot out of the bedroom before I finally find my voice. "Wait!"

He stops, his back to me. I don't know what I'd planned on saying after the *wait*, but that's all I needed from him. Just *wait*. Wait for me to get my thoughts together and my heart to catch up to my mind—to his words floating around in there—wreaking havoc, creating mayhem like they are. "Sit down."

He spins on his heels; his head lowered as he shuffles to the bed. He keeps it that way as he slumps down, eyes cast downward.

I sit sideways on his lap, my legs between his, and curl my arm around his neck. "Hi," is all I can think to say.

"Hi," he responds, his chest deflating as his arms tighten around me.

I lean into him, ignoring all the questions and uncertainty floating between us. "It was a pleasant surprise—seeing you after work."

He rears back, eyes meeting mine. "It was?"

I nod. "Are you going to tell me what's going on?"

He lowers his head to the crook of my neck before inhaling deeply. After a moment, he says, sounding almost defeated, "It doesn't even matter anymore. This..." He brings me closer. "This is what matters." He kisses me quickly before pulling away. "But I really do have to go. I don't *want* to. But I *have* to. I told my mom I was just picking you up from work, and I made a stupid promise to her that I'd be home on school nights, so..."

"It's okay," I say, attempting to get up. "You should go."

He only holds me tighter. "Come with me?"

"To your *house*? Why?"

He sucks in a breath, lets it out forcefully. And when his eyes settle on mine, I recognize the pain, the torment. "Because I need you, Jamie... I just..." He kisses me again. "I *need* you."

191

CHAPTER
THIRTY

JAMIE

I jolt awake at the sound of a phone ringing, and for a moment, I'm disorientated... because the phone ringing isn't mine and I'm not in my bed. "Sorry," Holden mumbles, reaching across me to flick on the lamp. "I have to take this." He sits up as he grabs his phone, pushing the covers down to his lap. "Mia Mac," he says in greeting, his voice scratchy from sleep. "No..." He shakes his head. "I wasn't sleeping... I was—yeah, okay, I was, but it's fine... how... how are you?" There's a sincerity in his tone that has me rolling to my side, placing a hand on his back to... what? Comfort him? I don't know, and I don't really know much about Mia besides the fact that he cares deeply for her.

"Yeah?" Holden says into the phone, and I feel his muscles relax beneath my touch. Just slightly. "Have you eaten?" His body slumps with relief at her answer, and I push the covers off me, get out of bed. It's obvious they need to talk, and I want him to do that openly. Freely.

As soon as I'm on my feet, Holden reaches for my arm, mouths, "Stay."

And I motion, with my hands, that I'm just getting water. I'm not thirsty, far from it. I'm also not fully awake or coherent because I don't even think as I make my way toward the lit kitchen. I have no concept of time, no idea how long we'd been asleep.

When we got here, Holden led me straight to his room and said to go ahead and use his shower. He told me he was going to check in on his mom, and when I got out, he was already in his bed waiting for me.

And then we…

We *slept*.

And I have to admit, there's something about simply *sleeping* with Holden—being wrapped in his arms, enveloped in his warmth, drowning in his scent—that competes with the notion of *sex* with Holden. Aaand now I'm contemplating returning and having sex with Holden. Even worse? I'm *remembering* what it was like. Which is probably the last thing I should be doing, especially since I just walked into the kitchen… where his mom is… sitting at the table working on a jigsaw puzzle.

Awesome.

I freeze in the doorway, quick to tug down at my shirt. I'm fully aware that my legs are bare, so I can't fault her for any possible assumptions.

"Hi, Jamie," she says, watching me a moment before going back to the puzzle. "Did you need something?"

"Hi, Mrs.—Miss—*Ma'am.*" I can't even look at her as I move past her and toward the kitchen sink. "I was just getting water."

"You can call me Tammy, and there's a tap in Holden's bathroom," she says. Then adds, "Though, not any glasses, so…"

Is she mad at me? For… being here? Holden did say he'd made a promise that he'd stay home, and maybe that extended to having girls over. Does he have girls over often? Is this new? "Yeah," I croak, heat burning my cheeks. I grab a glass from beside the sink and fill it with tap water. "He's on the phone with Mia, so I thought I'd give them some space…"

"He is?" she asks, and I somehow find the courage to face her.

After a nod, I search for the time, but there are no clocks in this room, and the microwave merely blinks 12:00 as if it had never been set. "Well... that's good."

I practically inhale the water, wash out the glass, and then I just stand there, facing the window above the sink. I don't want to go back to Holden's room just yet, and I don't really want to be standing here, awkwardly, with his mom judging me. Anxiousness swirls through me, elevating with every second that passes, each one filled with nothing but silence and the occasional sound of cardboard pieces shifting. Finally, Tammy speaks, "Holden says that you lost your mother recently."

Slowly, I turn to her, keeping my gaze on my feet as I grip the counter behind me. Heart in my stomach, I fumble over my words. "It was a while ago. I mean, late October, it'll be a year, so..."

"Well," she says, after a beat. "Grief has no timeline, right?"

I don't think I've ever really *grieved*, but she doesn't need to know that. "I guess."

"Jamie," she says, and I find the strength to look up. "I was wondering if you could give me some advice."

"Advice?"

Tammy nods. "On grief." I'm about to tell her I'm the last person to be dishing out *advice*, especially on that subject, but she speaks up before I can. "It's just that, I've never lost anyone super close to me, and Mia... she recently lost her grandfather, and she's going through an extremely hard time with it all. She's not eating. Not sleeping..." she trails off, and I look at her. Really, *truly* look at her. Her hair's a mess, similar to my mother's when she did nothing but fall in and out of drunken blackouts. Darkness circles her red, raw eyes as if she'd just been crying. And I can't help but look at her the way Holden did when I bared my pain to him—with pity.

I find myself asking, "Are you?"

Distracted with the puzzle piece in her hand, she asks, "Am I what?"

"Eating and sleeping?"

Her gaze snaps to mine, and it's clear I've overstepped.

"Sorry," I murmur. Obviously, I have close to zero social graces, but I remind myself that it's not my fault. I've never really been... *social.*

The silence stretches between us, and I push off the counter. "Well, goodnight," I mumble.

I make it to the doorway before Tammy says, surprising me, "Maybe I'm asking for the both of us, then. For Mia *and* me."

I pause, my stomach sinking at the desperation in her words. After inhaling deeply, I turn to her, give her the truth that'll do nothing to ease her anguish. "I wish, more than anything, that I could give you advice. That I could give you the answers you think you need, but I can't." I push through the knot in my throat, the sudden ache in my chest. "I feel like our circumstances of grief and loss are very different."

Tammy's slow to nod, her lips parting, but there are no words accompanying the action. I see it in her eyes, the blank stare, the bottomless void, and I can sense that she needs *something.* She just doesn't know what. And *I* don't know if I'm the right person to help her find whatever she's lost.

But... I know that *feeling,* that endless searching and hoping and praying for *something.* Even if that something is nothing. And that nothing lasts only seconds.

"The thing is..." I start, leaning against the doorframe, "my mom's death wasn't a shock to me. I'd been prepared for months. Maybe even years." I drop my gaze to my feet again, adding, "In a way, I think I'd considered her dead a long time ago." My words are harsh, but they're also reality—a reality I refuse to sugar-coat or wrap neatly in a bow just to spare the feelings of others.

Or myself.

"Maybe you're right," Tammy says, her voice cracking with emotion. "John—Mia's *papa*—he died of a heart attack. It was only weeks after he had an operation. He umm..." She clears her throat, so close to breaking. "He came here for the surgery, trusted in me to take care of him after, and..."

"I'm sorry," I whisper, pushing down my own heartache. Maybe I was wrong. Maybe our situations are more alike than I thought. Because the guilt? The guilt is worse than the grief.

"I shouldn't have let him go back," she whispers.

A single tear forces its way out of me, and I'm quick to wipe it away. *I shouldn't have forced Mom to leave.*

I still remember that day as if I'd just lived it. I remember the warmth of the tears as they soaked through my flesh. My pulse thump, thump, thumping through my bloodline. I can still feel the desperation… the hopelessness clinging to my words, to my pleas, to the very few parts of me that still held on to hope.

We needed to leave.

I was thirteen years old, and I'd just found the paperwork of her diagnosis in her purse—dated almost a year earlier. I was furious at her for not telling me, and so I cried, and I screamed and cried some more. I'd never cried as much as I did at that moment because I couldn't tell what was diminishing quicker: her body, her soul, or her will to live. And I couldn't fucking comprehend why she was so adamant about fighting me on it.

In my mind, it was simple.

We needed to leave.

If we stayed, she would die. She needed to break the cycle she was caught in: Beaker would hit her, she would drink. Around and around and around she would go.

We needed to leave.

The next day, while Beaker was at work, we packed a bag each and hopped on a bus to nowhere.

I never imagined that "nowhere" would be here, at God knows what hour, talking to a boy's mom about death. About loss. About *mourning.*

I stay quiet, my hands behind my back. I don't know what to say, how to react.

Tammy clears her throat, then asks, "How did—"

"Organ failure," I cut in, looking up at her.

She watches me, her hands paused mid puzzle placement. Tears well in her eyes, but she doesn't blink, doesn't let them fall. Then, beneath the table, she kicks out the chair opposite her, and I accept the offered seat. If my telling her about my experience will help her in any way, then I'll do it.

For her.

For Holden.

"Was there no treatment available?" she asks, pushing the half-complete puzzle to the middle of the table.

I scrutinize the image, try to make sense of it. I can't. I choose my words carefully, not wanting to lie. "By the time I found out about the diagnosis, the only solution was a transplant." I ignore the ache in my chest, the twisting in my gut when I add, "But they don't hand out organs to alcoholics."

"Oh, Jamie…"

"I tried to get her to go to AA," I rush out. Because guilt is a bitch no matter how much time has passed. No matter how many times I asked her—begged her—my mom never attended a single meeting. That doesn't mean I didn't read up on it as much as I could, and I made it my mission for her to complete all twelve steps.

The first step is admitting that you're powerless to alcohol and that it's caused your life to become unmanageable.

Obviously, the transplant never came.

Because she never made it past the first step.

I fight back the tears, the raw emotion threatening to explode out of me.

"It's not your fault, Jamie," Tammy says, reaching across the table. She grasps my hand in hers, gently squeezing. And it's such a simple act. Such a basic gesture, and yet… I look from our joined hands up to her face, where the remnants of her tears mar her beauty.

I cover her hand with both of mine, repeat her actions, and squeeze once. "It's not your fault, either, Tammy."

She lets out a sob so suddenly, I wasn't expecting it. Wasn't prepared. I don't know what to say, how to comfort her. When my mom cried, it was always for Beaker. It was pathetic, so I ignored her. I don't want to ignore Tammy, but I don't know what else to do. "You're right," Tammy says, nodding as she wipes at the onslaught of tears. Her shoulders shake, and she repeats, "You're absolutely right, Jamie."

A throat clearing has my focus snapping to Holden standing in the doorway. I don't know how long he's been there, how much he's heard. There's an emotion in his eyes I can't quite decipher, and then he's stepping into the room, his body rigid. To me, he says, "Let's go to bed."

And so I stand, squeezing Tammy's hand once more. "Goodnight," I say and wait for Holden as he settles his hand on his mother's shoulder.

"Night, Ma," he murmurs. "I love you."

Tammy reaches up, pats his hand. "I love you, too, baby."

"Try to get some sleep, okay?" He drops a kiss on top of her head.

I force myself to look away, the shared moment too intimate for my eyes.

"I will," she responds, and then Holden's taking my hand, leading me back to his room, where we crawl into bed, not a single word spoken, and he wraps me in his arms, envelopes me in his warmth, drowns me in his scent, and we...

We *sleep*.

CHAPTER THIRTY-ONE

HOLDEN

Jamie: I looked up the results on my break. Sorry you guys suck.

I smile as I read Jamie's text. It was the first game of the season, and after the physical beating from Lakewood High and the verbal beatdown from Coach, any form of communication with her is exactly what I need to pull me out of my headspace.

It's been over a week since Jamie and I have had any proper time together. We had the hour or so at Esme's on Wednesday, but Esme had gotten a delivery of sod, so we were busy working, and we couldn't even hang out when we'd finished because she'd picked up an extra shift right after. Besides the few minutes in the morning where I throw out wisecracks about her clothes, and she retorts with her usual insults, we don't really speak. We don't call. We don't text. Her schedule doesn't give her much time for a social life, and I guess I've been busy, too. The day after their little heart-to-heart, my mom and I had dinner, and we talked. It was the first time in months that she seemed fully present. Her eyes were clear, and maybe... maybe, her mind was, too. When we got to chatting about school and the Outreach Club, I told her all about Esme and the work Jamie and I are doing. A *tiny* spark lit up in her eyes, and she asked me to draft out the layout of Esme's yard and what I'd planned to do. She gave me advice, told me what I could change to suit the surroundings better, and because I hadn't seen her interested in much of anything lately, I jumped at the chance to show her in person. So, that's what we've been doing in our free time, Mom and me—working on Esme's yard. I don't know how long it will last, but even without the work itself, Mom and Esme seem to have formed a bond, and at least... at least she's doing something, and that's all I could've hoped for.

Sitting down on the bench in front of the lockers, I type back a reply:

Holden: *The team sucked. *I* did phenomenally. Check the stats.*

Her response is instant.

Jamie: *Pass. Even if I cared enough to look, I don't understand football. Big men fighting over small ball. What's to like?*

I laugh, then stop myself quickly, eyeing my surroundings. The locker room's still filled with my teammates, most of them in various levels of undress, and I really don't want to be *that* guy over *some girl* on the other end of the phone.

I school my features, shoot back another message.

Holden: *I'll have to teach you someday.*
Jamie: *Oh yay! Can't wait.*

I'm about to ask her what time she gets off work, but Billy Butler —the same motherfucker who literally *dropped* Dean on my front lawn—approaches, sits down right beside me. The bench groans beneath his weight, and he says, "What's the deal with you and Griffith?"

I shove my phone back in my locker and look behind me, where Dean's just getting out of the shower. "What do you mean?" Dean and I haven't said a word to each other since his little admission, and I haven't missed his presence in my life *one bit*. Personally, I don't give enough of a shit about him to talk crap behind his back. But maybe he doesn't feel the same. Either way, we have to play on the same team, so I've made an effort to keep things civil.

"That party at mine tonight?" Billy says. "I just asked him if he was going, and he said he'd go if you don't."

What a petty little bitch.

"I kind of want the whole team there," Billy adds.

"Fuck him, man. It's your house, your party. I'll be there."

He slaps my back. "Good man."

Once he's gone, I reach for my phone again.

Holden: *What time do you get off work?*
Jamie: *11*
Holden: *Feel like coming to a party?*
Jamie: *I'd rather shotgun copious amounts of horse tranquilizer.*

———

I'm high.

Maybe a little drunk, but mainly high.

The problem with having parties at Billy's house is that it's only two blocks from mine. Add that to the fact that it's been a minute since I gave myself permission to let loose, and well… I'll for sure be stumbling home tonight.

If I make it there at all.

A girl is standing in front of me, talking to me, her hands animated, and I have no clue what the hell she's saying. I don't even know who she is. Honestly, I don't even think it matters because she isn't Jamie.

Whoa. That realization hits hard, and I'm suddenly regretting my consumption of illicit substances because there's no way I can get to her tonight.

Sucks.

"I have to pee," I tell the random brunette and don't bother waiting for a reply before shuffling to the bathroom. Clearly, I'm not thinking straight because I don't lock the door, and it opens while I have my dick out, mid-stream. "Occupied," I mumble, and the door closes again.

But the person who opened it hasn't left. "You're doing the Outreach Club with that Jameson girl, right?"

My head *swivels* toward the voice. "Jesus, Bethany. I'm a little busy right now."

She doesn't move. "I'll wait."

I shift slightly, blocking her view of my cock. She doesn't say a word as I finish and flush. I'm halfway through washing my hands when she asks, "What's she like?"

"Oh my god," I whisper, rolling my eyes. I dry my hands in my hair and face her, my arms crossed as I lean against the counter. "This is very much a you-and-Dean problem and not at all a you-and-me-and-even-her problem." I don't know if that even made sense. I don't care.

"Just tell me," she says, her loose blonde hair swaying as she mimics my position, arms crossed, leaning against the wall opposite me.

"She's *good*, I guess," I almost laugh out. "She's..." *Not you.* And not at all in a bad way. "I don't know what you want me to say."

"Did you know about her?"

"I feel like I'm being interrogated."

"Did you, Holden?" she says, and I can't help but feel bad for her. "No."

"So Dean never mentioned it?"

"No."

"Would you have told me if you knew?"

I drop my head, close my eyes, and pretend to snore because fuck this.

"Holden!"

I heave out a sigh, look back at her. "Honestly, probably not."

She nods at this as if understanding. I don't know how she could. Lowering her hands to her side, she pushes off the wall, takes a step closer to me.

I narrow my eyes at her. If she's about to try to use me to get to Dean, then fuck them both.

"Do you know if she knew about me?"

"No," I state. "She didn't know you existed."

"So you've talked about it?"

"Bethany... I have nothing against you personally, but don't drag my ass into this. Like I said, this is a you-and-Dean problem. Talk to him."

She takes another step forward. "Did he love her?"

I rub my hand along my entire face vigorously. "Jesus Christ."

"He did, didn't he?" She's even closer now, and this—what she's doing—is the dictionary definition of "accosting."

Before I can come up with a response, the bathroom door opens again, and of course, it's Dean. He smirks, a disbelieving snort leaving him right before he pulls his phone from his pocket. "Oh, this is good," he says, snapping a picture of Bethany and me. "Jamie's going to love this."

CHAPTER
THIRTY-TWO

HOLDEN

B esides, you know, being an *adult,* I have never, not once, avoided anything.

Difficult situations? *Come at me!*

The harsh realities of life? *Let's fucking go!*

A freight train full of ninjas? *I'm ready!*

Jamie's possible reaction to a picture of me and her arch-nemesis alone in a bathroom at a party? *I'm noping the fucking out.*

I'd spent the entire weekend *avoiding* any and all potential scenarios in my head, which, yeah, is a pussy move, but I like my balls intact. Realistically, it wasn't all that hard to do. Jamie didn't call about it, didn't text, didn't email, didn't send any carrier pigeons or trained assassins my way. Which could mean one of two things: she's giving me the silent treatment or…. Dean never sent the picture. I'd prefer the latter, but it's been proven that Dean's a narcissistic asshole, and so, now, I have no choice but to wait it out.

Monday morning, and I'm the first of our tragic trio to get to our lockers. I'm *sweating.* And not from the heat. Dean's next, and he's wearing a smirk that I'd love to slam against a brick wall. I check the time—there are only a few minutes until the warning bell, and Jamie still hasn't shown.

Maybe she's avoiding, too.

Just as I'm about to shut my locker, hers opens.

Game time. I move around her to the open side of the locker and lean against the one beside hers. "Hi."

She doesn't look at me when she says, "Hi, back."

"So…"

She eyes me sideways. "So…?"

I suck in a breath, let it out slowly. And then I take her in from head to toe. Because it might be the last time I get to do it. Crisp white blouse tucked into a pale gray skirt, and honestly, her clothes are the only thing *meh* about her. Everything else is like a solar eclipse, and I don't know why I never noticed it before. "Did you get a text on Friday night… maybe a picture…?"

Jamie looks away, focuses on removing books from her bag and shoving them in her locker as she fights back a smile. "You mean one of you and Bethany alone in a bathroom?"

My stomach sinks. "That's the one."

"Yeah, I got it," she says, shrugging. "I just figured it was Dean being a dick." She slams her locker shut, revealing said *dick*. He's going through his locker, but it's obvious he's been listening in on our conversation, hoping to see his planned disaster come to life. Jamie looks back at him, then returns her focus to me. "Why? Should I be feeling a certain way about it?"

"Hopefully not." I shrug. "So, we're good?" I don't know what I'm asking. It's not as if we're dating. Or are we? Truthfully, I don't think either of us knows what we're doing.

She nods. "We're good," she states. "Besides, I've seen the way you are when you want someone." She says this loud enough for Dean to hear. "And that's not what I saw… you just looked annoyed."

"I was," I tell her, relief washing through me.

"So what happened?"

I give her a quick rundown, and when I'm done, I tell her, "It was weird, and I didn't like it."

She laughs, and I watch her, watch the way her smile reaches her eyes—eyes that twinkle beneath the harsh overhead lights, and I want to kiss her. I want to wrap her in my arms and lift her off the floor and spin her around the way guys do in the sappy movies Mom forces me to watch.

I don't do any of those things because that would be incredibly lame and entirely *not* me. Instead, I say, "You didn't call me."

"Phone works both ways, Eastwood," she says, and she's still smiling, and I'm still watching her every move.

"Jamie," Dean finally speaks up.

She rolls her eyes, ignoring him as she tugs on the front of my t-shirt. "I'll see you later?"

"Yeah," I breathe out.

And then she's gone, walking away, and I can't seem to take my eyes off her, even when she's no longer in view.

"She does that," Dean says, standing beside me.

"Does what?"

After a weighted silence, he says, "She takes over every part of you until there's nothing left. It's the greatest feeling in the world, but sometimes… the world isn't enough with her."

I look over at my ex-friend. "Were you always this much of a pompous asshole?"

CHAPTER
THIRTY-THREE

JAMIE

According to Holden, we're right on schedule for the work at Esme's. Though, I have noticed that a lot has been done since I was here last, and I don't know if she's paying someone to do the work. Holden would be pissed if she were. Or, at least interrogate her on who is doing it and how much they're charging. Obviously, Holden has a soft spot for her. Me too, apparently, because he asks, "Tough day?" He's standing by the bench in Esme's yard, staring at his empty water bottle as if he doesn't know how it got that way.

My eyes snap to his. "What?" And also: *how did he know?* I've been a little quieter than usual, but I've tried not to make it obvious.

Setting the bottle back on the bench, he motions in my direction before moving toward me, eyeing my legs. Since I returned Tammy's clothes, I've opted to wear denim cut-offs and a long sleeve tee whenever we come to Esme's. "Your leg," he states. "You've drawn on it, and you said..." he trails off, pulling out his phone from his pocket. He comes in close, and without permission, snaps a picture of my thigh.

"You realize how creepy that is, right?"

"I'm fully aware," he says, shoving his phone back where it belongs. "So what's up? Did something happen?"

I heave out a sigh. "Yes. And no. Not really." I look up, right into his eyes. "I know it's all in my head, and I need to just shake it off, but I don't know. It gets to me."

He stares at me, a blank expression trained on his features. "What the fuck are you talking about, Taylor?"

I half-smile, half-curse him for being able to force that single emotion out of me. "Bethany," I state.

"Ah." He scratches at his temple. "Before you tell me about it, am I simply listening, or are we problem-solving?"

I cock my head to the side. "Huh?"

"Well, I don't want to give you unsolicited advice if you didn't ask for it because that can be patronizing as hell, so if you just want to take an emotional dump on my chest then—"

"That's gross."

"It's a figure of speech."

"No, it's not."

He rolls his eyes, says, "Am I listening or we problem-solving?"

I ponder this a moment. "Listening."

Taking my hand, he links our fingers and leads me to the bench, waiting until I'm seated, before sidling up next to me. Arm around my neck, he brings me in closer, and I rest my head on his chest, staring at the small waves cascading along the pool's surface. "Spill it," he says, his thumb stroking my arm. It's such an intimate move, and I don't know how we got here.

"I had to use the little girl's room between classes, and when I got out, Bethany was at the sink. She was crying. And when she saw me, she tried to hide it, and then she kind of just stood there, intimidating me without meaning to, and I almost opened my big fat mouth to apologize for something that isn't even my fault." I take a breath and continue, "And then she left, and I swear I waited a whole minute before leaving the restroom. But she was still there, in the corridor. And the worse part? We were both going to the same class! Her legs are so much longer than mine, but swear, I felt like I was walking heel-to-toe just to keep my distance, and… *ugh*. It was just awkward and dumb, and I don't know. I keep thinking about it—like I should've said something, but what, you know?"

Holden doesn't respond, and so I pull back, look up at him. "Sucks," is all he says, shrugging.

I groan. "It's pathetic."

"Honestly? A little. Bethany is harmless, and the sooner you purge the whole situation out of your system, the better." He reaches up, flicks at my bun. "Can you take your hair down? I want to see it out."

I scoff. "You're telling me what to do now?"

"No. I'm telling you what I'd like to see and *asking* if you'll do it for me." He stares at me, challenging, his smile widening with each passing second. "You can always say no."

"No," I state, raising my chin in defiance.

His chuckle is soft, just loud enough for the butterflies in my stomach to hear, to move, to *flutter*. "You want to make out then?"

My grin is ridiculous. "Esme's home. She can probably see us."

Holden smirks, then drags both my legs over his. Arms around me, he settles his nose in the crook of my neck, inhales deeply before saying, "Esme can watch." His hand moves up the inside of my thigh —large and rough—sending goose bumps floating across my skin. I turn my head, just slightly, just enough to meet his mouth with mine. The moment our lips touch, his fingers curl, digging into my flesh. He moans, deepening the kiss. His tongue slides along mine as he grips my nape, holding me to him. Then he adjusts us, so I'm sitting directly on his lap, all so he can show me the effect I'm having on him. I push down, grinding against him. "God, I've fucking missed you," he says against my lips.

I pull back an inch, search his eyes—see the truth in his words beneath the lust setting the forest ablaze. "Me too," I whisper.

"I can't stop thinking about you, Jamie." He doesn't hold back when he kisses me again. And those butterflies in my stomach?

They fly.

Soar.

Right out of my chest and into his hands.

———

"I told my mom we'd be over for dinner, so I'll take you back to your place to get whatever you need for the night, and then we'll go."

That's way too much information in a single sentence, and I don't know which piece I want to pick apart first. I look around the diner, then lower my gaze to the burger and fries on the plate in front of me. "Aren't we having dinner now?"

Holden scoffs, his grilled sandwich poised halfway to his mouth. "This is a snack."

I push my plate toward him. "You eat it," I say. "My stomach isn't capable of handling both meals."

"Weak."

I watch him eat for a few minutes before asking, "We're having dinner with your mom?"

He nods.

"Why?"

He shrugs.

"And I'm staying at your house?"

He nods again.

"Why?"

He shrugs again.

"Did I agree to this?"

Holden sighs as he leans forward. "You can always say no, Jamie."

———

I didn't say no.

I couldn't.

I did, however, force Holden to call his mom and tell her we'll be bringing dessert, and then I went to the cold room in the diner's kitchen and grabbed an entire pecan pie. I added it to the list of products I bring home from the diner that Zeke *swears* he takes out of my wage.

I highly doubt he does.

We have dinner with Holden's mom—my first decent home-cooked meal in a while—and we discuss school and work and life. We don't go deeper than surface-level chatter, and we don't discuss *death*. But, when his mom brings up our future, mainly college, Holden shuts it down real fast.

Now, I'm dripping wet, just out of the shower with the towel wrapped around me, and I'm peeking into Holden's room, hoping to get a yes to my question. He isn't there, and so I grab my phone from the counter, my thumbs leaving rivulets of water in their wake as I send him a text.

Jamie: *Can I have a bath?*

I'd noticed the corner bath the first time I was here, and I'd wanted so badly to fill it, soak in it, maybe even cry tears of joy in it.

Holden: *Go for it.*

I don't even wait until the bath is semi-filled. I sit in the tub with my legs crossed, my hand under the stream as water cascades below me. I push aside thoughts of Gina, of tainted, murky water, and trembling bones caused by fear and shame.

When I feel as if the water's enough to cover half my body, I lie down, inhale deeply, and I then close my eyes. They're not closed long before they snap open at the sound of the bathroom door opening. Holden strides in, not a care in the world.

I *screech*, and he rolls his eyes. "Relax, Regina. I've seen it all before." He's cradling his arms, and I don't realize what he's doing until he dumps a bunch of candles on the bathroom counter. "Ambience," he says, sparking a lighter to life. He picks up a candle, lights it, and then sets it beside the tap. I silently watch as he lights each one, and when he's done, he flicks off the light and turns to me, saying, "I'll be back." No more than a minute later, he returns with a small step stool and makes a home for himself right beside the tub. "Hi."

The candles cast a dim glow across his features—nothing but striking lines and bold angles. I wonder how he sees me—too exposed? Too vulnerable? "The candles are a nice touch," I say, nervous energy pumping through my veins. "If I didn't know any better, I'd think you were trying to get in my pants."

With a smirk, he says, "Who says I'm not?"

"Yeah, about that…"

He quirks an eyebrow.

"I was just thinking that maybe… maybe we can put a pause on the whole sex thing? Just until—"

"Okay." He's too quick to cut in, and now I'm suspicious.

"Okay?" I ask, and he nods. "Just… *okay*?"

"Yeah, Jamie. If that's what you want, then that's what we'll do." He dips his hand in the water but doesn't touch me. "I have to say, though, it's incredibly cruel of you to say this while you're naked."

"Hold on." I sit up slightly. "You don't even want to know why?"

He shrugs, his gaze dipping to my breasts before meeting my eyes. "If I recall, sex for me is *fun*, and sex for you has to mean something, right?"

My eyes widen, and I jerk up, splashing water all around me. "You remember that?"

Lips curled, he says, "Yes, I remember, and you don't need to give me your reasons. Besides, telling someone how you feel shouldn't lead to an argument."

Who is he right now? "That's… true."

"Mia—she always says that *No* is a complete answer, and you don't need to justify it."

"I like Mia," I say through a smile.

He smiles back. "Anyway," he says, removing his hand from the water and flicking droplets on my face, "I was thinking about the whole you and Bethany thing."

I groan, roll to my side, and grip the edge of the tub.

"If it bothers you so much, why not just, like, drop out of school? You can still homeschool and get your diploma."

"I could," I sigh out. "But that would take away from one of the many reasons I enrolled in the first place."

"And what reason is that?"

I shift onto my back again and eye the ceiling, trying to come up with a response that will satisfy his curiosity. "I spent so much of my life being an outcast, or taking care of my mom, and once she was gone—" The ache in my chest is sudden and unexpectedly severe, and I blink hard, pushing past the pain. Through the knot in my throat, I manage to say, "I wanted something for myself. Something I'd craved but could never grasp while she was alive. I just..." I shrug. "I wanted to be a normal teenage girl."

Holden's silence is deafening, and I force myself to breathe, to settle the anguish twisting through my bloodline so I can peek up at him.

"You think it's stupid, don't you?" The crack in my voice betrays the strength I'm attempting to portray.

"I don't think it's stupid," he says, sitting taller, his gaze distant. "It's just that... I don't think you went through what you did and survived what you have so you could come out of it and be *normal*." He pauses a beat. "You're not here to be *average*, Jamie. You're here to be *extraordinary*."

I stare at him. At a boy lost in his own thoughts, in his own world, and he has no idea the effect he has on me.

Or the change he's creating inside me.

Gina used to give me her clothes to help fight my battles against my tormentors.

And now... now Holden's giving me his words to rage a war against myself.

CHAPTER
THIRTY-FOUR

HOLDEN

Over the next few weeks, Jamie and I fall into a routine that was never discussed—never outlined. On Wednesdays, we go to Esme's, then to the diner, and then to her house where she packs an overnight bag, and we go back to my house and have dinner with my mom.

Afterward, Jamie showers, bathes, and then I fuck her senseless against every surface of my room.

That last part is a lie.

On Saturday nights, I pick her up from work, and we go back to her house, where I fuck her senseless against every surface of *her* room.

That last part is also a lie.

Can you see where my headspace is at? And I realize that I'm being a dick but hear me out. We make out. *A lot*. We fool around. *A lot*. I see her naked. *A lot*. It's just that... I'm forcing myself not to do all those things at the same time.

It's... *awesome*—another lie, but it's what Jamie wants, so that's what Jamie gets.

On the upside, my dick and my hand are best friends again. *Yay!*

Besides those two nights a week, we don't hang out, don't call each other. Occasionally we'll send random, meaningless text messages, but apart from that, there's not a whole lot of communication going on.

And I can say the same for Dean and me, minus the text messages. We talk only when necessary, mainly during games or practices, and the rest of the time, I ignore his existence. I have other friends I can hang out with. So does Jamie now, too. Well, one friend. Some girl named Melanie from her art class who's notorious for hating *literally* everybody.

Besides Jamie, apparently.

I catch sight of the two girls at a table by the art room during lunch and make my way over to them. Jamie and I don't make a show of our... relationship *(?)* on school grounds. Not because we're trying to hide it or because we're ashamed, and *definitely* not because of Dean, but because—as Jamie puts it—it's no one's fucking business. I straddle the bench next to Jamie, startling her. "What the—"

"Hi," I cut in, baring my teeth with my smile.

She eyes me sideways. "Hi."

I point to her sandwich sitting on a Zeke's Diner paper bag. "Is that the grilled—" She's already offering it to me before I finish the sentence.

I take a bite, and then another, and when I'm done, I kiss the spot beneath her ear. The spot that makes her flinch, makes her laugh. "Stop it!" she hisses, but she's smiling. She's dressed the same as she is every day, and her hair's up in that perfect bun she can't seem to let go of. But... there's something different about her today. Something I can't quite put a finger on

I scoot closer to her, settle my hand on her knee, and slowly creep higher beneath her skirt. "What's with you?"

Her smile widens. "What's with you?"

"What's with both of you?" That comes from the girl sitting opposite us, her words completely monotone. I turn to face her—jet black hair with thick bangs covering half her bright blue eyes, and cherry red lips contrasting her pale face. She isn't like most of the other girls in the school, and, like Jamie, she doesn't make an effort to try to be. I dig it.

"I'm Holden," I say.

"I know."

I glance at Jamie, who's looking down at her food, trying to hide her amusement. Then back at Melanie. "You're Melanie, right?"

"Yep." She doesn't seem annoyed by my presence or happy about it either. Like her lack of inflection, her expression gives nothing away.

"Well, it's nice to meet you."

"We had three classes together last year."

"Oh."

Jamie giggles and I switch my focus back to her. "Are you working tonight?" It's a Monday, and from what she's told me, it's the only other day of the week that she *might* get off.

She nods. "I start at six."

"Do you want to come over after school?" I ask. "I have something to show you."

"His penis." Melanie deadpans, and my eyes snap to hers. She looks between us. "He's talking about his penis, Jamie."

Jamie snorts with her short laugh.

"I can see why you're friends," I state. "You're both obsessed with my dick activity."

Jamie backhands my stomach, making me choke on a breath. After recovering, I ask, "So wait for me after school?"

"Sure," Jamie replies.

Melanie again: "I bet it's for sex."

Jamie mumbles, "Oh my god," at the same time I tell Melanie, "You're charming."

With a completely straight face, Melanie replies, "Thank you. I try."

I turn to Jamie, press a kiss to the same trigger spot, and stand up before she can push me away. "I'll see you later," I say, then raise my hand toward Melanie. "It was a pleasure, Melanie."

"Likewise." She nods. "Enjoy your explosion of fluids tonight."

Shaking my head, I chuckle as I move behind Jamie and grasp the side of her face to tilt her head back. "Kiss me."

It takes her a moment to react, but then she's reaching up, cupping my nape as she brings me down to her waiting lips. She kisses me once. Twice. And as soon as she begins to pull away, I part my lips, deepen the kiss, which is a mistake, because I spend the rest of the afternoon sporting enough wood to build a treehouse. *Yay!*

―――――

"Where's your mama, sweet boy?" Jamie coos in a voice generally used on toddlers. It would be cute, *endearing* even… if her question wasn't aimed at me.

I glare at her as I pull into my driveway, causing her to snicker into her hands like a pre-schooler. "Why do I put up with you?"

"Because you *liiike* me," she sings, grinning over at me. "Seriously, though. Your mom's car isn't here."

"She's probably at Esme's. She's been doing some yard work there during the days," I tell her, hopping out of the truck. I make my way to her side to open her door, but she doesn't immediately step out. Instead, she raises her arms in the air, and so I bite back a smile, and lift her out of the seat. Her legs instantly wrap around me, her arms clinging to my neck, while my hands find her ass so I can hold her in place.

"So you've been spending your free time with Esme?" she asks, as I spin her toward the house.

"Yep."

"Maybe you do have a granny fetish?"

"Fuck off," I laugh out.

She giggles. "This is nice," she murmurs, nibbling on my neck. I carry her into the house exactly as we are, ignoring the constant sexual tension building between us. Stopping just outside my closed bedroom door, I lean her against it, just so I can look in her eyes when I ask, "I take it you've missed me?"

"A little," she says, flipping my cap backward before kissing me. Just once. She's the version of Jamie I've only witnessed recently— careless and calm, and it absolutely terrifies me to think that maybe... maybe I'm the reason.

She runs her nose along mine, kissing me again, and I push open the bedroom door and set her gently on my desk. She's in a plain navy dress with absolutely no shape, which works for me because it hides all the parts of her that only I get to see. Her short, little legs swing back and forth, and I turn away before she can see my reaction to that slight movement. It's *cute.* And I don't do *cute,* but on Jamie... everything is tolerable, and that, too, is terrifying.

I find the large, yellow envelope on the bookshelf and hold it out in front of her. "Here."

"Eeek!" she squeals, bouncing in her spot while making grabby hands.

"Don't get too excited," I warn, but she's already tearing into it as if it's the first and only gift she's ever received. That would suck. And it might also be a possibility. That *really* sucks.

Discarding the envelope to the side, Jamie looks down at the thick catalog in her hands, then up at me, again and again, and I don't know if she's confused or disappointed. Probably both. "I had my dad send it," I mumble, glancing around my room to hide my embarrassment. I'd never felt like this before, but then again, I've never really cared what people thought of me. Obviously, I care what Jamie thinks, and right now, I can't get a decent read on her.

"Holden..." she breathes out, but it's not enough to give anything away. She runs her thumb across the cover of the book, right over the Eastwood Nursery and Garden Center logo.

"It has all the products we sell in there. Pictures, too. I just thought..."

Her eyes meet mine. "Thought what?" she urges.

I shrug. "I'm sure it's nothing like the ones Gina had, but I thought you might like it."

Jamie's exhale is slow, forced, and then she's leaning back against my wall, a whispered "whoa" leaving her. For seconds that feel like minutes, she simply stares at the catalog, her breaths shaky, harsh against the silence around us. When she finally looks up, her eyes are filled with unshed tears.

I'm so quick to look away, my head spins. "Dammit, Jamie! You know I don't do crying girls."

I can *feel* her eyes roll even though I'm not facing her. "Well, you're going to have to," she says, tugging at my t-shirt to bring me closer. "Just this once."

I puff out a breath, my spine straightening as I roll my shoulders in preparation.

I can do this.

For *her*.

Shutting my eyes, I take one last courageous breath before facing her. The tears are still there—now flowing freely down her cheeks, and I don't even think before I reach up to cup her jaw. I thumb away her tears, let the liquid soak through my flesh and into my bloodline. "It's just a product catalog. I don't know why you—"

"Shut up," she whispers, pushing forward. After carefully setting the book aside, she scoots closer; her front pressed to mine, arms around my neck again. "This is a piece of you, Holden, and you're giving it to me, and that's—"

"Not a big deal," I cut in. It's really not. And if she makes it one, I don't know. It doesn't feel right.

"Maybe not to you." And then she's kissing me, her lips parting, tongue tracing my lips as one of her hands flatten against my abs, under my t-shirt. I tilt my head, drag my tongue along hers, and she's warm and wet and so fucking perfect. She tastes like she smells, like sunshine and solace, and my hands grasp at her thighs, fingers digging in as I bring her closer. My cock throbs against my shorts when I feel the heat emitting from her center. I slide my hand higher, just enough to feel the wetness pooling between her legs, and then I groan, reluctantly pull away. I nuzzle her neck, panting. "Maybe we should slow down. Or stop." I don't know if I can take another one of these "sessions" with her and not blow my load inside my boxer shorts.

She responds by covering my hand with hers, using two of my fingers to slide her panties to the side. And then she uses those same two fingers to trace a line down her slit, exposing me to the evidence of her need. Her want. "Fuck, Jamie," I moan, but I don't know if she hears me because she's too busy removing my t-shirt, then pulling the bottom of her dress up and over her ass, just enough to raise it over her head and discard it altogether. She sits in front of me, in only her bra and underwear, and she's *glorious*.

And mine.

Jesus Christ, she's *mine*.

And I don't care if I come in my pants from dry humping alone. She's so fucking worth it. Hands back between her legs, she guides my fingers inside her, her eyes rolling back when the heel of my palm rubs against her clit. "I'm wound so fucking tight, Holden, I just need…"

"Need what?" I push.

"I need to come," she gasps, her entire body writhing as she rides my fingers. She grabs onto my neck again as if she can't let go, her breaths warm against my cheek. A sheen of sweat coats her shoulders, and I lick her there, bite her.

She sighs, tilting her head back, and I reach up with my free hand, unclasp her bra from behind. I stop my worship of her just long enough to remove her bra and panties. Her tits now exposed; I flatten my tongue against her nipple before sucking on the hardened nub. I push my fingers back into her wet cunt, loving the way she uses them to bring her closer and closer to the edge, the way she pants, "Fuck fuck fuck.

"I can't wait for you to come," I murmur, making my way down her stomach. She leans back, her legs parting wider. "I want to feel this tight little pussy of yours clench around my fingers." I flick my tongue across her clit, watch as a shiver runs through every one of her limbs. "And feel your clit throb against my tongue." I taste her there, again and again, all while she moans my name between curses. Her fingers lace through my hair, tugging, holding me there. I lower my shorts, take out my cock, and stroke it slowly, just a few times, just enough to relieve some pressure. And then I'm back at her tits, squeezing, pulling, pinching. I feel the exact moment her orgasm builds, her pussy walls tightening around my fingers. She screams when she comes, eyes shut tight, head angled to the ceiling as her stomach contracts, riding out every wave. I'm right there with her, my movements never changing, never slowing, not until she's nothing but soft limbs coated in sweat beneath me.

"Fuck, you're like my personal paradise, baby," I say, my voice raspy. I wipe my mouth along the inside of her thigh before standing to full height, stretching out my back. I circle my cock again, stroke it more vigorously while I watch her chest rise and fall through her recovery, and I can't fucking wait anymore. "I'm going to come all over your tits," I tell her, and her eyes snap open. "No!" she yells, pushing me away.

I fall back a step, and it gives her just enough room to drop to her knees in front of me. She flicks at my wrist, and I release my dick from my hand and into hers. And then into her mouth, and *holy shit*.

Holy. Fucking. Shit.

I can't look away.

I'm too afraid to blink.

Jamie, naked, on her knees, her lips stretched around my cock, while her hands circle the base, her *eyes on mine…*

This girl will be my undoing. I have no fucking doubt.

Her lips are warm, wet, so is her tongue as she swirls it at the head while her fist follows her motions, in and out, over and over, and I force my muscles to tense, to not fucking move, because the idea of holding her head there and fucking her mouth… I almost come at the thought.

Almost.

Instead, I reach down, take that perfect bun of hers in my grasp and fuck it up when I force her to tilt her head back so I can see her eyes, her lips, the white of her spit mixing with my precum glazing the length of me.

The muscles in my stomach tighten, my jaw doing the same, my nostrils flaring with every inhale. Every exhale.

"I can't take much more, baby," I warn, and then I notice her arm shifting in minuscule movements, and I follow that movement to her hand, her fingers. She's rubbing her pussy.

Jesus Christ.

"Stop." I *force* myself to push her away because I don't know if she's ready for my load to slip down her throat. I pick her up off the floor and practically throw her onto the bed. She lands on her back, still playing with herself. I make quick work of grabbing a condom from the nightstand and slipping it on. When I turn back to her, she's on her knees and elbows, her ass in the air.

I groan, rub at my eyes—I swear I'm seeing things. This is too fucking much. Too fucking *perfect.*

"So this is how you like it?" I ask, strolling along the side of the bed. I run my fingers down her spine, causing a shiver.

"My ass," she pants.

"You want it *in your ass?*" I almost shout.

"No!" She actually does shout, head tilted to watch me move behind her. "I just want you to grab it. Pay it some attention."

Oh.

"Yeah, I knew that," I mumble. *I didn't.* Kneeling behind her, I give her what she asks. I splay both hands on her ass, spread them wide, and surprise her when I tongue-fuck her pussy, lap at the juices she's made just for me.

"You ready?" I ask, splitting her folds with the head of my cock.

"Please, Holden."

I mess with her. Because I can. "Please, Holden, what?"

She grunts into the mattress. "Please, just fuck me already!"

I push into her. All the way in. And then I still. Wait a moment for the need to come to ebb and flow. "I'm not going to last long," I groan, my thrusts slow.

"I'm already… holy shit." She grasps the covers beside her head, right before she jerks back, and then forward, and back again. It doesn't take long to find our rhythm, and the release comes only moments later. When we're done, I collapse onto my back beside her, gasping for breath. A second passes before she's rolling to her side…

and then off the bed and onto the floor. I bust out a laugh as I sit up on my elbow and look down at her sprawled out naked, covered in sweat, her hair a mess, lips and tits and ass and pussy red and raw from my assault.

"You good, Gladys?"

"Yeah," she breathes out.

And I don't know why I say what I say next. Maybe because she doesn't hear it enough. And maybe because it's the truth. "You're so fucking beautiful, Jamie."

She sighs, then reaches up to run her hand through my sweat-covered hair. "You make me feel beautiful. So thank you."

"You're welcome."

Her smile is lazy. "Want to shower with me?"

CHAPTER
THIRTY-FIVE

HOLDEN

I never really understood what couples did between dates and sex. I assumed at some point, they'd probably have to talk to each other or just… enjoy being in each other's presence? It had always been such an odd concept to me. But, lying in bed while Jamie sits with her back against the wall and her legs over mine, silently flipping through the catalog, I finally understand it.

The sunlight filtering through the blinds hits her eyes *just right*, capturing the lightness mixed with darkness, encompassing every-thing she is. She's in a pair of my boxer shorts—her underwear too wet to wear, so she says—and her dress replaced with the t-shirt I'd worn to school. And if this is *it*… if this is how people who *feel* things like spending their time, then yeah, I get it. I could watch her exactly like this, all day, all night, and never get sick of it.

"I can't even imagine growing up in a place like this," she says, showing me the double page spread of the catalog that's nothing but images of the farm. "I would sleep under the stars every night."

"Yeah," I agree. "I guess I took advantage of it."

Her focus moves from the catalog to me, my bare chest to be

exact, and her eyes narrow.

Mine do the same. "What?"

"The blinds are creating this shadow on you, and it's—" She breaks off on a sigh. "I wish I could draw on you right now."

"*On* me?"

"Yeah," she says, reaching over to stroke her finger across my torso. "You'd be the perfect medium."

"So why don't you?"

"Why don't I what?"

"Draw on me."

Eyes wide, she asks, already getting out of bed, "Are you serious?"

I nod, watching as she goes to her bag to grab a marker. She sits directly on my lap when she returns, her legs bent on either side of me, but there's nothing sexual about our positions. And while I'd love to be inside her again, the prospect of watching her create something excites me even more.

With the tip of the marker pressed into my flesh, she starts at the middle of my collarbone and makes her way down, tracing the outlines of the shadows caused by the blinds. "It's water-based," she says, glancing up at me momentarily. "It'll come right out."

I wish I could tell her that I don't care. That I'd almost *prefer* if it were permanent. But that would be weird. So, all I do is nod. And then I shift her loose, damp hair away from her eyes and behind her ear so I can watch her face as she creates magic with her fingers.

We don't speak as she works, the marker sliding across my skin effortlessly, and I don't look at what she's doing.

I look at her.

It's strange—this feeling of calm mixed with restlessness that beats through my chest and settles in the pit of my stomach. I've never felt it before, and I don't know if I want to feel it again.

"Why drawing?" I ask, cutting through the silence.

The marker pauses mid-movement, right above my breastbone, and Jamie peers up at me through her lashes. The setting sun highlights the embers of her eyes, the freckles across her cheeks. She clears her throat before refocusing on her task. "That's an odd question."

Is it, though? Maybe. And considering she doesn't live in my head, I can understand her confusion. I contemplate how to explain my need for her to answer. At least this one thing. "Mia has an eating disorder."

Her gaze snaps to mine and then right back down. She doesn't speak. I don't want her to.

"It's bulimia," I say, my voice cracking with emotion. "It came out when I was home for the summer... but I guess she's had it for a while, years now..." I push down the knot in my throat. "Ever since I left her."

Jamie's eyes are slow to meet mine. Hold them. "You mean when your parents divorced, and you had to move?"

"See, that's the thing," I'm quick to say, trying not to shift when she goes back to drawing. "I didn't *have* to move. It's not as if a choice was offered to me, but I could've fought to stay, and I should've because she wouldn't have left if I hadn't."

"You didn't know that would happen, Holden," she says so quietly I barely hear her.

"Yeah, but..." I sigh. "I could see a change in her, you know? And sometimes I think, maybe if I'd just asked the right questions, then..."

Jamie's eyebrows rise when she glances up. "What? You could've saved her?'

I shrug.

She heaves out a breath, warming my entire chest, and a moment later, she's moving lower down my body, her breasts near my junk as she focuses her attention on the spot right above my heart. Whatever she's working on now, it's far more intricate than what she'd been doing prior. I think she's about to ignore my question completely, and I'd be okay with that, but then her mouth opens, shuts, opens again. "When things were about to get bad between my mom and her boyfriend... she'd lock me in the closet under the stairs with nothing but paper and a pen, so I wouldn't have to see it, you know? But I'd still have to hear it. I'd hear the shouting and the screaming and sometimes the breaking of furniture… and those sounds were okay. I could handle those. It's when things got quiet—eerily silent—that's when I'd panic. That's when I'd draw. And I used it as an escape because I could control what I saw that way. I could see the ocean, or the stars, or a field full of daisies." She says all this, her voice low, filled with zero emotion. Maybe because I'm sucking all of it out of the room. I regret asking, but I can't regret knowing, because knowing is another piece of the puzzle.

"I almost hated when that closet door would open again because I knew what to expect. The smeared makeup and ratted hair and cuts and bruises and then came the reasoning. The excuses. The promises that it wouldn't happen again. And then the apologies…"

My entire body is rigid, and surely, she must feel that beneath her touch. "Did he ever—"

"Once," she says, pointing to the scar above her eyebrow. "Never again. My mom—she'd always step in to protect me."

I don't tell her what I want to—that *truly* protecting her daughter would mean getting them the fuck out of that situation.

"Anyway," Jamie says, cutting through my thoughts. "I think it happened so much that it's become second nature—like a coping mechanism. Some people bite their nails. Some people drink enough alcohol to slay a small horse. I draw. Because for so long, it was the only thing I had, and it was the only thing that made me feel *some-what* safe until…" she trails off.

"Gina?" I ask, and she's slow to respond, to look up and make me bear witness to her withheld tears. I run the pad of my thumb under her eyes—eyes far too delicate to be holding them hostage. "Yeah," she whispers, leaning into my touch. "*Gina.*" Her throat moves with her swallow as she adjusts herself on top of me, her voice kicking up in volume when she adds, "Now quit moving. You're going to make me mess up." And she's done with the talking, the exposing pieces of herself that are far too deep for me to even comprehend.

She goes back to her task, and I lie still while she works, watching her every move. The only sounds in the room are our breaths mixing with the movement of the marker. "Are you working on Thanksgiving?" I ask a few minutes of silence later.

Without losing focus, Jamie answers, "No. It's the only day of the year Zeke closes the diner."

"So you'll come here then?"

She chews her lip, but doesn't look at me, doesn't stop drawing. "If you want me to."

"I wouldn't ask if I didn't."

She attempts to hide her smile, but I see it. I see *her.* "Then I'll be here."

At some point while Jamie's drawing, my mom sends me a text, tells me she's on her way home. I reply, tell her that Jamie's here— a hint not to come into my room unannounced. A few minutes later, I hear the front door open and her moving around in the kitchen.

It's almost time to leave when Jamie completes what she declares, "might be her favorite piece yet."

I ask her to grab my phone from the pocket of my shorts, and so she does. After handing it to me, I open the camera app and snap picture after picture, from every space, every angle, making sure I don't miss a single thing. When I go back to inspect them, Jamie curls into my side, warming me there, while her head rests on the crook of my arm.

What she's drawn is nothing short of breathtaking, and I don't mean that in some bullshit metaphorical way. I mean, I literally can't breathe. She's used the shadow of the blinds like rays of sunlight across my torso, starting at my neck and making its way diagonally down my left side. Each beam is wrapped in vines and leaves and little flowers I have no doubt she could name, plus throw out a random fact about each one. But all of that isn't what's stolen all the oxygen away from my lungs. It's the centerpiece... the piece of the puzzle that connects all other parts, completes the entire image, the one she worked on the most. On the left of my chest is a compass similar to the one that she'd drawn in the anatomical heart that had slipped from the pages of her sketchbook.

I shouldn't ask.

Because the truth might destroy me.

I ask anyway. "What's with the compass?"

"It's right above your heart," she says simply, as if that's answer enough. It's not.

And I know I'm digging myself a hole I might not be able to get out of. Still, I ask, "But *why* a compass?"

She's quiet for a beat. And then: "Because it's where I feel the most found."

When it's time to take Jamie to work, I hand her my keys and ask her to wait out in my truck. Then I go to the kitchen, where my mom is standing by the sink, inspecting her little herb garden. "Ma," I call out, moving closer to her.

She spins around, the same smile I've grown up with lighting her eyes. "Are you taking Jamie to work now?"

I don't answer.

I just hold her.

Tight.

She's slow to respond—*understandable*—but then she's hugging me back, and I'm suddenly inundated with memories of all the other times she's held me like this. All the scraped knees and broken bones from being far too daring, far too young. Or every time she had to comfort me when I found an injured animal and couldn't save it, or the times Mia and I fought over nonsense. Or just the times when I needed to be held by my mother.

"What's this for?" Mom asks, and I'm too choked up to respond verbally. All the emotion I'd harbored while Jamie was speaking is coming out now, and I'm grateful that my mom's here to pick up the pieces.

"Thank you, Ma," I say over the lump in my throat.

"For what?"

It takes a moment for me to find the words. "For always being there for me. For giving up your life for me and always putting me first. For... for being my mom and always *protecting me*."

CHAPTER
THIRTY-SIX

JAMIE

"We're almost there," Holden says, squeezing my leg as we go over a particularly uneven patch of road.

I have no idea where "there" is.

He'd walked into my fifth-period economics class, and without even looking in my direction, made his way over to the teacher, handed him a note, and then he disappeared just as quickly as he arrived. Whatever was on the note excused me from the class, and I packed up my things and left. Holden was waiting just outside the room for me, and before I could ask what the hell he was doing, he took my hand and said, "Ready?" It wasn't a question.

But I answered anyway. "Yes."

I had zero clues where he was taking me, and I realized then—as he squeezed my hand and made a game of covertly sneaking out to his truck—that I'd pretty much do anything Holden Eastwood asks of me.

It's a dangerous feeling. Terrifying, really. And it's safe to say that I'm officially a goner for the green-eyed boy sitting beside me, leading me blindly into what he calls "an adventure."

It's strange how things can change in a blink of an eye.

Or a single kiss.

Or a single line drawn in black marker that has the power to change *everything*.

Now, Holden turns onto an unmarked gravel road led to him by his phone's navigator. We've been driving for an hour already. Asking where we're going would be pointless—something I figured out after the first five minutes.

A few more dips in the gravel, and me holding onto the dash for dear life, and we come to a closed gate at the end of the road. "This isn't sketchy at all," I murmur, looking behind me.

Ignoring me, he hops out of the truck, ordering over his shoulder, "Stay there."

I do as he asks, watching as he pushes open the gate and gets back in the truck. He drives, and I... I keep my eyes on his profile—at his full lips and sharp jawline covered in overnight stubble, high cheekbones slightly redder than normal, and is he... "Are you *blushing*?"

He glances at me quickly before refocusing ahead. "You keep staring at me like that, and I'll have to pull over and do dirty, filthy things to that smart little mouth of yours."

"Yeah, but where's the punishment in that?" I tease, and he groans, adjusts himself in his seat.

"You're bad." He hits the brakes. "And we're here."

I finally tear my eyes away from him and look around us. It's nothing but open space and green, green grass dotted in white and yellow. "What is..." I trail off when he gets out, makes his way over to my side.

He helps me out of my seat and onto my feet, and I take a few steps away, slowly spinning around to take in our surroundings. My breath catches the moment realization hits, and it hits *hard*. Heat burns behind my eyes as I crouch down, pick a flower by my feet and bring it to my nose. They're everywhere around me, these tiny little rays of sunlight. "A field full of daisies..." I breathe out. I'd mentioned it in passing only yesterday, and he's already delivering it to me.

Holden smiles as he steps up beside me, then drops a kiss on my forehead. "It hardly seemed fair that you have to draw what you want to see, Jamie." He takes my hand in his. "You deserve to experience it." Without another word, he leads me to the bed of his truck, where he pulls out a picnic basket and blanket.

He lays them out on the grass just by his truck, and we sit together, looking at nothing in particular. And we talk—something Holden and I rarely do. He tells me about his football season—all losses so far—which isn't a surprise, according to him. And I tell him about my plans for the upcoming weekend. "I found a thrift store online that I want to check out."

"That sounds *fun*," he says, the sarcasm in his voice unmistakable.

"Shut up," I laugh out, throwing a grape at his head. The picnic basket's filled with fruits and cheese and crackers, along with some bottles of apple cider and a couple of wine glasses. I'm sure if he'd brought any other girl here—one who doesn't have a shitty history with alcohol—there'd be *actual* wine.

He hasn't told me who packed the basket, and I don't ask, but I have a feeling his mother was involved.

"Is that where you get your grandma clothes from?" he asks.

"Some," I answer. "Mostly, they're hand-me-downs from Gina."

"Ah. The infamous Gina," he almost sings, kicking his legs out in front of him. "Tell me more about this Gina of yours."

It's getting colder out, the autumn chill just enough to float across my arms, to prickle along my flesh. I move closer to him, and he must notice the goose bumps, because he removes his Townsend HS Athletics hoody. "You don't have to—" I break off when he gets to his knees, holding the garment just above my head. He slides it over me, making sure not to ruin my hair, and it's such a sweet, affectionate move that when I finally push my arms through the sleeves, I'm... speechless. I don't know what to say or how to act. I've become so accustomed to taking care of myself, or others, that the mere act of someone else doing it for me has my chest aching. There's a burn behind my eyes that has me taking a breath, trying to hide my reaction.

"So Gina?" he asks, watching me, one eyebrow raised.

I clear my throat, speak through the knot in my throat. "Gina…" And then I exhale, releasing all my emotions out with it. "Gina found me at the bus stop when I was in second grade. I was filthy and unkempt and she… she took me into her home. The first time, it was to bathe me, but the next morning, she was there again, and I was in clothes that hadn't been washed in forever, and so…" I shrug. "She brought me back to her house and found some clothes for me to wear. I was still so little, so they were all too big, but she'd hem the skirts in a way that I could undo and alter the older I got." I run a hand along my skirt. "This is one of hers," I tell him.

We're both looking out at the field and not each other when he says, "So you just started dressing in her clothes every day?"

I nod. "I used to get teased a lot, but when I came to school in clean clothes, the teasing stopped being about the state of my wardrobe and switched to the style of it. And that? That I could handle because I felt like… I don't know… like I had something to be proud of."

"And now?"

"Now what?" I ask, turning to look up at him. He's already watching me.

"Why do you still wear them now?"

Another shrug. "Just because I grew up, it doesn't mean those insecurities go away. Especially as a senior starting at a new school. I'd rather have people talk about my shitty fashion choices than to be the poor, little orphan girl who scrubs dishes and lives in a trailer park."

After a beat of silence, he asks, "Where's your dad?"

I laugh once. "The only thing my mom knew about him was his name. And I'm not even sure if she got that right, which could be a disaster since she named me after him."

Holden says nothing.

"James," I tell him. "If you were curious."

He nods once. "Do you ever think that you're the only one who might see you that way? As the poor, little orphan girl who scrubs dishes and lives in a trailer park…"

"Maybe," I answer truthfully. "But it doesn't take the insecurities away."

He picks up a strawberry and inspects it a few moments before asking, "When was the last time you saw or spoke to Gina?"

"When we left. I was thirteen."

"And you haven't gone back to see her?"

"I can't," I reply, my heart suddenly heavy. "It's too dangerous."

His entire body stiffens against mine. "Why?"

"She only lives two doors down from Beaker, my mom's ex—and we didn't exactly leave on good terms, so…"

"Sucks," is all he says. And then he's quiet. Too quiet. And for far too long.

"What are you thinking?" I ask, even though I'm afraid of the answer.

"Nothing really." He throws a slight smile my way. "Just that… this suits you, being out here."

"Yeah?" I can't help but grin. "It *feels* good, being out here." I point to my head. "I just need a straw hat."

"Nah," he says, lifting his chin. "I'll do you one better. Come here." He pats his lap, and I don't hesitate to lay my head on there. Facing the overcast sky, I settle my arms at my side and stay quiet as I watch him reach across and pull out a bunch of daisies. He drops them on my stomach and, one after the other, starts joining them together. For minutes, we sit in silence while his large hands work delicately at making the chain longer and longer. Occasionally, he asks me to lift my head to measure the length, and when he's not satisfied, he taps his lap again. Over and over, he does this, his brow drawn, eyes focused on his task.

"How did you even know how to make these?" I ask.

"Are you kidding?" He scoffs. "Mia used to *literally* stand over me with a huge stick, threatening to beat me with it unless I made, like, fifty a day for her."

I giggle into his tight stomach. "I like Mia."

"She'd like you to," he murmurs, picking more flowers from the grass beside us. "I'm trying to convince her to fly over for Thanksgiving, so maybe you'll meet her then. My mom invited Esme, and my dad and his girlfriend will be here, too. And my grandparents."

I can't ignore the sudden racing of my pulse or the warmth that floats across my chest and into my heart. It comes out a whisper when I ask, "You want me to meet them?"

Holden shrugs. "Sure, why not?" He taps at my forehead, my cue to lift my head, and so I do. Carefully, he places the daisy chain around my head, and smiles when he's satisfied. Then he places his hand on my nape, holding my head up while he snaps a quick photo, a soft smile gracing his hardened features. When he's done, he lays me gently back on his lap. "You don't want to meet them?"

"No, I do," I'm quick to answer, sitting up and turning to him. "I just... I don't know." I sigh. "Sometimes I feel like you just say these things... throw them out as if they don't hold any meaning—"

"And sometimes I think you underestimate me," he cuts in. "Look, Jamie." He heaves out a breath, leaning back on his outstretched arms. "I'm not someone who needs to deep-dive into every emotion or scrutinize everything we do." His eyes meet mine, penetrating. "I say what I mean, and I mean what I say, and as long as you understand that, then nothing matters."

CHAPTER
THIRTY-SEVEN

JAMIE

I check the time on my phone. And then the day, *Wednesday.* Holden isn't at the lockers where we always meet to go to Esme's, and the more students that clear the corridor, the more confused I become. Just as I bring up Holden's number, someone calls out to me. I look up to see Dean walking toward me, his strides long and rushed. "There you are," he huffs. He's out of breath, his chest rising and falling rapidly. "I thought you met Holden out at his truck."

"No." I shake my head. "Why?" Then I look over his shoulder, stupidly expecting to see Holden. "Where is he?"

My first thought is that something horrible has happened, but before I let that fear fully set in, Dean answers, stopping just in front of me. "He didn't tell you?"

My patience for anything Dean-related ran out a long time ago. "Tell me *what*?"

"He had to fly home to North Carolina for some emergency."

"Is it his dad?" I ask, frantically dialing his number. "Mia?"

"I don't know."

Phone held to my ear; I listen to it ring out.

Dean watches, his eyebrows drawn.

I try again—the same result.

"Look," he says, stepping even closer, "the only reason I know is because his mom called the school and said he might be out for a few days. They told my dad, and my dad told me so we could work out some new plays for Friday's game."

"Right." I send Holden a text asking if everything's okay and then pocket the phone. "I should go," I tell Dean. "I have to catch a bus to Esme's."

"That's why I'm here."

Eyes wide, I ask, "To take me to Esme's?"

"Well, yeah. And the program—it has to be done in pairs, so…" he trails off, and I hate where he's going with this.

I rear back, my shoulders slumping. "So you're going with me?"

He nods. "Unless you want to call her and cancel."

"Yeah, that's probably best."

"Probably." He shrugs, and he doesn't look at me when he adds, "It's just that… with Esme, I don't think it's so much the work she looks forward to. It's more the company, so…"

I heave out a loud and somewhat frustrated breath. Dean's right, and he damn well knows it. "Fine."

We drive to Esme's in silence, and after a short greeting, we get bombarded with questions about Holden's sudden disappearance, which we answer as well as we can, which isn't well at all. I tried calling him twice more on the drive. He didn't answer either call. Once we get to the yard, I realize how useless it is to even attempt the work without Holden here. "Holden normally tells me what to do," I murmur, stepping into the pool house.

Dean scoffs as he examines all the tools on the wall. "Sounds like a great relationship."

"Hey, guess what?"

He turns to me. "What?"

"Fuck off. Like, all the way off."

He rolls his eyes.

But I'm not done. "And when you get all the way fucked, you should keep going."

After a defeated sigh, he says, "We're not getting anywhere with this."

"No shit."

"Maybe we should ask Esme if there's any other work we can do for her?"

I agree, and regret it ten minutes later when Dean and I are crammed in Esme's spare bedroom, going through Wesley's old clothes and bagging them up. "Are you sure you want to do this?" I ask Esme, who's standing at the doorway, her smile forced.

"It's time," she says, and then she's gone.

Dean and I work in silence while I check my phone every few minutes, sometimes seconds. Holden doesn't call back, doesn't respond to my texts.

By the following day, I've stopped calling him. Stopped waiting for a response. And by Friday, the only thing that consumes my mind is fear. I do web searches for Eastwood Nursery, but nothing shows up besides an outdated website and a few articles about the company. I try to search for news on Mia, but I don't even know her last name.

At the weekend, I skip going to the thrift store and go to Holden's house instead. His truck is there, but apart from that, there are no signs of life.

I spend what free time I have during the weekend at Esme's, helping her go through more of Wesley's things to donate. I hold her hand and console her and tell her she's taking a huge step and she should be proud. She cries on my shoulder, and I... I hold back my own.

· · ·

Dean and I spend another Wednesday afternoon with Esme. We don't do the yard work. We simply sit with her at her kitchen table and talk. Well, they do. I have nothing to say.

On the drive back to my place, Dean says, "Can I ask you a serious question without you telling me to get fucked or fuck off or threaten my life in any way?"

"Unlikely," I respond, staring out the window.

He asks anyway, "How are things going with you and Holden?"

It's the only question I'd feared he'd ask because the truth is what I tell him: "I don't know." I guess I thought we were something, but since I haven't heard from him since he hopped on a plane to another state says otherwise. *Holden means what he says, and he says what he means,* and the fact that he hasn't said anything means... everything.

"Is he good to you?" Dean asks.

I don't know why he's talking to me about this. *Now.* When all I want is to sit in silence.

"Does he treat you right?"

"Jesus, Dean." I rest my head on the window, let the vibrations scatter my brain even more.

Dean won't shut up. "Regardless of what you think of me, I care about you."

"Good for you," I mumble.

"And I want you to be happy."

"Will you *shut up.*"

"Because you deserve it, Jamie. More than anyone."

My eyes drift shut; my mind numb. "I know," I tell him. Maybe not *more than anyone,* but I at least deserve a semblance of it. And I don't know why I suddenly feel like it's slipping through my fingers.

I spend every night working and drawing and pacing and wondering. And by Thursday, over a full week since Holden disappeared, my middle finger has a blister on the side of the first knuckle from constantly gripping a marker.

"Here," Zeke says, handing me five takeout containers filled with food. "Try to get some sleep tonight, all right, kiddo?"

I take them from him, grateful, and open my backpack to carry them home. "How could you tell?"

He smiles, but it's sad. "The giant bags under your eyes gave it away." I've also been in a crappy mood, quieter than usual, and sucky at my job—though he won't say any of that. Zeke knows as much as I've told him—which is everything I know—Holden left. *That's it.*

I zip up my backpack, haul it over my shoulders, then pat the side pocket, making sure the pepper spray is there. "I'll see you tomorrow."

He watches me, the pity in his stare palpable. "Bye, sweetheart."

I push open the door, and I'm immediately blinded by headlights. I recognize the lights right away and the boy sitting on the hood of his truck. I don't think. I just run, and when I'm in Holden's arms... I take my first full breath in what feels like an eternity. I let him hold me, ignoring the fact that he hasn't called, that he didn't tell me he was even leaving. Because none of it matters. "I was so worried," I tell him, hugging him tighter. I've missed him, I realize, and maybe that's what the fear was... the dread... *losing someone.*

"I'm sorry," he says, and I don't even care what he's sorry for.

"Is your dad—"

"He's fine."

"And Mia?"

He pulls away. "Can we just go back to your house? We should talk."

We don't talk.

The second we're alone, we do anything *but* talk.

And maybe that's where we went wrong.

Because when I wake up the next morning, Holden isn't in my bed. I sit up, trying to adjust my vision, before flicking on the lamp on my nightstand. I startle when I see Holden in the room. Wearing only sweatpants, he's leaning against the dresser with his arms crossed, watching me. "You scared me," I breathe out, hand to my chest. "What the hell are you doing?"

His gaze drops. "I can't sleep."

"Come here," I say, patting the bed. He moves toward me, his head lowered, and he keeps it that way when he slumps down on the edge of the bed, his elbows resting on his knees. "What's going on? You still haven't told me what happened." I shuffle on my knees until I'm at his side, and then I reach up, run my hand through his hair.

"I don't even know where to start," he says, pulling away from my touch.

I sit taller, trying to silence the voices in my head warning me of what's to come, but when he lifts his gaze, those empty eyes searching mine, I know my fears are justified.

I don't know how long we sit there, only inches apart, while he says everything he means without ever saying a word. And with each second that passes, with each beat of my heart, I feel the dread in my chest become heavier, weighted by the barriers being rebuilt. Re-enforced. Wall after wall. Piece after piece. I'm quick to stand, to move to my dresser so I can remove his shirt I'd slept it. I replace it with my own and hand his back. "You should go."

"Jamie, just give me a minute—"

"It's okay," I cut in. Besides, I've heard it all before. First comes the reasoning. Then the excuses. Then the empty promises followed by the apologies. I turn my back to him and stare at the ceiling, hoping that gravity plays its part. I refuse to let him see me cry. See me weak. "You've been gone over a week and not once did I hear from you, so I kind of figured where I sat on the scale of importance in your life." I force out a breath, trying to remain calm amid the storm building inside me. "I just don't get it. Like, why come here and screw me, and "

"That wasn't my intention," he insists.

I scratch at my arms, try to rid the filth only I can see. "I feel so gross right now."

"Jamie." He sighs. "I came straight to your work from the airport to do... *this*."

I face him, see his regret staring back at me.

"I didn't mean for what happened last night to happen. It's just..." He stands up and moves toward me. I take a step back, and he halts, stops only feet away. "The moment I saw you, I felt like... like everything else disappeared, and maybe that's my problem." His throat moves with his swallow, his hands fists at his sides. "Maybe that's what you are to me, a distraction—"

I scoff, cutting him off. "I'm glad I could be of service to you."

His eyes drift shut, then snap open a second later. "That came out wrong," he says, shaking his head in frustration.

He starts to move again, but I stop him, my hand up between us. "You should go."

His chest rises. So does his voice. "So, you're not even going to let me explain?"

"What's there to explain, Holden!" I almost shout. "You were gone a week, and in that week, you realized you didn't want me anymore!"

"It's not about you, Jamie!" He points to his chest. "It's me! I can't..." he trails off.

"That's so fucking cliche, and I deserve better!" I laugh, fueled by bitterness and disappointment. "And I'm *trying*, Holden," I say, my voice breaking under the strain of my withheld sob. "I'm trying really fucking hard not to make this about me—but how can I not? Every fucking time I let my defenses down, I get..." I motion between us, "...*this*."

"Jamie," he groans. "It's not—"

"A big deal," I finish for him. I find what little strength I have left and raise my chin, holding on to the only thing I have left: my pride. "It's not like we were in love or anything." I lie... for the same reasons my mother always lied to me: to protect me from reality. "I'll be fine, Holden." I blink back the pathetic tears threatening to fall, ignoring the heartache pulsing through my veins. "You can go back

to being you, and soon enough, we'll both forget that this was once…
nothing."

He doesn't respond. He just stands there, staring at me, unmoving, unflinching. And then my alarm goes off, and Holden's head snaps to the sound. "Let's just go to school—"

"I'm not going to school today."

His eyes meet mine. "Why not?"

"I'd already planned to take the day off."

"Bullshit," he spits.

"I did!" Maybe if he'd called even *once*, he would know that. "I have a thing."

"A thing?" he asks, incredulous.

"Yeah, a *thing.*"

"What *thing*?"

"It's…" It hits me now. Hard and fast. Like the building of a dam right before the floodgates open. "It's not your problem anymore."

CHAPTER
THIRTY-EIGHT

HOLDEN

I'd woken up in the middle of the night and saw the drawings scattered on the kitchen counter—compass after compass after compass—and I knew what it meant. She was lost, with or without me. And I... I realized then that no matter how much it hurt, I had to face the truth.

And the truth was simple:

I couldn't be the one to find her.

To save her.

No matter how much it destroyed me.

I go home, shower, and then I drive to school because I have shit to do. Shit that can't wait. I call Mom on the way, who's now in New York with Mia until... until she gets the help she needs to make it through each day.

When I get to my locker, Dean's there, a single dahlia in his hand. He waits for me to open my locker before moving around me, using tape to stick the flower onto Jamie's locker. I haven't *wanted* to speak to him in weeks. I still don't. But I have to now. "What's that about?"

He faces me, eyebrows drawn. "You don't know?"

Obviously not because I wouldn't be asking. I bite back my agitation. "Know *what*?"

His expression changes to one of sadness and regret, and it's as instant as it is confusing. Because it's the same emotions I'm carrying. Only mine are buried deep, deep inside me. "Bro, her mom's name was Dahlia."

My heart plummets, finds a home by my feet. I'm afraid to ask. I do anyway. "And?"

"And today's the one-year anniversary of her death."

JAMIE

I finally got a headstone for my mother's grave. It has her full name, appropriate dates, and a small sketch of a dahlia.

I'd spent the better half of the past year trying to come up with the words to put on her final resting place, and I kept coming up blank. It was only recently that I realized that maybe... maybe she didn't need any last words.

Maybe her story is still unwritten.

Maybe *I* am her story.

I don't know what I thought I'd achieve by coming here. I guess it felt like the right thing to do. And I don't know why I decided to wear all her damn mood rings. They take up every finger, some with multiples. I guess, in my heart, it made sense to reunite the only thing she loved in the world with the only thing I can continue to love.

I sit down beside her plot and flick at the dirt around it, not knowing what else to do. The cemetery had only put the small headstone in yesterday so there's nothing to really clean. I don't even know if you'd call it a headstone. It's just a plaque stuck in cement and placed into the ground. Beneath it is what's left of her: nothing but ashes —fragments of her bones and flesh and those organs that failed her as much as she failed herself.

Liquid warmth trails down my cheeks, useless and unwanted, and I'm quick to rid their presence as I look over at Zeke. He's standing a few yards away, leaning against his truck, making it obvious that he *isn't* watching me.

I'd asked him to come with me because… because he's the only one in my life who knew her. Even if only for short moments, and even if those moments meant nothing to him—they meant something to me.

"I don't know what I'm supposed to say," I whisper, looking down at her name in raised copper. I try to push through the burning ache in my throat while more tears flee from my eyes, and this time—I let them flow. "I love you." But I don't *miss you*. "And I wish you were here." A sob escapes, and I suck in a shaky breath, and for a moment, just one, I let grief overpower my anger. And I let heartache control my pain. "A boy broke my heart, Mama, and I could really…" I sniff back the hurt. "I could really use someone to talk to about it, but you're not around. And even if you were… I don't know if you'd hear me. If you'd *understand* me." I'm quick to get back to anger, to disappointment. "God only knows what genius advice you'd offer. It's not as if you're known for making the best decisions when it comes to men. Or *love*." I take a breath. And then another. "You've made me so afraid to *love*, Mama. To care. To let anyone in. And maybe that was the purpose of all this… to teach me to keep my walls up, so I don't get screwed over like you did." I keep my voice low, my jaw tense. This isn't the place where people come to hear hatred or outrage. It's for longing and mourning and despair. Too bad I don't feel any of those things. "I just want you to know that I'm *not* okay. And I don't know if I ever will be." I get to my feet, swipe my hands over my jeans to clear any dirt. "Happy dying day, I guess." I start to leave but stop only a step away. Tears blur my vision while my heart throbs against my ribs. I turn to her, release one final cry. "I love you, Mama." And then I make a promise to myself that it's the last time I'll ever say the following words to or about her. "And I'm sorry I couldn't fix you."

· · ·

251

I cry in Zeke's truck, silent tears to go with my silent sobs, but he knows. He knows, but he doesn't ask. Doesn't push. He doesn't ask if I'm okay, and he doesn't force me to talk about my *feelings* or my fears that I have no feelings at all.

We simply drive.

And when we get to the bridge I knew we'd be crossing, I ask him to pull over.

Without hesitation, he does. As soon as the truck's stopped, I get out, already removing each and every ring from my fingers. And then I throw them all into the Tennessee River with just enough withheld rage to make me lose my breath.

I get back in the truck, and we drive.

We drive the winding roads surrounded by large trees, their leaves the perfect mix of oranges and reds and browns, and if I worked confidently with color, I'd paint those trees, those leaves, exactly like this—at their prettiest—right before they die.

"We can pull over if you want to draw them," Zeke says, and I face him for what might be the first time since I got in his car. It's like time hasn't changed him at all. He's still the same man who smiled down at me the first time we walked into his diner. Still the same backward ball cap. Probably the same flannel shirt and jeans, too. "It's okay," I croak, my voice low, harsh against my throat.

He glances at me quickly before looking away.

I face the window again, wipe the tears from my cheeks.

We drive some more until the leaves are gone and the trees are replaced with buildings and traffic lights. He pulls into the parking lot of a Staples and finds a spot. "I have to run in quickly and grab something for the diner."

I wind down my window and nod, breathing in the crisp, fall air, let it fill my lungs and bring me back to life. When he returns only minutes later, he sets a bulk box of markers on my lap—the same markers I use to draw.

"I figure you'd get more out of those than flowers," he tells me. "Flowers die. Kind of seems shitty to give them to you on a day like today."

252

I stare at him—the only reliable man I've ever known—a man who knows too much and sees too much. And I don't know why it's taken me all this time to realize how well he knows me. How much he must watch me. How much he *cares* for me.

"I pray for you every night, Jamie," he says and then clears his throat. "I still remember the first time I met you and your mama. You came in—this tiny little thing—nothing but skin and bones, and I saw in you then the same thing I see in you now. You were so lost, so afraid, but, *jeez*, you were determined." He smiles, his beard shifting with the movement. "You had a fight in you that your mama didn't, and I could tell—even then—that you were fighting for the both of you. And not once, through all the shit you've been through… from the beginning until the end of your mama's life… not once did I see that fight leave you. And I swear, Jamie, I hope it never does." His eyes hold mine, filled with nothing but clarity. "And you may feel like you're alone, that your life and your burdens are something that you need to tackle on your own, but you don't, sweetheart." He sucks in a breath, releases it slowly. "And I know that it's hard for you… and that you may not feel loved…" He pauses a breath. "But you are." He nods in affirmation. "You understand what I'm saying?"

I push down the lump in my throat, my heart beating out of my chest while my unshed tears make it hard to see. "Yes, sir."

HOLDEN

"I need to go to college in New York."

Mrs. Heller, the guidance counselor, looks up from my file, then right back down. "That's not exactly how things work, Mr. East-wood." With short graying hair and thick glasses, the woman's set for retirement any day now. I'm pretty sure she's over everyone's bull-shit, and then I walked in with one *demand*. How fun for her.

I heave out an exhale and square my shoulders. "Yeah, well, I'm going to need it to work like that, so what do I have to do?"

"Unfortunately, the only thing you have going for you is your athletics participation. I'd love to say *achievements* instead of participation, but let's be real, Townsend isn't known for our athletics program, so... how good is your college essay?"

My stomach drops. "I haven't started it."

Her face pinches as she leans forward, moving her lipstick-stained coffee mug to the side. "Well, that's probably a good starting point."

"And then? After that, what do I need to do? Quit sports and focus on academics?" I get more comfortable in my chair. "Just tell me what I need to do, and I'll do it."

Her outlandish sigh fills the entire room, fills my blood with nervous energy. "Why New York? A girl?"

"Yes," I state. "My best friend *is* a girl, and she almost accidentally killed herself last week, so yeah, I'd like to be there with her. *For* her."

Heller's eyes widen to saucers. "Okay, then..." She taps on her keyboard a few times, her aged face lighting up when the monitor comes to life. "Let's see what we can do for you, Mr. Eastwood."

A half-hour later, a backpack filled with brochures and a brain filled with way too much information, I'm walking out of her office... and directly into Jamie. She's sitting on one of the chairs just outside the door, spinning the stem of a dahlia between her fingers. Perfect bun in place, and not an inch of clothing astray, she looks just like she did the first time I saw her. "Hey," I breathe out.

She offers a tight smile while the red-headed middle-aged woman sitting beside her whispers something I can't hear.

Jamie nods in response, then stands when Mrs. Heller calls her name.

"Have you got a sec?" I ask her, even though it's clear she doesn't.

She turns to the other woman, now standing next to her. "You go ahead. I just need a second."

The woman smiles, first at me and then at Jamie. "Sure."

Once we're alone, I ask, "Who's that?"

Jamie looks up at me, her eyes clear. "She's kind of like a guidance counselor with the emancipation program. I'd forgotten I had the meeting set up, so..."

She's still twirling the dahlia between her fingers, and I say, "I'm sorry. I didn't know today was..." I trail off when Jamie shrugs, glancing at the office door.

"How could you have known?"

"Well, I'm sorry." I don't know what I'm truly apologizing for. For wanting to break it off with her? For her mother dying? Either way, I *am* sorry.

"I should um..." She motions to the door.

"Want me to wait until you're done?" I ask. "I can give you a ride home or work or—"

"Jameson?" Mrs. Heller calls out, standing in the doorway.

Jamie turns to her, holding up a finger. "I'm sorry. Just one minute?" She waits for Mrs. Heller to nod and then go behind her desk before looking up at me. "What are you doing, Holden?"

I stand taller. I thought it was pretty obvious, but maybe I'm as dumb as my academic history shows. "I'm offering to give you a ride."

Her shoulders deflate with her exhale. "You can't do these things anymore. You can't offer to give me rides or show up to my work." She takes a step back, saying, "Look, I need time to deal with this. I need space. And I need you to give me that."

I bite back my scoff. "So what? We can't be *friends*?"

"Holden," she says, looking at me in that *You Idiot* way she used to. "We were *never* friends."

My eyes narrow at first, and then it dawns on me... she's right. We went from her hating me to her kissing me, to whatever we were right before we ended it. There was no build-up, no in-between.

"I'll see you around." She holds the dahlia to my chest, and I take it from her. And then she's gone, leaving me grasping onto one final piece of her.

CHAPTER
THIRTY-NINE

HOLDEN

"**D**o you mind if I cut out early?" Jamie asks, already removing her gloves. It isn't the first time she's spoken to me today, but since we're at Esme's, she kind of doesn't have a choice. So far, we've kept the chatter to a bare minimum. And kept our distance.

I check the time on my watch. It's only five minutes until we're supposed to be leaving.

She says, "It's just—if I leave now, I can make the bus. Otherwise, I'd have to wait another forty-five minutes until the next one.

"Right." Because being in a car with me is too much for her even though we drove here together. She needs time and space—all things I've given her since she asked for it almost a week ago. "Sure, go ahead."

"Thanks," she says, handing me her gloves. "They're yours. I'll have a pair of my own for next time." I want to roll my eyes. I don't. Instead, I watch her haul both her messenger bag and her backpack with her change of clothes over her shoulders. "Say bye to Esme for me?"

I nod.

She leaves.

And by the time I finish up and drive away, Jamie's still walking to the bus stop. I slow down beside her—an instant reaction—and then I remember…

Time.

Space.

I keep driving.

And driving.

And driving.

I've been doing that a lot lately—driving around aimlessly. It's the only thing that seems to clear my head. It doesn't help much, but it's enough to make me reset and refocus.

When I get home, I go straight into studying. I do *homework* for the first time in my life, which—I've now come to realize—is too little too late. Then I research colleges in New York City, where Mia will be. I check admission criteria and enrolment costs, and the general cost of living there. And then I look up who I might need to screw to get me there in the place. When all that fails, I check how much I could earn from selling my organs on the black market. Not enough, apparently.

I call Mia.

I call my mom, who's still with Mia.

I call my dad.

And then, when my eyes fall heavy, and I have no one left to call, I crawl into bed and stare at the picture of a bright-eyed girl with windburned cheeks and a daisy chain for a crown.

It's the only picture I have of her face. Every other one I'd taken of her was of her legs or hands or other body parts, all covered in art.

I told her it suited her—being out in that field. But in my mind, in my heart, *there* meant back home…

Back to sunshine and solace.

I imagined surprising her with her own field of daisies one day. I would've planted the seeds myself.

It would've been perfect.

We could've been perfect.

In another time.

Another world.

Where mine wasn't falling apart.

And hers wasn't already in pieces.

———

I'd already told the appropriate people that I wouldn't be "trying out" for any other teams for the rest of the year. In other words, I quit all sports. But, when it came to football, Coach Griffith wasn't having it. In his words, it would look worse on my college transcripts to be a quitter than a loser, and he "strongly advised" I play out the rest of the season. So that's where I am. Under the Friday night lights of the football field while the entire school cheers us on.

For losing.

Again.

"Well, that wasn't *so* bad," Billy Butler says, sidling up next to me as we walk off the field. He's out of shape and out of breath, just like most of the team.

I remove my helmet and turn to him. "At least you're walking this time."

It's like a bottleneck to get into the tunnel toward the locker rooms with Coach front and center. He throws his clipboard to the ground, stomps on it a few times, and Billy stifles his laugh. "The man's losing his mind."

We start to move, slowly, slowly, while the crowd in the stands disperse the same way. The cheerleaders are on the sidelines, still cheering for no real reason. And all I want to do is shower and change and call it a night.

"Jamie!" The voice comes from the front of the pack—Dean, of course—and my head snaps up to the bleachers, eyes searching because he must be seeing things. Jamie's never been to a game before, so I don't know why she would now.

But she is.

Standing between a row of seats in dark denim and a leather jacket, loose hair blowing in the wind, she doesn't look at all like the Jamie I know. The guy behind her—someone I don't recognize—taps her shoulder, and she turns to him. *Smiles*. He points toward us, and she follows his gaze, those hazel eyes sparkling beneath the stadium lights. Then she turns back to him, shaking her head, and he... he puts his hands on her shoulders as they move out of the aisle. I watch their backs retreating as they walk side by side, and Billy shoves me forward. "What are you doing, man? Go."

I reset.

Refocus.

The tunnel ahead of me is clear, but my mind is not. I turn to Billy. "Party at my house tonight. Spread the word."

―――――

The music is too loud, the weed too strong, and the beer too plentiful. It's exactly what I need to clear my head. Or forget my mind completely.

Bodies pack my living room and the kitchen and flow out onto the back deck and yard. I'd called Mom on the way home and told her I was having a *few* people over. By few, I meant most of the senior class and at least half of the rest of the school. Dean's here, too. I don't know why he is, and right now, I don't care.

Leaning against the deck railing, I take another hit of the blunt and pass it to Billy. "This shit's good," I tell him. "Your brother's finally getting the right stuff."

He shakes his head. "This isn't from him."

"No?" I blink hard to fight off the effects of all the illegal substances I've consumed.

He leans in so he can shout in my ear. "It's from Melanie."

"Melanie, who?"

"Sanchez."

I stare blankly at him. "You know that hot-ass girl with the black hair, big blue eyes."

A girl walks toward me, offering me a beer, and I shake my head. To Billy, I say, "Oh yeah, I know Melanie." *Jamie's Melanie.*

"You should," he chuckles. "We had three classes with her last year."

"Wait." I turn to him. "She deals?"

He nods, handing the joint back. Before I can take a toke, Bethany's standing beside us, and what the hell she could possibly want... who fucking knows. If it's to ask more shit about Jamie, she can fuck right off. "What?" I ask, and she shrugs. *Games.* So many fucking games, and I'm not even the one playing. So, just to mess with her, I hold out the joint betwcen us.

A ribbon of smoke floats up as she looks from the joint to me, again and again. And then she sighs. "Why the fuck not?" She takes the blunt from me while Billy barks out a laugh.

"Damn, Bethany!" he hollers. "If there was ever a guy to pull that stick out of your ass, it *had* to be Eastwood."

CHAPTER
FORTY

JAMIE

M y hands are cramping, and I know I'm gripping the steering wheel way too tight, but I can't help it. Until last night, it'd been a while since I'd driven, and even then—the diner's old delivery truck isn't one I'm used to driving. Honestly, that's not even the real reason.

I'm nervous.

I spent most of last night tossing and turning, trying to convince myself not to get in the car to find Holden so I could explain why I was at his game with some guy. Not that he deserved an explanation, but it felt like… I don't know… the right thing to do?

I finally talked myself into sleeping on it, hoping I'd feel different in the morning.

So that's what I did.

And then I woke up.

And as soon as I opened my eyes, I saw him—Holden—his eyes to be exact. It was the same eyes I'd seen at the end of his games. First the confusion, and then the hurt. The *pain.*

So I got up, showered, got dressed, and now I'm pulling into his driveway. There's trash littering the front lawn, mainly beer cans. Obviously, he had a party last night, and I wonder, as I make my way to his front door, how many of these he'd thrown prior to me entering his world. Plenty, I bet.

I swipe my sweaty palms on my jeans, my hands shaking as I raise my fist. Knock. I'd gone over everything I wanted to say on the drive here, and so I'm ready. Or, as ready as I can be, considering we've barely said two words to each other since we broke up.

When no one answers, I hesitate to knock again. This isn't a good idea. Clearly, it's a step in the wrong direction. Besides, I was the one who needed time, who needed space, and now I'm forcing myself onto him as if—

The door opens.

And Holden is there, shirtless, eyes squinting against the sunlight. "Jamie?" he croaks, and his scent wafts between us and directly into my nostrils. He smells like… like something I haven't had the pleasure of smelling since Mom died. "What are you doing here?" he asks, opening the door wider.

I take a step back, trying to remain focused on why I'm here instead of fixating on the state of the clearly hungover boy standing in front of me, alcohol seeping through his pores. He's barefoot, in workout shorts, his hair flying in all directions. And even when he's like this.... even at his worst, I have to fight the urge to reach over and touch him. The truth is, I miss him. I miss the boy who brought me joy, pumped life back into my otherwise meaningless existence. "Jamie?" he says again, looking over my shoulder. "Who's car is that?"

"It's the diner's." I shake my head, clear the sudden storm brewing, and rid the memories of my past. "I uh… I wanted to talk to you about last night."

He licks the dryness off his lips and crosses his arms, his muscles bulging with the movement. Jerking his head, he says, "What about it?"

I clasp my hands in front of me while I take another step back. "I know that you saw me at your game with um… a guy."

He quirks an eyebrow.

"He's Zeke's nephew," I rush out, because standing in front of him like this has me antsy. "He's visiting from Europe, and one of the things he wanted to do was watch a high school football game. For some reason, it seems to be a big deal for foreigners. I don't get it, but..." I trail off.

Holden stares, and stares, and stares some more. And it's clear I'm crossing some invisible line by being here. I keep my gaze lowered and my defenses up. "Anyway, Zeke paid me to take him, and I did, and that's all it was." I'm rambling, but I can't seem to stop. "And I don't know why I felt the need to tell you. I just—I wanted you know that I wouldn't... or *couldn't*... move on from—"

"Holden?" My eyes snap up at the sound of his name being called. At the familiar voice calling it. "Have you seen my phone?"

Bethany's standing in the hallway to the bedrooms, dressed in an oversized Townsend Athletics t-shirt, and I'm pretty sure nothing else.

My heart stills... right before it plummets. I spin around quickly, gasping for air, but the only thing that fills my lungs is pain. Pain so overwhelming it blurs my vision, pounds at my flesh from the inside out.

"Jamie!" Holden shouts, and I can hear him behind me, his rushed steps getting louder and louder. I just need to make it to the car, and once I'm inside and far enough away from this hell, I'll be okay.

I *need* to be okay.

"Jamie, stop!" Holden grabs my elbow, turning me to him, and I don't know what happens next.

I don't know if it's the adrenaline or the anguish or the anger I've carried for far too many days now that has me *sobbing*. "You could have had any girl, Holden." I cry as the words tumble out of me. But the way Holden watches me, his empty gaze and stoic stance—I could've carved the words across his chest, and it'd be no different. I attempt a breath, but it doesn't calm the storm. "You chose her because you knew it would hurt me!" I wipe at the pathetic, useless tears. "Well, good job, '*friend*,' because it did!"

Holden stands to full height as he watches me—watching all the million

reckless,

fleeting,

emotions.

They fly through me, one after the other, racing through my bloodline before expelling with each harsh breath.

Holden's head tilts to one side as he steps closer, standing over me with his jaw tense. "Have you ever asked yourself why you're so fucking pressed about Bethany?"

My eyes narrow. "What?"

"You *just* said it: it could've been any other girl, but not her! Why?" He takes another step forward, pushing me back. "*Why!*"

I sniff back my heartache and lock eyes with him. I refuse to back down, to lose this fight. "What the fuck are you talking about?"

He shakes his head, looks down his nose at me. "She was with Dean last night!" he spits, his chest rising and falling with each sharp inhale. Each forced exhale. "Dean! Who you *loved*, right? And you said it yourself, it's not like *we* were in love! But I was, Jamie!" He points to himself, his arms moving, veins popping out of his flesh. "I was in love with you! I was so fucking in love with you that just the idea of hurting you ruined me!" He's yelling so loud, I feel each of his words inside me, beating me down, one by one. "And if you'd given me a chance to explain that, then you'd know exactly how I feel about you! But you didn't! And then you come here... *accusing* me... thinking that I would actually do something like that to you..." He laughs once, his eyes to the sky, and I don't take a breath. Not a single one. "That just proves how fucking little you think of me!"

Tears blur my vision, but I don't back down, don't allow myself the privilege of oxygen. There's a voice in my head, urging me, begging me to reach up, tap at the hand covering my mouth. But there is no hand, and there is no danger, and there is no Mom whispering in my ear, telling me it'll be okay. That *I am okay*.

"Jesus Christ, Jamie! Breathe!" The voice is distant, echoing through a tunnel, and three Deans are standing in front of me. "You can't talk to her like that, bro!" he says, and then he's shaking me, his hands on my shoulders. "Breathe, Jamie!"

My eyes widen as I gasp for air, again and again, until my vision clears and reality dawns on me like a heavy blanket, wanting to suffocate me and pull me back under. Three sets of eyes focus on me, staring, and I cry, and I say...

I say, "I'm sorry."

Because it was the only words spoken after each and every fight.

"I'm sorry."

CHAPTER
FORTY-ONE

HOLDEN

I have questions. Lots of them. Mainly why Dean knew to tell Jamie to do something so simple as *breathe,* and I didn't. It's selfish to want the answer to this over *why* he needed to tell her in the first place, but I figure I can get both answers with one question.

Unfortunately, Jamie doesn't show up to school on Monday or Tuesday, and sure, I could go to her work or her house, but I don't.

Now it's Wednesday, and she's finally here, standing at her locker right beside mine. I can smell her. Which is pathetic, really, but I don't think I'll ever get over her scent or the instant reaction I have to it.

I shut my locker and lean against it, waiting for her to do the same. It's the beginning of The Patience Game, but I'm the only one playing.

Jamie's locker slams shut, and she cringes at the sight of me, but before I can get a word out, someone's calling her name from behind me. Jamie looks over my shoulder, and I turn to see Miss Lockhart, the art teacher, practically running toward us, weaving through the students while waving a piece of paper in the air. She stops in front of

Jamie and me, her eyes as bright as her smile. "I'm so glad I caught you before class!" she huffs out, hand to her chest as she takes a few steadying breaths.

Jamie doesn't smile back. Doesn't brighten. She merely watches her with that same unnerving stare she used to bestow upon me.

"Your piece was accepted!" Miss Lockhart rejoices, waving the papers again.

Jamie remains silent.

And her reaction clearly isn't what Miss Lockhart expected because her shoulders drop, and her smile falters just a tad. "That art contest I entered you in, remember?" She's losing her steam. "They loved your work, and it's going to be showcased…"

I'm glued to Jamie's face, to any sign of a reaction. Nothing changes. Not until a single tear falls from her eye, trails down her cheek. It comes so fast and so unexpected that even Jamie seems surprised by its presence. She quickly swipes it away, and I don't know why my chest tightens at the sight.

"Oh, Jamie," Miss Lockhart coos. "I'm so proud of you." She settles a hand on Jamie's shoulder, her thumb stroking gently. "And I really hope that you are, too." After handing Jamie the papers, Jamie's gaze lowers, her eyes moving from side to side as she reads whatever's on there. "They had over two-hundred-and-fifty entries, and only six students' work gets showcased… and they chose you!"

I find myself smiling, even though it hurts.

Jamie's eyes are clear when she looks up, her chin raised. "Thank you," is all she says.

Miss Lockhart nods, her lips ticking up, before walking away.

Jamie's quick to shove the papers in her bag, discarding them completely. They should mean more to her, and I don't understand why she looks so… so *somber* about it. When she looks up, I say, my heart in my throat, "Congrats. That's huge, right?"

Jamie nods in acknowledgment but doesn't speak.

I push out an exhale and say, unsure if I want the answer, "So why don't you seem all that happy about it?"

Her gaze drops as she shrugs, and then she sighs, lifting those melancholy eyes to mine. "It doesn't really make sense without you, Holden."

JAMIE

I'd considered not going to school, like, ever again, but since I'd made it this far, I figure... what doesn't kill me makes me stronger, right?

Now, I'm sitting in the passenger's seat of Holden's truck, and as much as I want to pull out a marker and lift my skirt to draw, I don't. It's not just Holden's presence that makes me want to escape... it's also the fact that we're going to Esme's. The same Esme who opened her door for me on Saturday morning right after Holden and I fought, and I almost passed out in his front yard. As soon as I got in my car that day, I wanted to drive the four hours to Gina's house. But that would've been crazy. So I ended up on Esme's porch, tears flowing, my shame and remorse on full display.

I couldn't stop crying. Not even when she held me. Not even when she took my hand and led me to her couch and begged me to tell her what happened. I didn't tell her about Holden. Instead, I told her about my past. My life. Because I think, deep down, that's where the pain stems from the most. And the regret that I was harboring? It was merely due to my belief that things were starting to change for me. I didn't expect to be *fixed,* or healed, but... I wanted a *change,* and I felt like I was so, so close.

"Jamie?" Holden says, and I can feel his eyes like daggers on the side of my head.

"Mmm?" I respond, resting my head on the window. It hurts way too much to even look at him anymore.

"Why did Dean have to tell you to breathe?"

My heart sinks, and I push out an exhale. I could lie, make up something to spare both our feelings, but would be the point? "Beaker—my mom's boyfriend—he used to hate the fact that I existed. I wasn't allowed to speak when I was home. And on days when he was coming down from his high or going through some

271

kind of roid rage, even my breathing would bother him." I clear the lump in my throat, and sit taller, but still refuse to look in his direction. "So when he yelled, when he was angry, I tried not to breathe around him. It's stupid—my reaction—and it's not your fault."

He's quiet for a long moment, and then he says, his voice low, "I scared you enough to feel like that?"

"Not intentionally," I reply, hoping he believes me. "Look, Holden, my trauma is my problem, and it's my responsibility to heal from it. I can't expect the rest of the world to work around me. You didn't know, so..."

"But Dean did."

I glance at him and look away just as fast. I can tell he's hurting. So am I. And neither of us can *change* that. "Regrets are useless," I mumble. *And I refuse to hold on to them.*

He doesn't say anything more, and when we get to Esme's house, I step out of his truck and inhale my first full breath since I got in. Esme's sitting at the little table on her porch, and she stands as Holden and I make our way toward her. "Hi, sweetheart," she says, rushing down the steps to hug me. I don't like it, but I hug her back anyway. I don't want her to treat me any different, but at the same time, what can I expect? I bared my soul, and now my burdens are hers.

"Do I get a hug, too?" Holden cracks, and Esme releases me to give him the same treatment.

Once they're done, she stands in front of us, her smile sad. "No work this afternoon," she says, hands clasped. She looks between us, and I can see her nerves taking over. "I was hoping to take you somewhere?" She's looking at me, but she's talking to both of us.

"Where?" Holden asks.

"You'll know when we get there."

Since Holden's car is a two-seater, she has Holden drive us in her SUV to... her church. As soon as I realize where we are, I reach into my bag and make sure I have enough markers to last an entire...

what? Sermon? I have no idea how this works, but it's not really my thing, and if she expects me to *pray*, I don't know if I can do that. Not even for her.

Holden's the first to step out, and he rushes to her side, opens the door for her. I get out from the back seat and look up at the church. Besides the giant cross above the door, it looks like any other building.

"Where's everyone else?" I ask, looking around at the mostly empty parking lot.

"They're there," Esme says, linking her arm with mine.

I glance at Holden, questioning, and he merely shrugs.

Esme doesn't lead us to the main double door of the church. Instead, she walks us to the side of the building, and through a glass entryway that leads to a foyer. "In there," she whispers, pointing to a closed door. The closer we get, the more I can hear the murmured voices coming from behind it. Holden opens the door for us, and the moment he does, my blood turns cold. In the middle of the room there's around ten people—men and women, different ages, different races. They sit in a circle, all facing each other. I turn to leave, but Esme holds my hand, her frail grip making my eyes drift shut. Liquid heat forms on my lashes, and she whispers, "You don't have to talk, sweetheart. Just listen."

I inhale deeply, my chest rising with the force, and Esme's weak squeeze of my hand has my eyes opening and landing right on hers. Eyes red, filled with emotion, she says, "Please." And she reminds me so much of Gina. Wanting to help me. To *heal* me.

"Okay," I say, nodding as I clear my throat. We don't join the circle. Instead, we sit, all three of us, on a row of chairs against the wall, Holden on one side, Esme on the other, and I do as Esme asks.

I listen.

"My name is Tony, and I'm an alcoholic." An older man, likely in his sixties, looks around at all the faces in the circle as they respond, "Hi Tony."

"Most of you know me," Tony says. "I've been coming here for a while now, and the good news is, I haven't relapsed since the last time I was here. The bad news is… I've thought about it." His gaze drops, his legs kicking out in front of him. "As soon as the thought came to me, I called my daughter, and she was able to talk me out of it…" He continues to talk, and I continue to listen.

I listen to his entire story, and then the next man's—a man who got fired from his job and the stress of supporting his wife and kids had him looking for solutions at the bottom of a bottle. A man who's determined to fight this addiction *for his kids*.

I sit and I listen to everyone in that room list their fears and their accomplishments, their highs and their lows, and with each second that passes, I get more and more lost in every word they say. At some point, Esme takes my hand in hers, and I lower my head, hide my tears, my emotions. And when it's done, when they're all finished talking about their journeys, the woman running the meeting asks if anyone else has anything to say. I let go of Esme's hand and stand up. "Me," I declare, my voice coming out louder than I wanted. "I have something to say."

The woman, Layla, smiles up at me, her eyes crinkling at the corners. "Why don't you join us?" she asks, while Tony moves to the side to make room for me beside him.

Holden carries my chair over, and I sit, wait until he's back in his seat next to Esme before swallowing my nerves. Heart pounding, I look around the room, my nostrils flaring with my forced breaths.

"You can start with your name," Layla suggests, her tone gentle.

I nod, wishing more than anything that I had a marker in my hand, just so I can hold it. "My name is Jamie…" I sniff back my fears and look down at my hands. "And I'm *not* an alcoholic." A quiet, united gasp fills the room, and I add quickly, "But my mother was."

"We don't use past terms for addiction," Layla corrects. "Once an addict, always an addict."

I glance up. Not at her. But at Holden. And I see his eyes, eyes right on mine, and I wish I knew what he was thinking. He nods, just once, and then he smiles—a smile filled with pride and determination.

I clear my throat, square my shoulders. "My mom died… just over a year ago, so…"

"Oh, I'm sorry," Layla's quick to say.

"It's okay,' I assure. "She died of organ failure due to her addiction." I keep my gaze lowered. "And I understand that that's what it is: an addiction. A *disease*. And I think that's what scares me the most about this whole thing." I attempt a calming breath. But fail. "The truth is… I keep a bottle of her favorite whiskey in the house and sometimes I pour myself a glass, just to see… I don't really know why I do it, or what I'm hoping to feel or… *conquer*… because when I'd pour it down the sink, I'd feel nothing. No happiness or gratification, I'd just feel… empty." Nerves swarm though my veins, prick at my flesh, but I keep going. "The problem is I've been doing it more and more lately… testing myself… and *thinking*…" I look up, see a dozen sets of eyes all watching me, waiting. "I've been sitting here for the last hour listening to your stories, trying to somehow connect them with hers, but I guess you're all different. I grew up in an abusive household. My mom's boyfriend used to beat the shit of her, and drinking was her coping mechanism." I clear my throat, steady my voice. "There is something you do have in common, though. Most of you have kids, and I've sat here and listened to you all talk about them, saying that *they* are your reason for being here. For wanting to fight this disease. And you—" I turn to my side, face Tony. "You *call* your daughter when you feel as though you're about to relapse?"

Tony shrinks under my stare.

"Don't do that anymore," I grind out, my jaw tense, my chest tight as I fight back tears. "Don't you have a sponsor? Isn't that what this is? It's not up to your daughter to *fix* you. We're your goddamn *kids*. And the rest of you…" I spit, looking around the room, barely able to contain my resentment. "You're all doing this for your them, right? But please, for the love of God, don't tell them that, because if you relapse—" I break off on a sob, and fight to keep my composure. "If you relapse…" I repeat. "Your kids are going to think it's their fault. That they weren't *enough*. And they're going to question their worth every day for the rest of their life, and I know that because I *live* that. Every time I pour that glass of whiskey, I ask myself why… why did she have to continue down that path? Why didn't she leave? Why did she make me live through that hell?" I wipe at the fat and futile tears—tears full of anger and hatred. "Why did she love him enough to die for him, but she didn't love me enough to *live*!" I drop my head in my hands, my shoulders shaking with each sob that wretches through me.

"I'm so sorry," Layla soothes, her hand rubbing slow circles on my back.

I take my time, try to settle my breathing, but I can't seem to stop. Years and years of these pent-up emotions, these fucking *feelings*, all come out. Right here. Right now. I break down, and it's ugly and it's raw and it's in a room full of strangers, but I don't care. "It's not fair!" I cry. "It's not fair to me and it's not fair to everyone around me, because that's all I want in my life. It's all I'm searching for. Someone to love me enough to *stay*."

CHAPTER
FORTY-TWO

HOLDEN

> *Holden: This isn't easy for me, Jamie, and I want you to know that...*
> *Holden: Walking away from you was the hardest thing I've ever done.*

I'd sent the text a week ago, the night after Esme had brought Jamie and me to an AA meeting without us knowing. It was the last text I'd sent her, and she never responded. The only reason I'm punishing myself with seeing it again is because Jamie's not waiting for me at our lockers like most Wednesday afternoons. Instead, Billy Butler is here—standing as wide as he is tall. He grins from ear-to-ear as I approach, gripping onto his backpack straps like a pre-schooler. "What are we doing this afternoon, *boss*?"

My eyes narrow. "I don't know what you're doing, but I have that Outreach Club thing to go to." I look around us, searching for Jamie. She may not want to talk about what happened last week, and that's fine. I'll let it go.

"That's why I'm here," Billy says. "I'm the floater."

"Isn't that the girl who gives blowies to porn stars before shoots?"

Billy's face scrunches with disgust. "That's a *fluffer*."

"Oh."

Billy shakes his head. "Your partner had a make-up test, so you're stuck with me."

Watching Billy attempt to climb into my passenger's seat is comical. In fact, it's the only thing that's made me laugh in weeks. He's stuck, with one leg in and one leg out, cursing to himself as he tries to adjust the seat. After catching my breath from laughing so hard, I reach over, pull the lever under the seat, and slide it back as far as it goes. "Sorry," I tell him. "Jamie's the only one who sits there, and even then, she usually sits with her legs crossed."

I wait until he's strapped in before pulling out of the spot. Cars line the exit of the school, like every afternoon, and Billy says, "Jamie Taylor?"

I nod.

"I like Jamie," he almost announces. "She's cool."

I glance sideways at him. "You *know* her?"

"Yeah," he says, opening his backpack to reveal an entire McDonald's meal. He unwraps the burger, takes a bite, then offers it to me. I shake my head, not even surprised that he's been walking around with that for who knows how long. Around a mouthful of food, he adds, "She's in my art class."

"You take *art?*"

"Yeah." He laughs, finishes chewing before saying, "I thought it would be one of those subjects I could breeze through, but damn, that shit's hard."

I drive out of the parking lot and head toward Esme's house.

Billy says, "Pretty cool about her work being chosen for that art contest."

"Yeah, it is," I agree, then clear my throat. "Do you know what piece was entered? Is it good?"

He shifts in his seat, making my truck groan beneath his weight. "I assume it's good because, *duh*, it's Jamie, but no. No one's seen it besides Miss Lockhart. She keeps it locked in her office at the back of the art room, and Jamie works on it outside of class."

"Weird," I say, and Billy nods. "So, like, how well do you know her?"

"Miss Lockhart"?"

"No, you idiot." I chuckle. "I meant Jamie."

"Oh." He shrugs. "I don't know."

"Well, you said you *like* her, so you have to kind of know her, right?" I don't know why I'm pushing the issue, but it only really occurred to me now that Jamie has a life outside of me. She has friends, has all these other things going on that she never told me about. She never once mentioned Billy or her secret art project, and obviously, she didn't feel for me the way I felt for her, but now I'm wondering if every interaction we ever had was a different experience for her than it was for me.

That would suck.

"The first time I spoke to Jamie, I was whining about not understanding the work," Billy says, pulling me from my thoughts. "She was sitting next to me and she asked, completely straight-faced, 'Is Billy short for William or Wilma?'" He scoffs. "So I told her Wilma was a girl's name, right?"

"Right..."

"To which she had the *audacity* to respond, '*Then quit being a little bitch.*'"

I chuckle, imagining the interaction as if I were there, and I can see Jamie clearly. See her mind turning, waiting for the punchline, and then her eyes light up just before she delivers it.

"Anyway," Billy says, "when it was time to work on our projects, she said she would help me understand the work on one condition..." He waits, knowing he has me eating right out of his palm.

"What was the condition?" I ask.

"That I teach her about football."

My gaze slides to his.

279

He smirks. "She said some idiot jock who wanted to bend her over and bone her was on the team, and she just wanted to know the basics."

I look away, my heart picking up at the thought.

"I take it you're the idiot jock?" he asks.

My non-response is answer enough.

"And I take it things are over?"

I clear the sudden lump in my throat. "What makes you say that?"

"Well, she hasn't been the same the past few weeks. She used to come into class every day and say *Greetings, Wilma*, and now—" He breaks off on a sigh. "Now she just looks sad."

I stare out the windshield, my heart in my stomach. "She does?"

"Yep," Billy says. "Kind of like you right now."

CHAPTER
FORTY-THREE

HOLDEN

I'd almost forgotten what it was like to have both my parents in the same room. When I flew home a couple of weeks ago, I spent most of the time by Mia's hospital bed. Now, it's Thanksgiving, and everyone is here except the one person I wish was.

Mom floats around, making sure everyone is happy, and Dad does everything he can to ensure that his girlfriend, Maggie, doesn't feel out of place. The three of them spend the day cracking jokes at each other's expense, teasing to the point of tormenting, making everyone laugh around them, even Esme—who seems to have found new friends in my grandparents.

And me? I barely leave Mia's side.

Surprisingly, it didn't take a lot of convincing to get her here. All I had to do was ask. She and her dad flew from New York in a chartered private plane because that's who her dad is at his core—someone who throws money around to create false happiness. Luckily for me, he's staying in some lavish hotel because there was no fucking way I was letting him set foot in my house.

I knock softly on my bedroom door, where Mia is "resting," and when no response comes, I quietly open the door. She's curled into a ball on my bed, her eyes closed. I tiptoe across the room for my phone on the nightstand. As soon as it's in my hand, she says, "Expecting a booty call?"

I shake my head, looking down at her. "I didn't want it to wake you if it went off, you brat. And *no*. No booty call." I sigh. "I'm shelving that guy for a little while."

She sits up, her long, dark hair knotted on one side.

I ask, "Did I wake you?"

"Nah," she says. "I just needed to lie down for a bit. No one ever told me that pregnancy was exhausting. I always assumed it all went to hell after the baby was born, but damn. I can't make it through the day without a nap, and I'm only five months in."

I nod, not knowing how else to respond. "Well, I'll let you get some rest," I say, moving to the door.

"Holden?" she calls, halting me to my spot. She says my name the same way my mother does: One word. Two syllables. A million different meanings.

I turn to her, already nervous about what's to come.

"You want to tell me why you have a bunch of pamphlets for colleges in New York on your desk?"

My shoulders drop, and I heave out a breath. "Are you going back to sleep?"

Her eyes narrow. "Are you deflecting?"

"No." I shake my head. "I want to show you something. Come on."

Mia gasps, her hand to her mouth as we stand in front of the tire swing in my back yard. I'd put it up the moment she told me she was coming. It's similar to the one we had in her front yard back home, the one we used to play in for hours when we were kids. She pouts when she looks up at me, those big brown eyes of hers blinking back tears. "Don't cry," I warn. "You know I can't stand it."

She rolls her eyes. "I won't."

I bend down to pick up two rocks and hand one to her, then help her sit. She's in a loose shirt and jeans, so I can't tell if her belly's grown since I'd seen her last, but I don't want to take any risks.

Without hesitation, she uses the rock to scratch into the tire—a single vertical line, followed by another. Back home, you can find our names scratched into almost every surface in numerous places.

Holden + Mia.

She'd always write my name, and I'd always write hers, and that's just the way it'd always been.

Holden + Mia.

I sit down beside her and make sure there's enough room for her to complete my name before starting hers. "I'm going to move to New York," I tell her, focusing on the first stroke of the letter M. "I don't know how yet, but I will." I don't look at her because I know what I'll see, and I'm… I'm not ready to see it just yet. "I want to be there for you, Mia. For you and the baby. Emotionally anyway." I clear my throat, wait a few seconds to see if she'll respond.

She doesn't.

"I know your dad's a pro at throwing money around and thinking it will solve things, so at least I don't have to worry about that."

She quiet for a beat, and I know what she's going to say before she even opens her mouth. "He's changed, Holden." It's barely a whisper.

"I call bullshit," I say. "And even if he has, look at what it took to get him there—losing his dad and almost losing his daughter?" I scoff. "Stellar guy."

"He's *trying.*"

I heave out a breath, so fucking sick of everyone defending this motherfucker. "He's eighteen years too late."

"He's *my dad.*"

"Yeah, well, he's not mine," I blurt out. "So I guess I'm allowed to hate him enough for the both of us—"

"You mean the three of us?" she cuts in, and I shake my head, defeated. She knows me better than anyone, which means she knows my hot buttons, too, and damn if she's not a pro at pushing every single one.

"Please don't shoot the messenger," she says, her hand dropping mid-L of my name. "I caught them kissing—your mom and my dad…"

I'm not at all surprised. Disappointed, yes, but what the hell can I do about it? "Yeah, I figured as much."

"If they get married—"

"Stop."

"We could be brother and sister."

"We're already brother and sister, Mia Mac. Fuck genetics."

She's quiet for too long, and I finally find the courage to face her. *Tears.* "Dammit."

"I was going to name him Holden," she says, hand on her stomach.

I crack a smile.

"But then I figured it might be weird if you have a son someday, you might want to name him Holden the… fourth?"

"Fifth," I correct.

"It might be weird for him."

"Probably."

"So you're good being Uncle Holden?"

"Uncle Holden." I turn the words over in my mind, my smile widening with each pass. But then I think about the fucked-up circumstances that got Mia where she is today, and it doesn't sit right with me. "You know, he has, like, five other uncles…"

It's her turn to say, "Stop."

I know her hot buttons, too. "I'm just saying."

"Holden, you know why I can't tell his father. Or his *family*. It's hard enough for me to take care of myself right now, and then I find out I'm pregnant, and now you want to throw all that in the mix?" She's on the verge of sobbing, and I know that she's right, and I really, *really*, should've kept my mouth shut.

"I'm sorry," I say, my heart heavy, filled with guilt. "I'll never bring it up again."

"Good."

I'm already done with scratching in the three letters of her name while she works on the E of mine.

"So, what other names are you thinking?" I ask, kicking my legs out while leaning back on my outstretched arms.

She tilts her head. "I don't know."

"Well, what's the first thing you think of when you think of him?"

She finishes my name, adding the + in between, before settling both hands on her stomach. And then she turns to me, her eyes bright against the faint autumn sun. "Blessed."

"Blessed?"

She nods. "I hate to admit it, but… I don't know if I'd be here without him."

I suck in a breath, hold it. Because the mere thought of losing Mia… "Don't get all in your feelings, Holden, because I will, too, and you'll hate it," Mia warns, and if she had a stick, she'd be threatening me with it right now.

"I'm not!" I *was*. I pull out my phone as a distraction and type in the browser: *Boys names that mean blessed,* and scan the names until I find one I like. "Bennett," I say.

Mia leans into me, looking at my screen. "Huh?"

"Bennett. It means blessed."

"Bennett," she repeats, rolling the name on her tongue a few times. And then she smiles, just like she did when we were kids, and I'd give her the last of my ice cream. "Little Bennett."

"Baby Benny," I say, looking down at her stomach.

She reaches over and grabs my hand, places it right on her belly. "Baby Benny, meet your Uncle Holden."

I lift my gaze, push back my emotions—a mixture of pride and warmth and sadness and regret. I lock my eyes on hers—eyes belonging to the only girl I'd give up my entire world for. "I'll be good for him, Mia, I swear," I promise. "I'll get my shit together, and I'll help raise him, and I'll be whatever you need—"

She cries. Right into my chest, and I hold her there, and for minutes that feel like hours, we just sit together, staring at a tire swing—a memory of our pasts that we wish so badly we could go back to. But there is no going back. There's only the future, and the future means growing up and growing old, no matter how uncertain or terrifying it is.

"Holden?" Mia whispers, wiping her snot all over my shirt before pulling away. "Who's Jamie?"

Eyes wide, my lips part, stay that way.

Mia sighs. "Esme—she told me that it was a shame about you and Jamie, and I pretended like I knew what she was talking about, but... I guess I haven't really been the best friend to you lately."

I shake my head. "Mia, don't."

"So..." she pushes. "Who is she?"

I heave out a breath, trying to form the words. "She's..." I kick at the tire swing. "She's this..." *Sunshine and Solace.* "She's *home* to me."

Mia frowns. "So what happened?"

I shrug and give her a truth I'd admit only to myself. "I got scared."

CHAPTER
FORTY-FOUR

JAMIE

"Jamie!" Zeke calls, walking into the kitchen of the diner. "Someone's here to see you."

"What?" No one ever comes to see me. "Who?"

He shrugs. "I don't know. Some girl. I assume she goes to your school?"

The only girl I associate with at school is Melanie, and I don't even think she knows where I work. Dirty dishes and suds to my elbows, I ask, "Are you sure she's here for me?"

Zeke nods. "Asked for you by name."

Only slightly more curious than annoyed, I relieve my hands of their duties and dry them quickly before going out to the dining area. The girl stands out like a sore thumb amongst the truck drivers, and behind her, standing a few feet away, is a man dressed in a suit that possibly costs more than the diner itself. The girl's turned away, so I can only see her hair—dark, falling in waves around her shoulders. "Can I help you?" I ask, and she spins to me—light brown eyes and a smile so pure it has me instantly suspicious.

Occasionally I'll get this fleeting thought cross my mind that some random stranger does one of those ancestry DNA tests and comes knocking on my door saying they're my half-sister or something. "Jamie?" she asks, and I nod, look around for more troubling signs. "I don't know if you know who I am—"

"I don't," I cut in. Then add, "Sorry." Because obviously, she was about to tell me.

"I'm Mia."

Oh.

"I'm Holden's best friend…"

I know, I don't say. Out loud. Because I can't seem to breathe, let alone speak. So I nod, clasp my hands in front of me.

"I know you're busy right now, *obviously*, since at your work…" she trails off, and she looks as nervous as I feel. "I was hoping we could talk?" She watches me, her eyes uncertain—and *gosh*, she's beautiful.

I finally find my voice. "I can probably take a break now," I tell her, leading the way to an empty booth. She follows me, sliding in at the opposite side.

I motion to the man still standing in the same spot. "He your bodyguard?" I ask, and her eyes widen. Me and social graces? Not friends. Not even acquaintances.

"Dad!" Mia hisses. "Go away!" She shoos him away with a flick of her wrist, and the man rolls his eyes before nodding and taking up a stool at the counter. He glances at a menu without actually reading it.

"Sorry," Mia says. "He's a little protective right now."

I *think* I smile, but I feel like I'm grimacing, and this is weird. And awkward.

"So… this is awkward," she says out loud, and I can't help but laugh.

"A little."

"I just… I don't know where to start."

Funny. It's the same thing Holden said right before he ended it. Or I ended it, really. But either way, it was over. And now she's here, and I wish I knew why.

Fingers splayed on the table; she keeps her gaze lowered when she speaks. "I don't know how much Holden's told you, but um… he went to North Carolina that week because I needed him there. I uh…" She clears her throat, glancing up at me quickly before looking down again. "I haven't been in the best mental state lately, and my dad—he found me passed out on the bathroom floor surrounded by my own vomit, and um…"

"It's really not necessary for you to explain anything, Mia."

"No, I know," she says, sitting taller. "But I *want* to. A little for Holden, but mainly for me, and I know that's selfish, but there it is."

I nod, encouraging her to continue.

"After my dad called 911, he called Holden, and Holden dropped everything to be there. He sat by my bedside, held my hand the entire time." Her voice cracks on the last few words, and her eyes fill with tears while I fight back my own. I've realized, in the weeks since Holden and I split, that I really didn't know that much about him, but I knew this: his love for the girl opposite me is unwavering, and I'm glad she sees that—that she recognizes and acknowledges it. "He didn't say a lot. He's not all that good at communicating how he feels." She smiles to one side. "He's a lot like his dad in that way. Not much talk, all action."

Silence falls between us because I don't know if she has more to say, and I… don't have anything. I pull out a napkin, spread it out on the tabletop, but I don't have a marker. I don't have my crutch. "I appreciate what you're saying, but…Holden and I—it's over, so…"

"I know," she says. "And I'm sorry. Because it's kind of my fault."

"Because he left to be with you?" I ask. "I don't…" I don't get it.

"He broke up with you because he was scared, Jamie. I don't know if he's told you about my dad and his mom, and the way he's treated her… and the way he's treated *me*. And then my whole eating disorder thing and now the pregnancy—"

"You're pregnant?"

"He didn't tell you?"

"No."

She smiles. "I am. We found out while he was in North Carolina with me." She scrunches her nose in disgust. "And before things get gross, no, it's not his."

I stifle my giggle at her reaction. "I wasn't thinking that."

"Good," she breathes out, getting more comfortable. "The point I'm trying to make is... Holden—he's had to watch some pretty shitty things happen to the women he cares about, and I think it just got him thinking about the choices he makes and the consequences of those choices. And he got scared, Jamie. He's afraid because he doesn't think he's mature enough to handle being responsible for anyone else's emotions or actions or *reactions*..." she trails off, unable to speak through her emotions. "Especially when he cares so deeply about those people. When he *loves* those people. And the love that Holden gives... God, if you're lucky enough to be on the receiving end..." She pulls out a napkin, dabbing at the tears welling in her eyes. "It's such a privilege... and an honor."

I sit still, forcing myself to breathe through the pain of watching her, witnessing a girl fight for strength through her weaknesses.

"Sorry," she says, taking a minute to get herself together.

I lower my head, push back my own tears. My own heartache.

After clearing her throat, she shifts in her seat, bringing my focus back to her. She's digging through her purse and then pulling out the product catalog Holden had his dad send for me. I'd left it at his house, not knowing it would be the last time I'd be there.

She opens it to a specific page and slides it across to me. "I think this belongs to you." Leaning over the table, she points to a picture of her and Holden, a picture I'm familiar with. It had stuck out to me the moment I saw it, and for days, I couldn't get it out of my mind. They're only kids in the picture, standing in front of a wooden play-house with their names painted above the door. *Holden + Mia.* He's smiling, proud, looking at the camera, while she looks at him... the way I've looked at him. "My papa took that picture of us on his phone," she tells me. And then she sniffs. Just once. Just enough so that she can continue to speak. "I can still see his smile when he looked at it..." Mia's so lost in her emotions, she can barely get the words out, and I'm right there with her. Right on the edge of losing it.

"He showed Tammy, Holden's mom, and I'll never forget what she said." She sucks in a breath before releasing it slowly. "She said '*That girl looks at him as if he sneaks out every night and hangs the moon just for her.*'" She stares longingly at the photograph as if reliving every moment of it. "I was only six or seven when I overheard it, and I didn't really understand what she meant. I thought Holden *literally* snuck out at night and pulled out a ladder from my barn and hung the moon *just for me*. Some nights when I couldn't sleep, I used to look out the window expecting to see just that, because to me, back then... and even now... it isn't *that* unbelievable." She laughs, but it's filled with so much sadness I wish I could hug her.

I don't.

Instead, I reach over, take her hand in mine, and squeeze once before pulling away and hiding my hands beneath the table. I don't speak. I don't have anything to say.

Mia looks down at her hand, her breaths shaky. She doesn't look up when she says, "He asked me something yesterday that reminded me of that picture." Her throat moves with her swallow. "He asked if he could've changed the course of my life had he asked the right questions at the right time."

I nod because at least I know this piece of him.

"And I told him the truth," she continues. "I told him that it wouldn't have changed anything. That I would've lied to him as much as I lied to everyone around me. As much as I lied to myself. I kept trying to convince myself that I was okay, but I wasn't." She pauses a beat, contemplating her next words. "Jamie, I spent so many years living in those lies, drowning in them, that eventually, I started believing them myself. But through all those lies, all the hurt and all the pain, I held on to one undeniable truth." Her eyes meet mine again—eyes full of strength—even beneath all the tears. "Every day, the sun would go down... And the moon would rise. *Just for me.*"

CHAPTER
FORTY-FIVE

HOLDEN

For hours now, I've sat on the edge of my bed with my shoulders rigid, my head bowed, and my entire body shaking with nervous energy. Occasionally, I'll glance at my desk where the package sits, imploring me to open it, while my mind, my heart, beg me not to.

The gift was on my doorstep when I got home from school, the last day before winter break. It's wrapped in plain white paper with daisies drawn on every corner, and I knew immediately who it was from. It's the only reason I didn't rip into it the moment it was in my hands. Whatever is in there—it could mean nothing. But it could also mean everything. *Change* everything. And that's what I'm scared of the most.

I'd been good. Whenever Jamie and I were around each other, I kept my distance. I spent almost every second of every day reminding myself that my end goal wasn't going to change, so bringing up our past would only dig up the pain. And that pain had the power to ruin me.

I get up. Pace. Stop. Start again. And then I stand by my desk, looking down at the package as if it's a ticking time bomb waiting to explode... and I'd happily let it destroy me. "Fuck it," I whisper, slumping down on my desk chair. I peel back the tape slowly and carefully, not wanting to damage the paper. I'd already worked out from holding it that it was a framed picture. A drawing. A piece of her. It's face-down when I finally peel back the paper, and so I take a moment to collect myself, to level my breathing.

I'd only felt like this once before: when I was at Mia's bedside waiting for the doctors to return. To tell us that she'd be okay. At least physically. Mentally? That was a whole other journey.

I suck in a breath, push out an exhale, and then I flip the frame over. My breath falters as my lips part, and my chest tightens... right before it expands, bringing new life into every cell of my being. It's a sketch of Mia and me as kids, sitting on the fence beneath the Eastwood Nursery sign back home. Mia's looking at me, holding a giant stick, while I make a daisy chain so long it goes from the front of the drawing all the way to my hands. Jamie's managed to capture every detail—from the faded sign to the greenhouse behind us, to *us*: *Holden + Mia*.

And while it feels like home. Like happiness. Like better days spent playing in the yard, dirty and sweating, not a care in the world —my heart grows heavy with the realization that it's missing one thing... the final piece of the puzzle.

It's missing *sunshine and solace*.

JAMIE

The days pass, turn to weeks, and not a lot changes. I go to school and I go to work and I live my life the best way I can. *For now*. I don't tell Holden about my conversation with Mia or how that conversation changed me in ways they'll never know.

It took a few days to let Mia's words sink in, and when they finally did, I came to one simple conclusion.

I am privileged and honored to have been loved by Holden Eastwood. Even for a couple of months. A few weeks. A single day.

Even if I didn't know it at the time.

People have the ability to *change* you, and I'd been so wrapped up in the way my mother was changed that I never thought that something *good* could come out of it.

And I understand it now.

I understand that the whole of him belongs to her, but I can still hold on to pieces of him.

I pick up daisies whenever I see them and store them between pages of sketchbooks as a reminder of who he was and how he loved me. Not just the "average" me, but the "extraordinary" he saw *in* me.

"I'll see you tomorrow!" I call out to Zeke, pushing open the door to the alleyway.

I halt the moment I see him, my breath catching, muscles tensing. At most, I'd expected a text from him. A simple *thank you* and nothing else. I surely didn't expect to see him sitting on the hood of his truck. "It's like deja vu," I breathe out, stepping toward him. "What are you doing here?"

He waits until I'm standing in front of him before replying, "I just wanted to say thank you in person." After clearing his throat, he adds, "You have no idea what that gift means to me, Jamie."

I have some idea, but I don't tell him that. "You're welcome."

He smiles to one side, but even through the darkness around us, the moon our only source of light, I can see the uncertainty in his eyes, the hesitation in his words when he says, "Do you have time to talk?"

I swallow my nerves. My problem isn't time—my issue is fear. Holden and I are at a calm right now, and I'm not sure that I'm ready to face the storm of whatever he feels he needs to say to me. Still, I find myself answering, "Sure."

He motions to the cab of his truck. "Maybe in there," he says, rubbing his hands together. "It's fucking cold."

I nod, removing my backpack as I follow him to the passenger door. He opens the door for me, waits until I'm settled before going to his side, sliding in behind the wheel, and turning the car on. The heater comes to life, blowing warm air across my flesh. For a moment, Holden just sits there, staring ahead, his head in his hands, and he seems so… *small*. So lost in an ocean of unease. And then he turns to me, his eyes right on mine, but his focus is scattered—as if there's wave after wave knocking him in all directions. After a beat, he says, "I'm not here to give you an explanation of why I wanted to end things… I just wanted you to know that it really wasn't about you, Jamie." His gaze drops momentarily, and a knot forms in my throat, blocking all air from my lungs. "I don't want you going through life thinking that you weren't enough because—"

"It's okay," I cut in.

"And I wasn't lying when I told you I loved you."

"Holden, *please*." I don't know if I can hear this. Not now. Not when I'd just come to terms with losing him.

"I did," he urges. "I *do*, Jamie. I love you."

I inhale sharply, push back the sudden tears threatening to fall. His words are everything, but they can't *mean* anything.

"And I wish that I hadn't thrown it in your face the way I did."

I shake my head, fight against the heartache. "It's okay," I say again, and I don't know if I'm saying it for him or for me.

His touch is warm as he takes my hand, holds it palm up between us. I don't look at our connection when he says, "I got you this. I've had it for a while, but I never knew the right time to give it to you." Something cold lands on my palm, and I take a moment to settle my nerves, calm my erratic pulse. And then I look down, my stomach flipping at the sight. He says, "I realized a few days after we broke up that you weren't wearing the mood rings anymore, but I'd already had it made, so…"

It's a silver pendant with a mood ring center and dahlia petals all around it. I close my fist around the cool metal and bring it to my chest, a single sob escaping me. And it's not even about the gift or the boy giving me the gift. It's a reminder of what I loved, what I lost. He's giving me a piece of my heart back—a piece I thought I could live without, but I couldn't.

Through tear-filled eyes and a shattered soul, I ask, "How did you know?"

"Know what?"

"Her name," I say. "I never told you her name."

He's quiet a beat before answering, "Dean. He put the dahlia on your locker that day…"

"But that was after we'd already…" I trail off.

"Just because we weren't together anymore, it doesn't mean I don't care about you."

I nod, lower my hand before opening it again, revealing the beauty of the jewel. Before I get a chance to inspect it closer, Holden says, "I got you something else."

"No, Holden. This is too much already." *So* much.

He reaches beside him, revealing a white box, and I can tell what it is before it lands on my lap. From the sound alone, I know what's in there: tiny cardboard pieces. "You said you've never done a real one before, so now you have your own."

I lift the box closer so that I can see the final image on the cover.

He says, "They're all the pieces of you I've collected since we met."

The completed puzzle is a collage of my drawings. Some I don't even remember doing, and ones I'm positive I'd balled up and discarded because they meant nothing to me. But Holden had taken them, kept them, because they meant something to *him*.

My tears flow fast and free now, anger mixed with sorrow, for wanting something—*someone*—so badly, and knowing, deep in my soul, that I can't have him. Can't *keep* him. "Holden…"

And just when I think my heart can't take anymore, he gets a dagger and *impales* me with it when he says, his voice harsh as he fights back his emotions, "You're the only puzzle I couldn't complete, Jameson Taylor."

My eyes snap to his, my stomach sinking… because it suddenly dawns on me that throughout all of this… I'm not the only one left with questions. I sniff back my sob and square my shoulders. "I lied to you," I tell him.

His eyes widen. "What?"

I look down at the metal dahlia in my palm and say, my heart in my throat, "Remember that day when we were in your room, and I was drawing on you?"

"Of course, I remember, Jamie. I think about it all the time."

I lick the liquid regret off my lips. "I told you that I'd never felt safe until—"

"Gina." he cuts in.

I nod, my mind spinning, trying to come up with a way to explain it, so he never has to question his worth. "It's funny…" I start, lost in my thoughts. "The first time I met you, I was afraid of you because you reminded me so much of Beaker. Your build, mainly." I exhale, shaky. "I remember the first time I hugged you… that day when I kissed you… I went to bed that night thinking how solid you were against me. How strong. And how that strength had the power to destroy me… but you never did." I look up at him now, make sure he can see the truth in my eyes, the declaration in my words. "And I don't know when things changed, but they did. I felt safe with you, Holden. *Completely.* When I was in your arms…" He pulls me to him, his arms wrapped so tight around me that I feel the same as I did all those nights we spent together. "I felt *indestructible.*" I release a sob. Just one. "No matter what happens," I say into his chest. "Just know that those moments with you… being in your arms… you gave me something I'd never had before. You completed me then like you're completing me now, and I'll never forget that."

He rears back slightly, his eyes red as his nose brushes along mine. Our breaths merge into one as our eyes lock, and we're there now… in the eye of the storm, and then he's kissing me, his mouth warm and wet, merging with the tears that won't seem to quit. I kiss him back, my body melting into his as his tongue parts my lips. And I surrender to the moment, to the need, to the *love,* and I accept this for exactly what it is: a Holden *for now.*

I flinch at the sound of glass shattering, shards of it falling all around us. We pull apart just as the truck doors open, and then comes the screaming and the yelling and the metal crunching, and it's everywhere—no matter where I look or how loud my pulse pounds in my ears. "Jamie!" Holden yells, reaching for me, but we're being pulled apart and out of the car, and all I see is a rush of bodies, all dressed in black… and baseball bats.

I try to scream, but a hand covers my mouth while I get dragged by my hair, my feet kicking uselessly at the loose gravel beneath me.

My face is smashed against the hood of the truck, the pain searing through my entire side, blurring my vision. "Holden!" I scream when I see him being held up by two guys while one takes a bat to his stomach.

"Don't touch her," he shouts, earning another blow to his face. And then his legs. And then he's no longer there, no longer standing.

Blood rushes to my ears, and I shut my eyes tight, fist the pendant so hard it digs into my flesh. The truck rocks beneath me, and I cry into the cold metal as a fist slams against my jaw. I keep my eyes closed when I get flipped onto my back, cop a hit to the stomach. Blood fills my mouth, and I gasp for air.

And then a door opens, a single gunshot sounds, and my attacker releases me. "Where's the goddamn money, Jamie!" he shouts, his unfamiliar voice like a tidal wave, turning my blood cold, halting everything inside me.

Car doors slam shut and tires squeal, and I fall to the ground, my eyes barely open, my breaths barely there. Zeke's talking, his words panicked, but that's not what has me grasping for air, for my need to survive. "Holden…" I can see him beneath the truck, lying on his side, his eyes closed, blood oozing from his mouth, his noise, his chest barely moving. "Holden," I sob, and I find what little strength I have and crawl to him.

In the distance, sirens blare.

"Holden," I cry out, coughing up blood. I lift his arm when I get to him, but he doesn't move. Not willingly. "Holden, wake up!" I lie down beside him, put his arm over me, and hold him close.

"Jamie," he whispers, and I cry into his chest, relief swarming through me when his arm tightens around me. "It's okay, baby. You're *safe*."

EPILOGUE

5 YEARS LATER

"H olden…" *I can see him beneath the truck, lying on his side, his eyes closed, blood oozing from his mouth, his noise, his chest barely moving.* "Holden," *I sob, and I find what little strength I have and crawl to him.*

In the distance, sirens blare.

"Holden," I cry out, coughing up blood. I lift his arm when I get to him, but he doesn't move. Not willingly. "Holden, wake up!" I lie down beside him, put his arm over me, and hold him close.

"Jamie," he whispers, and I cry into his chest, relief swarming through me when his arm tightens around me. "It's okay, baby. You're safe."

I gasp awake, sitting up in an unfamiliar bed, an unfamiliar room. Sweat coats every naked inch of me, pooling at my hairline as I struggle to breathe. I flinch at the warm hand landing on my shoulder, while the mattress shifts beside me. "Another nightmare?"

Blinking back tears, I force air into my lungs and fight to come back to reality.

"Jamie?"

I swallow the ache in my throat and turn to the man sitting next to me.

"You okay?" he asks, big brown eyes blinking away his fatigue.

"Yeah, Dean," I mumble, getting out of bed and taking the covers with me to hide my shame. "I'm fine."

To be continued…

WANT TO READ MIA'S STORY?

You can read all about her epic story in Leo, A Preston Brothers Novel #3. Leo can be read as a standalone, but why not get to know all the Preston boys?

PESTON BROTHERS

- Lucas
- Logan
- Leo

ABOUT THE AUTHOR

 Jay McLean is an international best-selling author and full-time reader, writer of New Adult and Young Adult romance, and skilled procrastinator. When she's not doing any of those things, she can be found running after her three boys, investing way too much time on True Crime Documentaries and binge-watching reality TV.

She writes what she loves to read, which are books that can make her laugh, make her hurt and make her feel.

Jay lives in the suburbs of Melbourne, Australia, in her dream home where music is loud and laughter is louder.

Connect With Jay
www.jaymcleanauthor.com
jay@jaymcleanauthor.com

Printed in Great Britain
by Amazon